What Do You Fear?

Book One

by

E. L. Jefferson

To Clyme
enjoy and much
success to you
E J Jeff

RoseDog Books
PITTSBURGH, PENNSYLVANIA 15222

ISBN: 978-1-4349-9305-2
Library of Congress Control Number: 2008937166

Printed in the United States of America

First Printing

For more information or to order additional books, please contact:
RoseDog Books
701 Smithfield Street
Pittsburgh, Pennsylvania 15222
U.S.A.
1-800-834-1803
www.rosedogbookstore.com

This book is dedicated to all you motherfuckers who said I wouldn't amount to shit.

What do you fear?

Webster Dictionary defines fear as the idea of intense reluctance to face or meet a person or situation and suggests aversion as well as anxiety. Loss of courage, intense apprehension produced by newly perceived awareness of immediate danger, the implication of shuddering or abhorrence or aversion before a sight, activity, or demand that causes fear.

So having defined fear, ask the question of yourself, "What do you fear?" Does that thought make you uneasy? It's only a question, and questions are nothing to be afraid of— or are they? I guess that would depend on the response, wouldn't it? And only you know the answer.

Do you understand the nature of your fears? That you cannot hide from them? The fact that you refuse to acknowledge them doesn't make them any less real or threatening, because they are always with you. Your fears are a physical manifestation of those things that exist within you. Hiding from who you are and what's in your heart is foolish and ultimately self-destructive, but there are ways to deal with your fears. Act on them, let them guide you to what you want, and all your desires will be fulfilled.

Contents

When desires turns deadly and you conquer your fear, retribution can be a beautiful thing.

Turnabout

Karen didn't feel like having lunch with the girls today. The day was too beautiful, with sunny skies and pleasant temperatures. Besides, the office gossip had gotten old, and she didn't feel like fast food today. She wanted to go home and have lunch with her friend. She liked training days because of the extended lunch breaks, which allowed her and her roommate, CJ, to get together. As Karen pulled up to her home, she got a warm feeling inside, the kind of sensation that comes with knowing this is your home.

Karen thought to herself that, at twenty-four, she'd done pretty good for herself. She was buying her own home, and she had a good government job, a relatively new car, and the best friend anyone could possibly ask for. CJ was almost everything to her. She would die for Karen, and Karen felt the same way about her. At this point, the only thing missing in her life was a steady man. Sure, she could get dick any time she wanted it. She knew how attractive she was. But having a boyfriend also meant putting up with a lot of unnecessary bullshit. CJ was always trying to fix her up, but she'd always pass. So for now, she thought it was okay that she didn't have a steady man in her life.

Karen pulled up to her driveway, parked, and went into the house using the side carport door. Over the past two years, they'd found it easier to come in the house using the side door off the carport. In the warm months, this offered shade and quick access to the kitchen and dinning room.

Karen opened the door and noticed the chime didn't go off. Oh, well, she thought, *CJ must have forgotten to turn it back on. girlfriend is always complaining about them and doesn't see the need for them, but I re-*

mind her that my father installed them so that we'd know when doors or windows were opened.

Karen closed the door and headed for the kitchen. She figured she had about ninety minutes left before she had to return to work. She went to look in the fridge and saw that their lunch had been prepared, but CJ wasn't home. Okay *I can wait*, Karen thought. *CJ probably had to step outside for a minute*. As Karen closed the door, she looked down the hall and saw the downstairs bathroom door open. She said, "Hey, girl, I thought you were..." and stopped in mid-sentence when she saw a man emerge from her bathroom. Her heart almost leapt from her chest as she turned to run. She was too slow. He grabbed her by the hair, yanking her head back, and threw her to the ground. He raised his foot and brought it down hard on her stomach. The pain shot through her body like a wave. She found it almost impossible to breath, let alone scream or cry. She felt only pain.

"Try to run again, you black bitch, and your fuck'in dead," her attacker said. He reached down and snatched her up by the hair. "Come here, bitch," he said. He got behind her and put his arm around her throat. Karen found it difficult to breathe as he started to choke her. She grabbed his forearm and said, crying, "Please, don't hurt me. I'll give you money, and I promise I won't tell anyone." Please, she cried, "don't hurt me."

Her begging only enraged him. "Bitch, I don't need your fuck'in money." as he said this, he punched her hard in the back. Karen thought, Oh, God, as another wave of pain shot through her. She fell to her knees, but he snatched her up again and shoved her up the steps and down the hall to the first bedroom on the right. As he did this, he said to Karen, "I'm gonna take what I want out of your sweet little pussy and that tight asshole." Karen could only cry as he pushed her through the door and against the bed. "Yeah, bitch," he said as he moved his arm from her throat to her breast. He then put his hand under her skirt and ripped her panties off. He brought them to his face, inhaled deeply, and said, "I'm gonna love this." Standing there in pain and terrified, Karen noticed he had a thick Hispanic accent, but before she could react, he said, "Let me soften up the pussy." He spread her legs and kneed her in the groin. She fell to the bed, the pain numbing her whole body. Her only thought was that she was going to die. He forcefully ripped the clothes from her body and removed his own. He turned her toward him so she could watch him stroke his dick until it was hard. He grabbed her by both legs and pulled her toward him.

Karen lay there crying and praying that she'd survive this. He straddled her upper body with his knees, holding his dick between her breasts and asked if this is what she wanted. When she only cried and turned away, he slapped her and said, "Bitch, tell me you want this dick." Karen said yes, "Say it like you mean it, whore," Crying, Karen said "yes, baby, I want it." Before he positioned himself between her legs, he said, "I like fucking you pretty bitches," and brutally forced his dick in her. Karen cried out in pain, and that excited her captor. He began to push in harder and harder. As he battered her pussy, he felt her tightness as her juices lubricated his dick. "Tell me you want me to cum in this tight pussy, bitch. Say it."

Karen's response drove him wild. As he pushed harder and faster in the pussy, he watched her reaction to his motion and pushed harder as he felt her pain and himself cumming. He exploded in her, unable to hold back. He let his cum flow into her. Karen was frozen with fright and the pain he'd inflicted on her. He pulled out of her and looked down on her captive form, still unsatisfied with his torture of her, he said.

"Now come here and suck my dick clean." At that moment, he pulled out a large knife and said, "Bitch, if you bite me, I'll cut out your pussy and stuff it down your throat." The thought of what she was being forced to do made her sick, but she couldn't take the beating anymore, and if she did this, maybe he'd leave. She moved toward him, took his dick in her hand, put it in her mouth and began to gently suck his dick. As he stood over her, watching with perverse pleasure as she sucked him, he had to fight the impulse to cum in her mouth. He pushed her off him and said, "bitch, I don't want to cum now. I just want to get hard again." And he smiled with such evil, she knew what he meant, and she cried like a helpless child. He looked down on her and said, "Oh, bitch I'm just getting started."

CJ knew she was supposed to be home twenty minutes ago, but the guy at the market was irresistible. Besides, lunch was almost ready, she just needed the stuff for the salad, so they'd have plenty of time to spend together before Karen went back to work. As CJ entered through the side door, she noticed the chime didn't go off when she opened the door. She thought her girl finally came around and turned those annoying chimes off.

CJ walked into the kitchen and thought she heard voices upstairs. She walked toward the steps and noticed the door to her room was opened. The attacker told Karen to turn around. "Now I want to fuck that ass. Turn over, bitch." CJ did not intend to eavesdrop, but they were in her room. Even though they'd always respected each other's privacy, CJ thought that it was damn strange and totally fucked up for her to take a guy to her room. They'd have to have a serious talk about this later, CJ thought to herself.

I'll just leave them alone, CJ thought as she prepared to leave. At that moment, Karen cried out, "Please, don't do this. Let me finish the other way. I can't take it there." He slapped her hard and said, "Bitch, by the time I'm done with that asshole, you'll be begging for it." He forced her around and pulled her by the waist, he took his dick in one hand and began forcing it in her ass.

Karen cried out loudly, "Please, don't do this to me." She felt him penetrate her asshole, as he brutally pushed his dick in her ass. Just then, with her head turned toward the door, she saw through teary eyes a blur of motion come in the room. As her assailant was pulled off her, she involuntarily cried out as his dick was ripped out of her.

Karen's assailant felt himself being pulled off her. He was grabbed, from behind, and he felt a hand at the back of his neck. He then felt his face was being slammed into the wall. He felt as though the bones of his face had been shattered into a dozen pieces under his skin, and his whole head went numb. He felt himself being lifted off the floor, and he was body slammed hard to the floor. Then he felt a foot crash into his side. He almost passed out from the pain.

Karen stood up on very shaky legs, crying, bleeding, and in excruciating pain. She said, "CJ, he raped me. He hurt me bad." The rage on CJ's face was inhuman as he looked at the broken, bleeding thing on the floor. CJ said, "baby girl, call the police before I kill this motherfucka." Holding on to CJ's arm for support, Karen looked down on her assailant who himself was totally at their mercy. Something happened to her at that moment, something she couldn't explain nor comprehend. She looked up at CJ, and they both came to an unspoken understanding.

Karen left the room. CJ looked down at the thing on the floor curled up in a fetal position, crying, and thought, *In a minute, I'm gonna give you a lot to cry about.* CJ heard loud music coming from the living room. It wasn't loud enough to carry outside the house, but it would mask someone screaming. Minutes later when Karen returned to the room, she seemed unnaturally calm and said, "I called the job and told them I wouldn't be back today." She looked at the thing on the floor. CJ had taken off his sweat suit and was holding his captive from behind and around his throat. CJ said, "What is your name, bitch." "I want to know who it is I'm about to fuck." Stuttering, he tells CJ his name is Miguel, he said, sobbing like a baby. Miguel felt CJ's chest and stomach against his naked back. He also felt a large bulge. Karen left the room again.

"Miguel," CJ said, whispering in Miguel's ear in a mock female voice that terrified Miguel. CJ said, "Do you have any idea what you did to my girl motherfucka?" Do you understand how you've fucked her life up? Do you MIGUEL? CJ shouted. Feeling the powerful arm around his throat and hearing the fury in his voice, Miguel could only say he was sorry and cry, as he began to speak in Spanish. He could not comprehend what was going through his mind, the thought of another man fucking him. He tried to pull away, but CJ drove his elbow into the back of Miguel's neck and that took the fight out of him. As he fell back to the floor, he knew he couldn't escape.

Karen re-entered the room wearing a blue robe and sat down in a chair facing both men. She noticed her assailant crying as he was being held down by CJ. Karen screamed, "How does it feel to be the victim, motherfucka?" "How does it feel to know you're about to be raped?" Karen kicked him in the stomach as hard as she could. Miguel coughed and wanted to double over, but CJ wouldn't let him. Karen said, "Pull him up now CJ. Play with your dick, bitch. I want to see if you can get it up now motherfucka."

Miguel was sobbing like an infant and shaking uncontrollably. CJ grabbed him around the throat and said, "You heard her, Bitch. Jerk it off for her. Miguel took his soft, little dick in his hand and started to stroke it, but as scared as he was, getting it hard wasn't on his mind." Oh, poor baby can't get it up for us. maybe we can help. "Karen grabbed the knife Miguel pulled on her and said, "Maybe if you suck a real dick, your little shit will get hard."

CJ smiled and said, "Get two belts from the drawer behind you and tie his hands." Karen tied one hand to the leg of the bed and one to the dresser. CJ moved in front of Miguel, who was on his knees. Karen positioned herself so that she had a side view, kneeling at Miguel's side, holding the knife he threatened her with. "Now bitch," Karen yelled. "Suck his dick. And if you bite him, I'll shove this knife in your ass."

Karen put the tip of the knife against his asshole. He knew she meant what she said. CJ said, "Open your mouth, bitch." Holding his huge dick in Miguel's face and wiping away Miguel's tears with it, CJ said again, "open your mouth, bitch." He opened his mouth and took the head of CJ's dick in his mouth. Karen's anger grew more intense. "Suck his dick like you mean it, bitch," Karen said. "Suck it the way you wanted me to suck your little dick." Miguel took more of CJ's dick in his mouth, and CJ helped him by pushing it in further. Miguel started to gag, and CJ pulled out, wiping his dick across Miguel's face. "Maybe he'll get better after I fuck him," CJ said.

Miguel cried and pleaded for CJ not to do that, speaking in Spanish and broken English, but they would hear none of that. CJ position himself behind Miguel and laid his dick on top of Miguel's naked ass. "Baby girl give me that KY on the dresser," said CJ. Karen smiled as she handed the liquid to CJ and watched as he lubricated his dick. She felt no sexual desire for his penis, but she thought, *that dick is gonna split his ass wide open,* and she smiled. Miguel tried to struggle against his bonds, but Karen punched him in the face with everything she had. "No bitch, you're not going anywhere. By the time we're done, you'll be begging to suck that dick."

Miguel screamed and began speaking in Spanish as CJ started to work the head of his dick in his asshole. Karen watched as the veins and muscles in Miguel's neck strained and bulged as the dick went in slowly. CJ strained and began to sweat as he pushed in and out, working his dick in Miguel's asshole. He said, "I've never had a ass this tight" and smacked Miguel's right cheek so hard Karen could see a hand print form.

Miguel made strange crying noises as he felt it being pushed farther in. Tears streamed down is face in rivers as he felt his asshole tear with more dick in his ass. Karen said, "Come on, CJ. I want all twelve inches in his ass." "OK, baby girl," CJ said as he repositioned himself behind Miguel to put it all in. "Oh shit, baby girl. this tight ass is good." As CJ fucked him for the next hour, Karen said "Enjoy it baby" as she looked at Miguel, who was as red as blood. She said, "Say you like that big dick in your ass, bitch. Say it, motherfucka."

Karen grabbed his face, but he could only scream and cry as CJ shredded his ass. "Say you want his dick in your mouth, and we'll give your asshole a break." CJ pushed his entire massive dick in Miguel's ass and came just as Karen finished talking. "Oh shit, baby girl" CJ said, and he closed his eyes as his cum pumped into Miguel's ass. CJ held Miguel's tight against his dick, which was completely in Miguel's ass. CJ hollered as he came again, sweat dripping down his face and onto Miguel's back. "Did you like that, bitch?" Karen said as Miguel collapsed to the floor, crying and bleeding. His pain was so great, he couldn't think or speak, blood and cum running down his ass and legs.

CJ pulled out very slowly, breathing heavily he took a towel and started to wipe himself. Karen stopped him and said, "He's gonna suck your dick clean." Sobbing uncontrollably, Miguel laid on the floor, his legs bent close to his chest, his arms stretched out and his head resting on the floor. With his eyes closed, he managed to say, "Please, God, no more. I'm sorry. I'm..." he couldn't stop crying. As he looked at CJ, Karen was stroking CJ's blood stained dick, getting it hard again. They both looked down on him, and with the most evil smile he'd ever seen, Karen said "come on bitch, suck this dick now. We're just getting started. But soon you'll be dead."

Fulfilling your desires is the only way to make yourself happy. Leave the fear behind you.

Family secrets

"I am so sick of her fucking excuses. Every day and night, it's the same shit. I'm telling you, Tony, I honestly don't know what to do anymore."
"Do you love her, Frank"?

"I'm not sure anymore, bro." At first, everything was fine. Jennifer was my princess, and Francis was my sunshine. I thought I had the best marriage and daughter in the world. But like I told you before, as Fran got older, she started the change most young girls go through, and we grew apart. Sometimes Fran would act like I wasn't her father at all. And later, after Fran moved out, Jen started to become more and more distant."

"When Fran came to us and said she didn't want to go to college, I was upset. But after high school, what could I do? She's old enough to make her own decisions. Then two years later, she got a job and moved out on her own. But prior to that, they both became almost secretive about something they kept between them. Fran and her mother would bump heads sometimes on issues and pretty much shut me out."
"Fran disappointed me, yes, about the college thing, because she was always a smart student. It took a while, but I got over it. But what hurts is that she won't even let me visit her at home, but Jen sees her often. Why not me? I'm her father so, what the fuck did I do wrong?"

"Then Jennifer started these goddamn mood swings. I always believed when the kids moved out, it was party time for the parents. You get to walk around your house naked with spontaneous sex all the time like before the kid came. We used to have a lot of fun. Now we're just totally fucked up, and I don't know why. I do know I haven't changed."

"I mean we have problems like most couples, but we've always managed to work through them. It's almost like when we first had Francis, and Jennifer slowly pulled away from me sexually. But I knew that was because of child birth, and it didn't last long. Now our sex life is non-existent. We're pleasant with each other, but there is also a lot missing between us."

"Look, Frank, you're my brother, and I know you're feeling a bit fucked up now, but it's like I've said before, you and Jennifer need to talk with a counselor."

"Don't you think I've tried that? Jen won't even talk about it."

"Well if that's the case, then there is always my temporary solution."

"What? Cheat with a hooker?" Frank said to Tony.

"Why the fuck not? You aren't getting it at home. You're sick of jerking off, going to bed with a hard dick, and you're miserable. What's wrong with letting off a little steam? And besides, it's not like you've never done it before," Tony said. "But that was when I was in the fucking military, over 25 years ago. I'm forty-five years old now. My daughter is twenty-one and out of the house. I shouldn't have to resort to that kind of thing," Frank responded.

"I knew you would say that Frank. You shouldn't have to buy pussy anymore, but things change and people change and you're not the first married guy to experience this shit. I'm just tired of seeing you so miserable. Look, just hear me out." "I care about you, and I hope you can work this thing out with Jen, but what I've suggested to you can help in the short term if you just give it a try," Tony said.

"Every now and then, I visit this little place just outside of town. It's a health spa, but they provide extra services, if you know what I mean."

"Yeah", Tony, I know what you mean", Frank said, laughing.

"Listen," Tony continues. "there's this one chick there who can suck the skin off your dick and fuck you blind. She'll give you the ride of your life." Frank started laughing again. "She'll blow your mind, she's so good. I don't want to give too much away, it'll spoil the fun, but it's the way they set you up that's mind blowing."

"What is there to give away? You pay, you fuck, you go home," Frank said.

"No, little brother, it's much more to it than that, and that's what I want you to find out for yourself."

"I'm telling you, once you've had some of that pussy, you'll feel better. And this really will help you work through your problem. "Before you say fuck off, take this."

"What is it? Frank asked.

"A VIP pass I picked up for you just in case, and they don't come cheap, so don't trash it."

"Look, I'll take it, but I won't promise anything." "You don't have to. Just use it if you need to, it's okay". "Oh by the way, the girl you want is Jade. I had her about a year ago. Actually I got a two- for- one deal. Jade gave me some awesome head, then I got some of the best pussy I've ever had in my life after Jade sucked my dick. The point is, I'm still blown away thinking about it." "What, is Jade Asian or something?"

"No all the girls have one-word names, and they are all extremely hot." "Good, because if I decide to use this pass of yours" Frank held up the pass as he spoke.

"Not mine anymore little brother yours."

"All right, Frank. Let me take you home."

"Okay Tony. And I'll try to talk with Jen this evening."

"You do that, little brother."

"And thanks again, Tony, for listening."

"Hey, no problem, man. That's what big brothers are for."

***

"Princess, I'm home." "Hey honey, I'm in the kitchen."

"Hey, something smells good. What's for dinner?"

"Meatloaf and mashed potatoes," Jennifer said. "What's the occasion? That's one of my favorites."

"No occasion. I just wanted to fix you a nice dinner."

Tony got behind Jennifer and put his arms around her waist and kissed her neck as he brought his body next to hers. He thought to himself that maybe this was the start of something. He felt ashamed of himself for even considering his brother's suggestion. He felt his dick start to get hard as he held his wife closer. He thought, *This is the way it's supposed to be*.

Jennifer put her hands on top of his, pushed them straight down, and pushed him away, saying she needed to concentrate on fixing dinner. Tony felt his hard-on fade away and said, "okay fine, I'll go watch TV."

Frank felt rejected and sorry for himself that his wife of twenty-two years was treating him like she can't stand to be touched by him. He didn't understand why. He told himself as he turned on the TV that tonight he would find out what the fuck was going on. *Maybe she's seeing someone else. Fuck if I know*. Anger and rage suddenly filled him. He found the sensation of his being angry about this situation curious, and then he realized his dick was rock hard.

***

During dinner, they sat across from each other, eating and not saying much. The food was good, but Frank couldn't take this silence anymore.

"Jennifer, can we please talk about what's bothering you?"

"What do you mean? she responded."

"Princess, you know what I'm talking about. Us, our sex life, hell, our whole relationship. Can you please tell me whats bothering you?"

She looked at him as if he were an alien and said, "How many times do we have to go into this? You want to talk about sex. Is that all our relationship is built on?" she said with frustration in her voice.

"No, dear it's not, but we haven't had sex in more than six months."

"Jennifer, I love you, and I've tried to be understanding about what's happening, but I honestly don't know what's going on."

"Like I've told you before, Frank, I have some things on my mind that I'm trying to work out."

Frank cut in and said, "Baby, maybe we can work on this thing together."

She looked at him and said, "No I'll be okay" She took her plate and went into the kitchen.

I give up, Frank thought to himself. *What more can I do*? Frustrated, Frank took a shower and went to bed, leaving his wife to clean up. The next day at his office, Frank called his brother. "Hello, Tony. Are you busy?" "Hey, what's up, Frank?" Tony responded. "No, I'm not busy. What's on your mind, Frank?"

"I didn't get anywhere with Jennifer last night, and I've decided to visit that place we were talking about."

"Good, glad to hear it," his brother said. "Just go, relax, and have some fun. It'll make a world of difference." "By the way, I tried a new girl the last time I was there. Man, was she hot. "I fucked her until I was shoot'n blanks."

"Tony, one question: "How much does this cost?" "The VIP pass will get you one hour with Jade for straight massage action, and anything extra will start at about five hundred bucks. But, man, I'm telling you, it'll be worth every dime. And you're not hurting for money, so enjoy," Tony said.

"Frank, listen to me. I don't want you to feel guilty for doing this behind Jennifer's back. It's not like you didn't try to work this shit out." "Hell, if she can't take care of you, someone else will. And besides, what she doesn't know can't hurt her," Tony said. "Besides it's not like I'm there all the time," said Frank. "I agree. Gotta run, bro. But remember, ask for Jade and have fun."

***

Frank got off work at five o'clock and decided that he would pay the spa a visit. Months of frustration had built up in him, and he was tired of jerking off and being rejected by his own wife. *Fuck that bitch*, he thought to himself as he justified in his mind what he was about to do.

As Frank drove down the highway, he thought to himself about "how good it was going to feel to actually fuck a women again and not have to think about it while he jerked off and how he had a lot of frustration and cum built up to release. Just thinking about it made his dick hard. He found himself excited about the prospect of doing this, knowing it was morally wrong and probably illegal, but he decided before having come this far that he didn't give a fuck and that it was too late to turn back now.

***

Frank drove another ten miles down the interstate until he spotted the neon sign for Joan's Sauna & Spa. Frank thought that the name of the place didn't give any indication that prostitution went on there. He pulled his car into the parking lot and went inside. The place was tastefully adorned in Asian décor. The woman who greeted him wore a very flattering Asian: style dress that hung tightly on her every curve.

"Hello, sir, my name is Vivian. How may I help you?"

"Hello. I want a rubdown." Frank handed her the VIP pass, and she took it and turned it over and told Frank to follow her. They walked through a doorway that led past several steam rooms, saunas, and several smaller rooms. Frank noticed the place seemed to be pretty busy for a whore house, unless only special customers get that kind of treatment.

Vivian led Frank through another doorway and into a room with a large padded table, a bed, and other comfortable-looking furnishings. Vivian asked Frank to sit down.

How did you hear about the spa?

"My brother comes here, and he bought me this pass."

"If you could wait here just one moment I'll be right back."

Vivian returned a few minutes later. "Alright, Frank, let me explain how this works. These passes are for a select clientele. I checked the code, and it shows your brother is indeed a client of ours and he purchased this for you. You guys must be close. That's good. I had to verify that you got this from a member."

"This pass is good for a steam bath, massage, two drinks, and a shower." Frank seemed confused. He didn't care about any of that shit. He wanted to fuck. "After you've had a steam bath, your masseuse will notify me and I'll arrange for your other activities. So how does that sound?" Vivian said.

"Sounds good to me, but there is one more question." In a low voice, he asked how much the other activity cost.

Vivian replied in a very sexy voice, "Five hundred dollars to start, baby." And it'll be worth every penny. "You'll leave here drained and very satisfied." That thought pleased Frank. He was instructed to undress and take a hot shower and given a choice of drinks. He choose white wine.

***

Jennifer sat home brooding all day. She thought about her family and what was happening to those relationships- most of all, how she had been treating her husband for the last few months. Frank was a good man and provider. He made enough money that she didn't have to work the entire time they'd been married, and he was a good father to their daughter.

What Jennifer couldn't put her finger on is how things went so wrong. Frank never asked her for much, and he almost never complained about anything. She knew he was disappointed about Fran's decision to skip college, but they had gotten over that years ago. But the events of the last couple years had a profound effect on Jennifer and her state of mind.

The things she'd done and the secrets she'd been forced to keep from her husband affected her so much that she didn't care about her husband or how he felt about anything. She knew he wasn't going anywhere, so she became indifferent toward him and his needs.

Last night, though, as they ate dinner, she sensed something different about Frank. The look in his eyes told her something was on his mind, that he was waging a war within himself and that it was about her. She knew withholding sex from him was wrong, but she had made her mind up that she didn't give a damn about his needs and feelings. But what she thought she sensed was that maybe he no longer cared about her feelings either, that he had had enough of her shit.

Even when they went to bed, something was wrong. Even though her passion for him had temporarily gone away, he would still hold her at night from behind like he'd always done. Jennifer would tolerate his hard dick against her body, but that's as far as she would let it go. When it went down, he was sleep, and like she had done for months, she'd pull away from him and go to sleep. Last night, he never touched her.

Something about last night frightened Jennifer into realizing that she needed to wake up and come to her senses before she lost the man she loved.

All Jennifer could do over and over again is to apologize to Frank in her mind. She finally came to the conclusion that what she had been doing was not only wrong but destructive. After all her soul searching, she realized Frank didn't deserve to be treated the way she had been treating him.

She knew this, and she also knew she needed to talk to someone, that she couldn't keep this to herself any longer. *This situation is destroying everything*, she thought to herself. *My home, my marriage. And now my life is falling apart, and I allowed it to happen*. All these thoughts and many others ran through Jennifer's mind. The secrets she'd kept from her husband and the way she'd treated him the past few months had been horrible. She realized that now, and she also realized it couldn't continue.

Jennifer thought she needed to speak to someone close before she talked to Frank that evening, so she figured she'd call Tony early in the day before he left work.

"Hi, Tony, it's Jennifer. Do you have a minute?"

"Sure, doll, what's on your mind?"

"Tony, I really need to speak to someone close to me about something that's been bothering me for a while now."

"Sure, Jen, whatever you need. Would you like to have a late lunch?"

"No, this is more private family stuff," Jennifer said. "Frank won't be home till late. Can you swing by about 5 PM? That will give me time to air this out with you before I talk with Frank later this evening."

"Sure, Jen, I'll be there at 5 PM sharp. See you then."

Jennifer thanked Tony then hung up.

***

Frank finished his shower and put on the robe provided for him. He noticed the five hundred on the dresser had been taken, and his clothes had been neatly folded and hung up in the closet for him. He thought, *Now that's classy*, and he poured himself a glass of wine that had been brought in for him.

A few minutes later, Vivian came in wearing a red, two-piece nightie and a shear robe. Frank found himself instantly turned on. He saw she had a beautiful body, large full breasts, and curvy hips he'd love to explore.

Vivian explained that she would be his facilitator, and that she would guide him through his encounter. He had a choice of six women, and she would bring his choice to him. She explained that for the next two hours, they were there to please him, and that there was no limit to the number of times he could cum or the ways in which he could be satisfied-oral, anal, straight, two on one, anything he wanted. She said, "You'll be begging us to stop." But first, she said he had to wear a face-mask that completely covered his eyes and blocked his vision.

At first, this made Frank nervous, but he thought, what the hell, he'd play along. Vivian explained that the woman he'd choose would also were a feminine version of the mask he was wearing. The reason, she explained, is that this protects the woman's identity and his and that once he established himself after a few visits, the masks would no longer be necessary, if that's what he wanted.

Frank put on the mask and found the fact that he couldn't see to be exciting. He asked Vivian if he already knew what girl he wanted, could he just request her now? Vivian said, "Absolutely. Who would you like?"

"Jade," he said. Vivian told Frank to wait one moment while she went to get Jade.

Standing naked in the dark wearing a mask and a bath robe seemed stupid to Frank, but he was willing to go along with it, remembering his brother had come here. He heard someone return to the room. Vivian stood in front of Frank and removed her robe, panties, and bra. Facing Frank and whispering softly in his ear, she instructed him to gently put his hands on her shoulders. She then said in a very sexy voice, "Now, Frank, explore my body using both sides of your hands. Don't squeeze. Gently touch my whole body." Frank did so.

Frank began moving his hands gently down Vivian's arms, feeling the softness of her skin. He put his hands on her shoulders and came down to her breasts. They felt wonderful. As he cupped her large firm breasts in his hands, he instantly got a mental image of them. He felt himself getting hard.

Vivian then guided Frank's hands with hers over the rest of her body. Her ass was firm and her pussy soft and warm. These sensation excited Frank even more. Her scent drove him wild. As his dick made contact with her body, Vivian said, "Yes, baby, your big dick feels so good against my body, with her breast against his chest, she whispered to him," This is how we see, baby. We don't need our eyes, and from here on, we don't talk. We use all our other senses."

Moving to Frank's back, Vivian pressed her body against his while another women took his hands and placed them on her hips. Vivian whispered, "This is jade. I'll leave you two alone now, unless you want me to watch. Explore her body with your hands, Frank. Let her guide you."

Frank heard the door close as Vivian left the room. As before, Frank used his hands to explore Jade's body. She felt so good. Touching her shoulders told Frank she was taller than Vivian. Her breasts were warm and full, as he touched her body. Her hands found his dick. Her touch was warm and gentle, and she used both hands to massage him, stroking the full length of him and bringing his dick to full erection.

She put the head of his dick in her mouth and slowly worked it, using her tongue to lick the head and her lips to bring more of his dick in her mouth, using very slow, deliberate motions. She took more of him in her mouth, working slowly. The pleasure she gave was mind blowing. His groans of pleasure grew louder. She put a finger to his lips to silence him. He understood, and his moans of pleasure got silent, but he couldn't control his breathing, which got heavier and heavier.

She had more than half his dick in her mouth. She adjusted herself so that she could slowly take more of him down her throat. Like a snake swallowing its prey, she took the full length of his dick into her throat. This went on for what seemed to Frank like hours, but it had only been thirty minutes of the slow, methodical bobbing of her head, feeling his dick in her mouth and in her throat. Frank was driven wild as he felt his large dick swallowed and taken down her throat. He felt his dick start to throb uncontrollably, feeling himself start to surge to climax like an exploding volcano. He felt as if he was going to explode any second. There was no way he wanted this to end.

Jade felt the length of his dick start to throb in her throat. She quickly but gently pulled back, sliding her mouth off his dick. As she did so, he started to cum. The first wad filled her mouth. She guided his dick to her breast as he unloaded. Frank felt as if he'd come for hours. His cum flowed out of him in what felt like rivers, and her left breast was covered with his cum. She slowly rubbed his hard dick over both her breasts, cum flowing down her stomach. Frank couldn't control his moans of ecstasy as she rubbed his cum over her now completely covered breasts.

***

Tony arrived at Frank and Jennifer's a little after five. She opened the door for him, and he could tell when he saw her she was bothered by something.

"Hi, Tony," Jen said. "Come in. Let's go to the living room and talk. Do you want something to drink?"

"No, I'm fine. How have you been Jen?"

"Alright, but there are a lot of issues I've been dealing with that I need to get off my chest before they drive me crazy."

"You talk, I'll listen," Tony said as he sat in the chair across from Jen and listened as she told her story."

"Tony, I don't know how much Frank has told you about what's been going on between us lately, but whatever he's told you, it's okay. I'm going to tell him everything I'm about to tell you, I just need to talk to someone I trust."

"Sure Jen, I'm here for both you guys, you know that."

Jennifer told Tony that everything started about two and a half years ago. Remember when we let Fran go on her high school senior cruise to the Caribbean? Well, when she came back home, she wasn't the same person we sent away. I began to notice how quiet she'd become and how her attitude changed toward not only us but to her friends as well, even you, in the space of six months. She'd pretty much cut off contact from everyone she knew, and she no longer cared about college, which she made clear to us in no uncertain terms.

"Frank tried to talk to her in every way he knew how. Nothing worked. Fran told me she wanted to work and that she'd found the perfect job. She wanted to save enough money to move out on her own. She didn't want our help and didn't care about our advice or how we felt. She was certain at nineteen she could make it on her own."

"After a while, Frank gave up trying to talk to her. She began treating him like a stranger, and over the next two years, she did exactly what she said she'd do. Now, you have to understand that Fran is my daughter, and I love her. There was no way I was going to let her just up and leave without telling me something, and I got tired of being treated like a stranger."

"The year before she moved out on her own, I followed Fran as she left to go to work, I'm her mother, and I had no clue where she worked or what she was doing to earn her money, and she wouldn't talk about it. She'd only say it was a good job and she enjoyed her work."

"The place where she works is called Joan's Spa. It's a new place just outside the city. "Tony's heart started to beat a little faster at the mention of the Spa." I figured, at least now I know where she works. I waited outside for an hour after she went in, trying to decide if I should go in or not. I decided not to, if this is where she wanted to work, it was fine with me. Then I became upset the longer I sat in my car, thinking, *This is what she gave up college for? To work in a health club?"*

"I changed my mind and went inside. I asked to see Francis. About twenty minutes later, Fran comes into the lobby and asks me what I was doing there. She wasn't glad to see me. There was an almost controlled fury about her when she saw me. I said, "Baby, I just wanted to see where you worked." She accused me of meddling in her affairs. I tried to tell her otherwise but she wouldn't listen. At that point, I just left."

"A week later, Francis calls me at home and asks me to meet her at the spa at five o'clock. She said she wanted to show me something. I get there, Fran meets me in the lobby, we go into a room, and she tells me that she wants to explain something to me but first she wanted me to see what it was she did.

"A woman named Vivian came and got me. She explained that what I was about to see may be shocking, and if I couldn't handle it, we would leave, but that either way, we'd talk afterward. But while in the room, I was not to talk for any reason. She led me to a very dimly lit room. Two people came in, a man and women, both wearing masks. The women sat on the bed with the man standing over her. I was shocked to my core. The only thing I could think was, *I know I'm not about to see what I think I'm going to see.*

The man was wearing only a robe. The woman started to stroke his penis. I was totally shocked. I couldn't believe I was watching this live. Then it dawned on me, even with her hair pinned up and wearing the mask, I knew it was Fran. She started to suck the man's penis. She had to know I was watching. She invited me here to watch her.

"I was appalled watching her do this and ashamed to admit I was turned on too. I was speechless, but I kept watching. The women who was there, Vivian, didn't say a word. I was so intent on watching Fran suck this man's dick and all the shit that was going through my mind, I didn't realize Vivian had her hand on my thigh.

"I was disgusted at first, and I was gonna bolt the hell out of there. Vivian pushed down on my leg and whispered to me how pretty I was and started trying to kiss me. She whispered, 'This is what Fran does and she's good at it.' Her lips found mine in the dark, and it was like something took over me.

"She had her hand in my jeans before I knew what was happening. I'm so ashamed to admit this now. I'd never been with a woman before but I couldn't control myself. I actually got so turned on, I let her do what she wanted. Her hands were all over me. We watched touching and kissing as the man came in Fran's mouth and she drank it down. Vivian then asked if I wanted to join my daughter, Jade. Before I knew what was happening, I was naked and wearing a mask. I was lead to the bed. I got on my knees in front of him and let that bastard take me from behind."

Tony sat there flabbergasted as he listened to Jennifer's story. His heart was racing as his mind went back to the time he had recently told his brother about, the time he got a two-for-one. There was no way Jen could describe what she just did and what he experienced unless she was there. Only someone who was there could describe what he experienced. The realization hit him with such force, he could barely catch his breath or stand.

***

Jade crawled to the middle of the bed on her hands and knees, Frank gently held on to her ankles, following her to the middle of the bed, his dick rock hard and ready to enter her. Closer to her now, he let his hands find her pussy. It was so wet, ready to receive him. He couldn't see her, but the warmth of her body guided him to her.

With one hand on her left hip and his dick in the other, he positioned himself to enter her from behind. His dick found the lips of her pussy, and he pushed forward. Frank thought to himself that she felt so good. Her pussy was wet and hot as he went further and further inside her. He felt her react to him as he went deep inside her. The feeling drove him wild.

She accepted his entire dick inside her, and as he began to stroke her, thrusting harder and harder he could hear her try to stifle her moans of pleasure and pain. Her breathing became short and fast with each thrust. She buried her head in the pillow to drown out her cries as Frank punished her soft, wet pussy.

The wet sounds his dick made as he fucked her told Frank she was extremely wet, and the feel of her walls against his dick let him know that he filled her and she loved it. She began to counter thrust in tune with his stroke. Frank was in heaven.

***

Tony was speechless and in shock as he realized it was his niece who sucked his dick and his sister-in-law he fucked. He desperately tried not to let his shock show as Jen continued to speak. He could barely contain himself. She continued to speak, but he didn't hear her. He needed to get out of the house. He felt himself getting sick to the point he wanted to throw up. He had violated his brother's family, and just as that thought hit him, he realized where his brother was and whom he was with.

Tony bolted straight up and ran for the door. He hastily apologized to Jen, telling her he had forgotten about an urgent matter and had to leave. He ran to his car thinking, *How could this have happened?* The panic and shame he felt was almost too much to bear. He had to get to his brother.

***

Frank couldn't control himself. He became lost in his desires. It had been months since he had some pussy, and Jade felt so damn good to him. Even the smell of her sex turned him on. As he came in her, holding her tight against his dick to completely drain in her, he whispered, "Oh, God, princess, where have you been? I've missed you so much. "Baby, I love you. You're my princess."

Jade froze and her heart almost stopped with the shock of hearing those words, the tone of the voice, the way he said princess. She thought, *This can't be*. As she pulled away from him, she could only repeat one word in her mind, *No...no... no... no.*

She turned to face him in the near darkness of the room, backing as far away as she could. She took off her mask and turned on the light. When she saw her father kneeling on the bed, she put her hand to her mouth to block out the scream that was to follow. She was in such a state of shock that no sound emerged. Frank removed his mask, and Jade grabbed the sheet to cover herself.

Frank found himself staring into his daughter's tear-filled eyes. He began to tremble as his mind went totally blank, getting off the bed and backing away from her. His heart pounding in his chest, trembling so bad he could hardly stand. With his eyes starting to water, he screamed and screamed louder with every breath he took, as he stared at his naked daughter, the daughter he just fucked.

He was still screaming when the police took him away.

Fear and stupidity, when unleashed, often have lethal consequences.
If you don't conquer your fear, it'll destroy you.

Night Drive

Imagine you're driving alone at night and your car is the only one on the road. You check your rearview mirror, and there is no one behind you. You're cruising at 65 mph. There's lighting in the distance. It had rained earlier in the evening. Another flash of lighting startles you out of your daydreaming.

You realize you've always been afraid of lightning, ever since you were a kid. Now you're an adult, and the shit still scares you, even when you're at home with the family, though you'd never admit it.

Anyway, you have about twenty-five miles to go, and the road is a little wet. As you drive down the highway, the sky is pitch black of course, and the lightning is everywhere, it seems. But the sky doesn't feel right. It doesn't look right. But how the fuck could you possibly know that?

It's 10 PM. That gives you an uneasy feeling as you speed down the highway toward home and safety. A flash of lightning directly in front of you scares the shit out of you as you make your way toward home. You think to yourself how happy you'll be when you reach the comfort of your home.

You check your rear-view mirror, and you notice another vehicle behind you. You can barely make out the headlights, but another vehicle is there. That gives you comfort for some strange reason, so much so that you almost wish the other driver were closer to you.

You continue on, knowing that every minute brings you closer to home. That thought gives you comfort now more than ever. There are no more cars on the road, and that bothers you. That fucking lightning is flashing with more frequency now, but there is no thunder, just constant flashes that, for an instant, illuminate the sky and those horrible looking clouds. They appear as black, ominous, shapeless, hideous things in the sky, which are made more terrifying because now you feel as though the lightning is chasing you. Of course you know that's silly, but you can't help being a little frightened.

You take comfort in the fact that at least your not alone on the road. The other car is still behind you, but you notice it neither gets closer nor farther away. Your speed is constant, so you assume the other driver's is too, but you'd feel a little better if the other driver we're closer, almost like an escort. You don't have that much further to go, just a little while longer and you'll be safe at home.

***

You think to yourself how much you fucking hate lightning and can't wait to be out of this shit, and it seems like at that precise second, just as you finish that thought, a long, jagged bolt of bright blue lightning splits the sky directly in front of you, the thunder so loud it feels as if it shook the ground. In that instant, you let out a startled cry and tense up. You grip the wheel tighter. You feel as if your heart is going to go into overdrive. The feeling quickly passes. You still feel a little tense, but it's passing.

You look in your rear-view mirror and notice the other driver is still there, and you wonder to yourself, *Is that person scared of storms too, or is it just me?* You continue on your drive home. Less than ten miles now and you'll be safe.

Fuck this storm, you think. A double flash of lightning gets your attention, and you lose focus on your thoughts, but you are aware of the fact that you are scared and that goddamned thunder reinforces your fear. As you drive toward home and safety, it seems as if the fucking sky has gotten darker, but that's not possible. You think, *Fuck this, I just want to get the fuck home*. You try to suppress childhood fears surrounding thunderstorms and remember to think like the intelligent person you claim to be, but all you can think about is home and safety. *Home and I'm out of this fucking storm*. At least you're not the only person on the road in this mess.

You see the other driver is still behind you at about the same distance. That at least gives you a little comfort. Another flash of lightning, this time to the right of your car. You think if you can just hold it together you'll be fine. *I don't have that much further to go, and I'll be safe. Just over three miles to go and this fucking storm can kiss my ass.* As you approach your exit off the highway, memories of your childhood come to you.

For some strange reason, they all involve thunderstorms- running in the house, hiding in closets, covering your ears to protect them from the house-rattling thunder. All of those memories were still scary, and those particular memories were some shit you could have done without at this moment. But you can rest easy, you're almost home. Fuck the lightning and the thunder. One more overpass, and you're home free. All you have to do is drive to the top of the hill, turn right, and you're safe. You look in the rear-view mirror, and your companion on the road is still there, no closer and no further away.

The car's headlights give you the comfort of knowing you're not alone. At least there is at least one other fucking human being on the road on this miserable night. You return your attention from the rear-view mirror to the road, and in that millisecond, as you face forward coming to the top of the ramp with your exit in sight, lightning flashes in what appears to be an almost strobe-light flash pattern. It locks your attention. Fright seizes your muscles, and in the cloud pattern, for the briefest of instants, you think you see something.

You can't make it out. It happened too quickly. You're scared out of your mind. You have to get away. You step on the gas hard and jerk the wheel to the right hard. The face in the clouds is almost on you. Your car hits the guardrail at 75 mph. The rail acts as a ramp, deflecting your car at an angle into the air and over the ramp. You scream on the way down. It seems to take forever. You continue to scream. You can't feel your body anymore. All your mind can process is blind terror.

The road is getting closer, and you continue to scream. Your car comes down with the front windshield facing oncoming traffic in what appears to you to be slow motion. You see a vehicle coming toward you. Although you're suspended in your car upside down, you see the approaching vehicle has two female passengers in the front. You see the terror in their eyes and the silent screams on their faces as they barrel toward you at highway speeds. You can't even cover your face. You're so terrified, the only thing you can do is scream as the two vehicles meet. The last conscious thought you have before death is, I'm sorry.

It's a damn shame people go through life never knowing what they really are. Was it failure to face their own fears that blinded them?

35,000

Jay thought to himself often that he didn't know how much longer he could continue on this job. Sure, the money was damn good, there were no supervisors breathing down your neck, no uniform to wear. But he didn't feel comfortable when he sat on those damn airplanes, cooped up in that small space with all those fucking people. Being a flight attack mitigation specialist had its advantages though: the travel, different cities every day, beautiful women everywhere. But Jay knew he didn't have the heart to physically engage another man, women, or fuck'in rag head terrorist for that matter in combat of any sort.

He knew in his heart that if shit hit the fan on his airplane, he'd bitch out and let his partner and the other passengers handle the shit. He'd talk his way out of his cowardice like he'd done in the past at his last department. Being a cop on the streets of Washington, D.C. was no joke, and he always thought there were way too many niggers on the force. But he did work in D.C., and at least there were other officers there for backup when the need arose. The "brothers" would break their dumbass necks backing up white cops. As a flight attack mitigation specialist, that luxury didn't exist. He also laughed to himself when he thought about that stupid job title.

Jay figured, he's gotten by this long, so what if he was a coward? He could admit that to himself. No one else had to know. Like he'd said to himself many times, *I'm in this for the money.* Yeah, the shit that went down on September 11 was fucked up, but he wasn't the cause of it, and if it opened opportunities for him, he'd take them.

He'd constantly remind himself that he didn't give a fuck about serving anyone but himself. If this fucked-up agency was willing to pay him one hundred grand a year to basically fly around the country and fuck flight attendants, he was more then willing to take advantage of everything the job had to offer. And he knew that he had a few advantages. He thought to himself, *I'm relatively young, good looking, and white. And there is one other huge advantage with this agency. Ninety-five percent of our organization's management is white, and at least we knew how to watch out for each other. So I'm not putting my ass on the line for anybody.*

Jay arrived at Reagan National Airport at 8 AM. He had an early flight to Dallas Texas. He'd worked with the guy he was partnered up with today on several occasions. He was a pretty big guy, ex-SWAT officer, and black. Jay thought, *That's another thing. I didn't like about this job. You never knew who your partner is going to be from day to day.* And he preferred working with the "brothers." They all thought he was cool, which was because of the bullshit he learned to perfect working for the DCPD for five years.

As soon as he got to the ticket agent's desk, his cell phone rang. He looked at the display and saw it was his operations office calling. He was informed that his scheduled partner had called in sick today, and he was given the contact information for his new partner.

Jay hoped his partner would be black, but he knew he probably wouldn't be. Most likely it would be someone he didn't know. That's the way this place worked. At 8:15 AM, he made contact with Mitch Kramer.

Jay was rather disappointed when they met. Mitch was a much older guy who had been with the U.S. Secret Service, he'd found out, and he didn't look to be in the best of shape. *Another problem with this place is they hire a lot of fat, out-of-shape guys.* He also spoke with a slight Southern accent, which Jay found to be a bit irritating. *Oh, well,* Jay thought. He'd make the best of it. After all, they were gonna turn around and come right back when they landed in Texas, and he was off for the next three days when they got back home. So, thankfully, it was going to be a short day.

The plane boarded at 9:30 AM, and they had to pre-board in front of everybody at the gate. Jay absolutely hated doing that, but his partner insisted so that they could brief the flight crew. After talking to the pilot and lead attendant, Barbara, who by the way didn't care much for their being there, Jay and Mitch took there seats. "Boarding," the announcement came over the PA.

A few seconds later, the passengers started to come on board the plane. This was the part Jay hated the most. All these people saw him come on board first and may have guessed who he was. Try as he might, he wouldn't or couldn't make eye contact with any of them. He kept thinking to himself, *do they have an idea who I am?*

Jay wondered if today would be the day he would have to do what he was hired to do: prevent another 9-11 or some other crime onboard the airplane. He felt scared and alone. What would he do if something happened? Dozens of scenarios ran through his mind. His heart began to beat a little faster, and he felt himself tremble. He glanced at his partner, who was casually reading a magazine as the people walked by him. He seemed completely at ease, but all Jay felt was apprehension.

Jay noticed Mitch would look up every few seconds, making eye contact with the passengers as they boarded. Jay faced forward and tried to calm himself down. A man who appeared to be of Middle-Eastern descent sat next to Jay, and that made Jay even more nervous. Jay thought, *why the fuck did he have to sit next to me?*

The flight attendant made her announcements to the passengers, then the captain, and a few minutes later the airplane was heading for the taxiway and then to the runway for takeoff. Once in the air, Jay started to calm down. He thought, *We have almost three fucking hours to go. Maybe some music will help me to calm myself the fuck down.* Jay thought to himself that one of the best perks of this job was sitting in first class and having to do absolutely nothing other than sit back, relax, and enjoy the ride, food, drinks, and if you're lucky, you'd get at least one good-looking flight attendant with a nice ass to watch. He felt himself relaxing as the sky waitress, as he called them, took his drink order.

The raghead sitting next to Jay still made him a little uneasy, but he thought, *Fuck it. As long as he sits down and doesn't cause any trouble, it'll be okay*. Jay hated all those fucking people. Jay thought as the flight progressed. *It's been an hour and a half since takeoff. We've eaten already, and now we're watching a movie, and as usual, nothing's happened so far, so chances are nothing will.* That thought really made Jay relax.

Jay was watching the overhead video screen when he noticed Mitch look away from his magazine and up at the front section where the attendants sat. This was an Airbus 320, so there were always two attendants up front. Mitch put his magazine down and started to watch the attendants in the front galley.

Jay noticed that the lead attendant, Barbara, had a worried look on her face as she was talking to someone on the phone and looking toward the rear of the plane. Another attendant came walking up front very quickly, and she did have a worried look on her face. She and the lead attendant went to the corner of the galley, out of sight, and started to talk.

Jay saw the lead attendant make a hand motion asking for Mitch to join them in the galley. Now Jay became very nervous. He had no idea what was going on, and he didn't care. He said to himself, *Whatever it is, Mitch is gonna deal with it.* Then another attendant came toward the front and stopped at the entrance to the first-class cabin. Jay heard one of the younger attendants up front say she wasn't going back there again.

Jay noticed one of the attendants was looking at him with a very concerned look on her face. This made him tremble. Now he knew some shit was gonna go down, and he wanted no part of it. Mitch returned to his seat, but before he did he slipped Jay a note. No one saw him do it. Jay didn't want to read it but he had no choice, he opened the note, and it read: Get ready. We may have an arrest in seat 22D.

Jay heard shouting coming from the rear of the aircraft now but couldn't make out what was being said. The attendants looked nervous, and the lead attendant got on the phone to the captain. A man in the rear of the plane shouted something Jay couldn't believe, but he could only make out part of what was said- "Man, what the hell do you think your doing?" Mitch turned around to see what was going on and looked at Jay, who was looking at the attendant on the phone to the captain. She hung the phone up and walked toward Jay. She told him the captain said "to go to the back of the plane and handle the situation."

Jay asked what was going on. She told him that the man in 22D pulled out his penis and told the rear attendants to suck it. "He grabbed her, threw her in the back, and now he has her trapped back there. We think he may be high on something." Jay froze in his seat, and he got so nervous he became lightheaded. At that moment, there were sounds of a struggle coming from the back.

Mitch turned around and saw two men fighting. Apparently, a passenger got up to confront the man causing the problem, and they started fighting. There weren't a lot of people back there and quite a few of them were elderly. The man exposing himself was much bigger than the passenger who tried to help the attendant, and the smaller man was getting pounded. Another man got up to help and he was beat down. Now there were women screaming and children crying back there.

Mitch looked at Jay and got out of his seat and said, "Come on, partner. Let's go deal with this." Jay said nothing to his partner. He looked away. Again Mitch said, "Jay, we need to deal with this. What the fuck is wrong with you?" Mitch said. Jay said nothing. Mitch looked at him with disgust and went to go deal with the problem. Jay was terrified, and he said to himself, *Mitch is on his own. I'm not getting in a fight with that motherfucker.* And he stayed planted in his seat, trembling like a bitch. He heard Mitch Identify himself as he approached the man. As Mitch walked down the aisle, he saw the frightened looks on the faces of the passengers. They were terrified both the men and the women. He could see the one causing the problem. Walking toward him, Mitch could see he still had his dick hanging out of his pants, and he saw the two men he already bludgeoned, one on the floor, bleeding from the nose and mouth, his wife or girlfriend next to him crying for someone to help him, the other guy in his seat looked to be unconscious and was bleeding from a cut under his eye.

Mitch was frightened, but he had to do the job he was paid to do. He turned to see if his partner was behind him. He didn't see Jay, and this made him angry. All he could see was the flight attendants cowering up front. The closer he got to the guy, the more scared he got, as Mitch realized how big this guy was and how crazy or high he had to be to act this way.

Mitch identified himself to the lunatic passenger again as he moved forward. It was the look in his eyes that truly frightened Mitch. The closer he got to him, the man's eyes told Mitch there was nothing he can do to him and that he'd kill him or anyone else on this plane. This was the look of a crazed lunatic. These thoughts crossed Mitch's mind in a split second.

Mitch was terrified but tried not to show it as he approached the man. A woman stood up as the assailant passed her seat. She didn't seem scared but angry as she said, "Why don't you sit your crazy ass down and put that ugly little thing back in your pants?" At that moment, the man turned around and backhanded her across the face, blood flying from her mouth. He then moved to grab her, and the woman's companion shouted, "Brenda," as she fell backward. The crazed man then swung on the women's companion, catching him square on the jaw. The sound of the man's jaw breaking was sickening. He was out cold before he fell back into his seat.

Mitch made his move. He got to within a few feet of the man, again identified himself and removed his cuffs, trying to sound as tough and authoritative as he could manage. He told the assailant he was under arrest and ordered him to turn around and place his hands on top of his head. The man looked at Mitch and closed the short distance between them so fast Mitch didn't have time to react. He was on top of him, slamming his fist into Mitch's face. After the fourth blow, blood covered Mitch's face and he fell onto the deck of the plane, unmoving. His assailant continued pounding him in the face, his fist now covered in blood.

The rear attendant shouted for someone to help him, but instead everybody closed their eyes or stayed glued to their seats, turning away from the carnage that was taking place. Just before he was bludgeoned into unconsciousness and then death, Mitch's last thought was that he probably should have shot this motherfucker.

The lead attendant with the two younger attendants standing behind her looked at Jay and in a truly hysterical voice told him his partner needed help. "That guy's beating him in the face and he's not moving." Jay looked at her and said nothing. She clearly saw the fear in his eyes, and he was too scared to even respond. She looked at him and said, "You have a gun. Shoot this motherfucker before he kills your partner."

Jay managed to say in a trembling voice that disgusted her, "It's in my bag," and he pointed to the overhead bin. She said, "You sorry piece of shit" and looked away from him, disgusted. The crazed man saw her talking to someone and started to come toward the front of the airplane. One of the attendants quickly got on the phone and told the captain what was happening. One officer and three passengers were down and the remaining officer up front refused to do anything.

The captain was furious. He told her he was coming out and hung up the phone. His co-pilot stopped him. "Sir, you can't go out there. We need to land this plane now," his co-pilot said. As the assailant passed Jay's seat, he sat there frozen and cowered like a scared rabbit when he looked into the crazy man's eyes. The assailant continued forward toward the remaining flight attendants and attacked them. The captain and co-pilot heard the women outside the flight-deck door screaming as they tried to fight their attacker off and were totally powerless to help them as they rushed to land the airplane.

Jay watched as one of the attendants ran past him, blood streaming from her mouth. He watched as the assailant threw another women around the galley like a rag doll. She fell to the floor unmoving. The passengers in the front of the airplane all looked toward Jay, but not one of the six people seated in first class raised a finger to help the now battered women, and the person assigned to prevent just such an event from occurring did nothing.

Eventually two older passengers tried to help the unconscious flight attendant as she was thrown from the galley. They pulled her away from the galley and put her in an empty seat. Meanwhile, the last attendant in the galley was screaming and trying to fight off her attacker. He knocked her against the galley wall and forced her down to the ground. He straddled her shoulders with his knees and tried to force her to suck his dick. She violently turned her head and screamed "no." With her legs kicking, he grabbed her head and shoved it hard against the wall. She fell silent. He then pulled her head up and opened her mouth with his hand. While sitting on her chest, he put his dick in her mouth, moving her head forward and back as if she was sucking his dick.

The flight attendants in the rear were screaming for someone to help Barbara. But not knowing what the crazed passenger did to the others, no one stood up or tried to help their colleague. Jay could only see her legs from where he was sitting, and they weren't moving. He could barely see the guy's back, but he knew he was sitting on her chest. His mind was a blank. He didn't know what to do. He felt like a scared, trapped rabbit. He was so frightened, he pissed in his pants, thinking that guy was going to come after him next, and Jay still couldn't move from his seat.

Barbara came to, gagging, and found it very hard to breath, the taste of cum in her mouth, the man was holding her by the head, and she realized his dick was being forced in her mouth. She thought, *Fuck this* and bit down with every bit of strength she had. Now she tasted blood as it filled her mouth. Her assailant screamed so loud, it was heard over the roar of the plane's engines, he tried to stand. Barbara got to her knees holding his dick with her hands and teeth. She was determined to bite it off. He hit her in the face as he fell back screaming, slipping in his own blood.

She opened her mouth and freed him, spitting out his blood. He was now bleeding profusely. She saw that his dick was bitten almost in half but still connected to his body by the skin. His drug-induced high no longer effective to kill the pain he felt, his screams filled the cabin. Carol saw Barbara stumble forward into the middle of the galley and ran forward, determined to help her. She got to the officer lying on the floor unmoving. She saw when she moved his coat that his gun was still in its holster. She took it out, holding it with both hands, pointing it in front of her as she moved forward. When Carol got close to Barbara, she thought she looked like a vampire that had just feasted on its victim.

Carol looked at the man on the galley floor. His blood was everywhere. He laid there curled up in a fetal position, bleeding like a gutted pig and screaming. Barbara screamed with a rage that frightened

Carol to her core. At that moment, Barbara snatched the gun from Carol, pointed it at the bleeding thing on the floor, and shot it until it stopped that damn screaming and it no longer moved.

Carol was not shocked or saddened at what she had just witnessed, even though she had never seen someone shot before. She had no feelings for that maniac who had just hurt and killed people on her airplane. That piece of shit deserved every bullet. She just wished at that time it was she who shot that piece of shit.

Barbara looked down the aisle, and the first thing she noticed was the body of the officer on the floor. Her eyes focused on his bloody face, the pool of blood under his head, his body unmoving, then a new, uncontrollable fury filled her. Something else needed to be put out of its fucking misery.

She walked to the seat where the other piece of shit sat, the motherfucker who reeked of cowardice and piss. In an instant, Carol knew what she was going to do, but this one she couldn't go along with. She ran to the phone and called the captain.

Barbara pointed the gun at Jay who was still cowering in his seat, and she said, "You no good piece of shit, give me one reason why you need to live." Barbara commanded that no one move. The other passengers up front obeyed as they sat frozen in there seats, too afraid now to even breath. "Motherfucker, you couldn't even move to help your own partner. At least he tried to do his job. And it cost him his life. Why the fuck should I let you live? What are you willing to pay to stay alive, motherfucker? she shouted. "Answer me, goddamnit!" she shouted even louder.

Jay couldn't move or look at her. Barbara thought about what he allowed to happen to her, the other passengers, and his partner. Barbara thought to herself about how she was beat damn near to death, knocked out, sodomized, that animal's filthy dick forced in her mouth, having to bite that filthy thing off to save herself. But it was the taste of his blood and semen that temporarily drove her insane.

Jay watched like a deer caught in headlights as she pointed the gun to his face, slowly pulling the trigger back. His eyes focused on the trigger as it moved backward, further and further. He watched, paralyzed as the hammer rose. He saw this all in slow motion as the barrel of his partner's weapon grew larger before his eyes.

He saw the disgust for him on Barbara's face as she looked him in his eyes and continued her slow pull on the trigger. The last three sensations Jay experienced were the sounds of the captain's voice as he shouted, "Barbara nooooo!" and the sound and flash of light that heralds death is approaching.

Bang.

Childhood fears never really leave you, and until you face them, they always come back.

Mirror, Mirror

I hate this fucking job, Walter Jackson thinks to himself as he sits at the same security post he's worked for the last year. He is miserable. Today was like every other day for him, and he can't wait to get off and go home.

He hates working as a security officer. His assignments are always the same, and he sees absolutely no future for himself as a security guard. Patrolling office buildings and sitting at posts for a living is not why he went to college, he complains to himself.

He watches the clock, waiting for his shift to end and for the relief guard to show up. He doesn't like the government workers in his building, because in his opinion, they are all arrogant assholes who all think they're better than him, everyday he feels like saying the hell with it and walking off this fucked up job.

As Walter waits for his relief to show, he hopes today maybe he'll get some news on one of the dozens of applications and resumes he's sent out. He knows leaving his job right now wouldn't be a smart move though. As much as he hates his job, it pays his bills.

The other thing Walter hates about the building he works in is all the mirrors that decorate the lobby. He's always had a dislike for mirrors. As a child, he was cut badly by a mirror as he and some friends stood in front of one playing a game. The mirror they were using fell of a wall and he tried to catch it, cutting his hands badly and sending him to the emergency room.

Even more disturbing to Walter than the injuries to his hands were the stories his grandfathered use to tell him and his friends growing up in an attempt to scare them. Stories about how mirrors not only showed your reflection, but were gateways to a world of monsters. To set them free, you had to recite silly-sounding spells while standing in front of them, which is what he and his friends were doing when he had his accident, he hadn't thought about that in years, he thinks to himself as he prepares to leave for the day.

When Walter's relief reports for his shift, he doesn't greet the other security officer. He simply grabs his gear and leaves for the day. Walter is aware he's not the most likable guy around. He doesn't have many friends and spends a great deal of time alone. It's been that way for him since high school and throughout college. His circle of friends has always been small, and what friends he does make don't stay around long, and he's fine with that since he doesn't like being bothered with many people. He hasn't had a girlfriend in years, which he knows is sad for a twenty-eight-year-old man, but he thinks that's okay too.

As Walter gets into his car, he decides to go have a beer at his favorite bar, which happens to be a strip club. He can at least look at the dancers while he drinks a beer before he heads home. It's the same routine he's followed for months now.

Walter gets to the bar at 4:30 PM, goes inside, and orders a beer. He sits alone in a corner, which gives him a decent view of the stage but is just far enough away so that he doesn't have to tip the dancers.

In all the time he's been coming to this particular bar, he thinks he'd be a more popular customer, but the waitresses and the dancers avoid him when he comes in.

No one greets him and he does the same, which is why he doesn't tip any of these skanks, he thinks. *What the hell? I'm not fucking any of them, and I don't owe them shit. As long as I buy a drink, the show is free as far as I'm concerned,* and he finishes his beer. Besides, it's not his fault these bitches can't do anything else but shake their asses for money, and he leaves an hour after he got there, having satisfied his needs for the time being.

***

Walter gets home and has no particular plans. He simply wants to unwind and relax. The place is quiet and peaceful, just the way he likes it. He looks around his place. His furnishings are simple, but he has no need to impress anyone. He likes his home as it is. He settles in and starts to change into more comfortable clothes when he gets an eerie feeling. It's nothing that he gives much thought to at first so he continues to undress out of his work clothes and into something more comfortable.

That feeling hits him again, and this time he takes notice. He knows there is no one here with him, but he can't shake the feeling he's not alone. He figures a drink to calm his nerves after a fucked-up day at work is all he needs and a little TV to occupy his mind.

He notices his living room seems a little dimmer than usual, but that makes no sense because the living room lights are all on one switch, and there are three light fixtures. He chalks it up to fatigue. He finishes his drink and continues to watch the 6 PM evening news reports.

The main story is a report on a neighborhood shooting where three young men were gunned down, apparently gang related. He thinks to himself, *Fuck'em. They probably deserved to die. All those fucking niggers are criminals anyway*. With that thought, Walter wonders to himself why he suddenly, feels alone, not just alone but secluded as if he were a child who was abandoned by his mother.

He doesn't know why, he feels this way but he does, and now his home seems darker and menacing somehow, and he knows that makes no sense but he can't shake the feeling.

He pours another drink and slams it back and decides to go to bed. It's early, but what the hell? *I don't have shit else to do.* He feels ridiculous because he knows what he's feeling doesn't make sense. Slowly at first, he feels a tingling sensation run down his spine. He thinks to himself, *What the fuck is wrong with me? I'm a college-educated adult. There is nothing to be afraid of in my own home.* The more he tells himself that, the more like bullshit it sounds because he's afraid and the feeling is getting stronger.

***

He takes off his clothes and lies on the bed. He reaches for the light switch, but something stops him from turning it off. It's a sensation he barely perceives on a conscious level, an almost primordial fear of darkness. He swings his feet to the floor and sits up on the bed and thinks to himself, *Fuck this shit.* Feeling both ashamed and embarrassed of himself, he decides to take a shower to try to calm himself.

Crossing the room, he's startled when he thinks he sees something move out of the corner of his eye. He looks quickly in that direction and sees nothing. Walter's eyes focus on a picture of a woman hanging on the wall, and the eyes seem to be watching him. His heart is beating a little faster now, and he notices his hands are shaking. He tries to get a hold of himself and get in the goddamn shower. Looking at himself in the mirror, he recalls a particular game he played as a kid with mirrors.

The game required him to stand in front of a mirror and repeat some silly phrase. No, it seemed like more than just words. A spell, yes. And he was reciting a spell in the hope of conjuring up a spirit or demon who'd only show itself at a certain hour and under certain conditions.

That frightens him now, and although he doesn't want to remember the words to the spell and he wants to pull away from the fucking mirror, he can't, and the words he is desperately trying not to remember break through his jumbled thoughts with perfect clarity.

Demon in the dark who hides in shadow and owns the night, I summon you now into the light. Join with me and give me your power, here and now this very hour, and in return I pledge my soul. When the light passes and the night is cold, I am now and forever to be owned by he who lurks in shadow.

He feels like he's ten years old again, frightened and helpless. His knees get weak because he doesn't want to be there. He doesn't want to see what's going to show itself in the fucking mirror. He knows he's trembling but can't find the strength to pull away, he closes his eyes and remembers the stories his grandfather used to tell him. When he opens his eyes, the only thing staring back at him is his own reflection.

He thinks to himself that this shit is crazy. He gets in the shower and closes the curtain. During his shower he feels uneasy, but the water feels good and he relaxes just a little. Returning to the bedroom, he still can't shake the feeling he's not alone, but he knows that makes no sense. He lays on the bed and looks at the clock. It says 10 PM. Now he realizes he's tired and wants to sleep.

The sleep he wants eludes him for what seems to him like hours. The more he thinks about it the more uneasy he becomes. Now he's not just uneasy, he's afraid, and he knows he shouldn't be, but he is. He makes up his mind not to turn out the light. *Just lay here and go the fuck to sleep.* He closes his eyes, and he thinks he hears something. His eyes snap open, but there's nothing there. He turns over on his side, but he realizes that turns him away from the door, so he shifts to face the door. He looks at his clock and it still says 10 PM, he thinks that can't be right.

This goes on until he knows he can't sleep, then another sensation hits him, a mortal terror that overpowers him with dread and a single thought: Get out of here. Go anywhere but get out of this place now. Get the fuck out of this apartment. He bolts up to get out of bed, but he's so frightened now he can't move, and now his heart is beating so hard he can hear it. There is a presence here other than his own. He can feel it.

He looks down the hall and remembers leaving all the lights on, but now the whole apartment is dark, with the exception of the lights in his bedroom. And in all his mind's confusion, he starts to hear a voice in his mind that's not his own.

The words come through in short phrases. *Demon in the dark, who hides in shadow and owns the night.* His mouth goes dry when he realizes what the words are. *I summon you now into the light.* He hears this in his mind, and he knows it's not his voice. *Join with me, and give me your power.* He can't move off the bed, the words won't stop. *Here and now, this very hour, and in return, I pledge my soul, when the light passes and the night is cold.* He looks to the door to run, and still those fucking words won't stop coming. *I am now and forever to be owned by he who lurks in shadow.* The voice in his mind is harsh and malevolent. He senses it's evil, but he's so frightened he can't move.

His heart is beating so hard, his chest hurts, and the pain starts to spread all over his body, and still those fucking words taunt him. They get louder in his mind. *He who lurks in shadow.* At that moment the lights go out. He feels a warm wetness run down his legs and tears flow down his cheeks.

He is frozen in place. He feels a foul, warm breath on his neck, and he hears something move behind him. He can't move or hide. He needs to run, but there's nowhere to go. He needs an explanation as to why this is happening to him, but there is none. He can feel every pulse in his body beating so hard the pain is terrible. His heart feels like it's racing out of control, as if it's going to explode from his chest any second.

Something touches him in the darkness, and he screams with all his might, all his rage, and all his fury. And in the split second before he dies, he realizes no sound came out of his mouth.

We've always been told crime doesn't pay to instill fear in us, but we know that's bullshit. It can be quite lucrative, depending on who benefits.

Three Blind Mice

"We've been watching this damn house for a fucking week now," Chuck said, "and it's the same shit every day. Every morning at 9 AM sharp, these same workers show up, do whatever the fuck it is they do, and leave at 6 PM. Not a damn thing has changed since last Monday."

"There is a reason, dumb ass," "Tony said." We watch this shit to learn what's happening and when, and to check out the hood. We know they've been installing shit for a while now. We don't know what it is, but when they're done, we're gonna steal everything in that motherfucka, whether it's nailed down or not."

"We know the owners are long gone and won't be back from their fucking vacation for another five days. I hate these rich motherfuckas," Tony said. They come in here flashing their fucking money, buying these big fucking houses. We're gonna rob this motherfucka blind." "Yeah, well, I hope that dumbass ho you're fuck'in' at the bank is right about the shit she told you about the motherfucka who live's here," Rob said.

"It's been right so far, she works for the motherfucka that owns the house. He's the bank manager or some shit. I seen him. He drives that Jag in the driveway to work in the mornings. We saw him drive away in the BMW to the airport with his fucking family." Rob thinks to himself, *I would love to lay dick to his wife though. Maybe next time,* I come by myself and fuck the shit out of her."

Tony continued, "He's a short, fat ass grayboy, always wears a suit and fucked up ties." Carla says he's a fucking dick to all the workers at the bank, and that he's a weird motherfucka. He's into some shit called wicken or wicked or some shit like that, whatever the fuck that is. Says he was bragging about taking his fucking family to some fucking place in Europe for two weeks, and how he wanted to get away from everyone before he fired them all. He's gonna be surprised like shit when he brings his fat ass home."

"Hey, Tony, how do you know this bitch isn't going to rat us out when word gets out that his crib got broken into?"

Look, Rob, that's not gonna happen. All that dumb ho cares about is this dick up her ass. I got tired of her talking about how fucked up her boss is and how she'd like to fuck him over, so I asked the bitch about the dude. She filled in all the blanks. Don't worry, motherfucka, she doesn't know shit, least of all what we're up to. And even if she did, I'm tappin' that ass every night. She won't say shit, dumbass ho.

"So when are we gonna do this thing? We've cased this place long enough, and we got about five days before fat ass comes home. Everybody knows the workers are gone at 6 PM. Chuck already scoped them out, asking about if their company is hiring installers because he's looking for work, and dude told him they'd be done here by noon today and gave him a card to call the company, so this is the last day of the job."

"We'll hit that motherfucka today about 2 PM. People in the neighborhood won't suspect shit. All they'll see is the same three coverall uniforms working in the house until 6 PM, as normal. The van won't be a problem because they've used different unmarked vehicles the whole job, and by 6 PM, we'll have handled our business and got the fuck out.

"Chuck, you get the same type uniforms as they have on right?"

"Yeah, man, no problem. You can buy that shit anywhere cheap."

"We're ready then, let's go get something to eat, come back and go to work." They return at 2 PM.

"All right, this is the plan. We'll park our van in the front of the house like normal. Chuck, you and Rob go around to the back of the house under the deck with the toolboxes. We know there's a key box under the deck. That's how the workers got in every day."

"Rob, you cut the power cord to the key box and smash it open with the sledgehammer. Go through the house and open the garage door. I'll back the van up in the driveway, and then we go to work."

Tony backs the van up in the driveway. Chuck and Rob proceed to the back of the house. Like clockwork, all goes as planned. The lockbox is deactivated and broken open. Chuck and Rob enter the house under the deck and hurry to the garage entrance. Laughing, Rob says, "Man, this is too fuck'in' easy."

"Yeah, like taking candy from a baby," says Chuck.

Opening the door for Tony, Rob and Chuck place their toolboxes in the back of the van and go back into the house.

"Alright here's the plan," Tony says. "We have three hours tops to do our thing and get the fuck outta here. Rob, you take the upstairs. Check every room. We want cash, jewelry, electronics, bonds, any shit like that. Chuck, you take the basement, and, man, tie your fuck'in' shoes before you bust your ass."

"Fuck you, man, This is a big fuck'in' house," says Chuck.

I know, motherfucka, that's why we're here," says Tony. "Same thing for you, Chuck, plus all small electronics, computers, phones, game systems, all that type shit, and we take every flat screen in this bitch. I'll take the middle level, the van is in the garage, and the garage door is closed, so go get busy niggas."

Tony thinks to himself, *Yeah, this is a big fuck'in' house, and it's well furnished. Too bad we can't take all this shit, but this is a one-time deal, and what we can't take, we're gonna trash anyway.* Just then, Tony noticed the statues, ugly little motherfuckas about six-inches tall. He'd never seen shit like this before. He gets a closer look at one of them, and they look like little, hairy shrunken people or some shit. *Ugly motherfuckas. Oh well, fuck these rich weird fuckers. They'll be buying all new shit when we're done.*

As everyone splits up, Tony stops for a second to admire the kitchen, notices several appliances that will be coming with them, and thinks. *Man, this is some nice, top quality shit*, and goes over to the fridge.

Opening the door, and seeing all the food inside reminds him of a time growing up when, as a kid, his fridge was damn near always empty, and it never had this much food in it. That thought makes him angry, how some fuck'in' people had it so fuck'in easy, and he and his always had to struggle and always barely had enough to eat. A bowl of strawberries sitting on the center shelf catches his attention. He's not sure why though. He's never liked those motherfuckas. The damn seeds always got caught in his teeth. And then thoughts of childhood return. He can remember times asking his mother to buy certain things, and she would have to say no because they couldn't afford it. That makes him angrier, looking in this very well-stocked fridge now.

Tony again thinks how much he hates these rich, arrogant motherfuckas and how they've always looked down on him, like he's a piece of shit. *Well, I'll show these motherfuckas.* He unzips his pants and pulls his dick out, thinking to himself, *I hope I have a gallon of piss in me so I can spray all this shit.* He pisses all over the contents of the fridge. No level of the fridge is left unsprayed. Every corner of every shelf is now dripping in piss, and he purposely saves a little just for the uncovered strawberries. He laughs as he watches his piss cover the fruit and settles in the bowl. Putting his dick back in his pants, he slams the door and laughs as he walks away, shouting, "Fellas, stay out of the fridge."

Rob is quick about his work. Knowing the family has two kids, he walks quickly through the rooms and notices that each child has his own huge, fully furnished room with an adjoining bathroom and a lot of ugly-ass statues everywhere. He thinks, *Well, they can keep these motherfuckas.* He quickly spies the PS3 game systems and computers in each room and carefully unplugs the consoles and computers and moves them to the hallway. He takes a pillowcase off a pillow and stuffs every game he can find inside. He takes all the computer software in each storage rack from each room and all the music CDs he can find and the piggy banks off each dresser and thinks, *Damn, these are some heavy-ass piggy banks for kids.* He finds enough shit to fill four pillowcases.

He carries everything downstairs to the waiting van. He calls out for Tony, but he doesn't answer. He thinks, *This is a big damn house, but he still should have heard me. I heard him say some shit about the fridge. Oh, well, fuck it.* Putting the pillowcases in the van, he returns for the computers and game consoles he left in the hall and loads them in the van. Now he thinks to himself that he'll go back and get those 40-inch flat screens and go through the master bedrooms. Laughing, he says, "We hit the fucking jackpot."

Returning to the van with the TVs, he sees other goodies inside. He thinks, *The fellas ain't bullshitin'. The van is half-full with shit, and we've only been here about an hour.*

Well, let me go through the master bedrooms and see what we got, he thinks. Running up the stairs, Rob heads straight to the bedroom on the right across the hall from the kids rooms. He opens the door and says to himself, *"Goddamn, this one room is bigger than my whole fuck'in' shitty ass apartment.* Rob also notices more of those fuck'in' statues. He quickly pulls out every drawer in all four dressers and realizes that this must be a dude's room because all the clothes are men's.

He crosses the room and opens the closet door. Looking around quickly, he finds what he's looking for- a safe. But it has an electronic lock. *No time to fuck with that, he thinks. We'll just take the whole damn thing.* He runs into the hall and calls for Tony. Leaning over the banister, he yells, "Tony, I found a safe. Hey, man, where the fuck are you?" He sees Tony and Chuck returning from the van.

"What?" Tony says.

"I found a safe, man, in the first master bedroom. We can't open it now. We'll have to take the whole thing."

"Cool. Chuck, go to the van and get the dolly," Tony tells him. "Bring the safe down, and we'll load that last."

"Cool," Chuck said.

Looking at his watch, Tony tells Rob. "We're almost full, man, It's four 'clock. Check out the other bedroom so we can get the fuck outta here."

Running through the first master bedroom, Rob sees what must be an adjoining bedroom door. He turns the knob and finds it's locked. He laughs out loud and thinks, *These motherfuckas don't even sleep in the same damn bedroom. Why the fuck be married if you don't even sleep with the bitch?*

Running out of the first bedroom and down the hall, he opens the door to the second master and hits the light switch. The first thing he notices is the smell of the room. It's sweet, but not overpowering. He thinks it's almost like a light rose-type smell. The room is feminine in it's furnishings and very well decorated, like the rest of the house.

He sees what must be jewelry boxes on one of the dressers and heads right to them. Rob sees the wife's pictures on the dresser and a few on the edges of the mirror and thinks. *That ho is fine as hell. The only way a soft-assed faggot like her husband can get a bitch like this is if he's payin' for that pussy. Hell, dude is payin' and ain't even hittin it.* That thought makes him laugh out loud and think. Stupid motherfucker.

Opening the boxes, his eyes get wide. *Look at all this shit. Gold necklaces, big-ass diamond rings, and some more shit. Fuck this. We're taking all this shit.* For an instant, he thought to himself, *If they have all this shit lying around, why didn't the real workers take any of this shit? Oh, well, fuck it.* The though quickly passes.

Opening the drawers to the dresser, he quickly tosses out the contents of the first four. Nothing there of interest. Coming to the top middle drawer, he pulls it open, and it's full of her underwear, folded and neatly placed. He goes to scoop them out, and as he touches them, he feels the softness of the garments, and again he notices a very pleasant smell that momentarily distracts him. Rob also notices another of those weird-ass statues, but he could have sworn it wasn't there a moment ago. He hears a loud thumping sound coming from the stairs and jerks his head in that direction, then realizing it must be Chuck taking the safe down to the van.

Returning his attention back to the dresser and its contents, he finds himself holding many pairs of the underwear in his hands and notices that some are thong underwear and that the colors seem brighter. Again, he thinks, *I didn't notice that before.*

Looking at that hos pictures and holding her underwear in his hands, he thinks to himself how much he'd love to fuck the shit out of her. He thinks, as he looks at her picture, *I'd give you all this shit back for a piece of that pussy.* Looking at a picture of her in a bikini at the top of the mirror arouses him as he holds her underwear in his hands. He feels his dick getting hard as he stares at her picture, and the smell of the room excites him. He thinks, *This is what this bitch must smell like.* He drops her underwear in the drawer and puts his hand on his growing dick, rubbing it through his pants as he stares at her picture on the mirror.

He unzips his pants and pulls out his dick. The cool air feels good on his dick as he begins to stroke it. His dick fills his hand as he begins to pull harder but gently, imagining that it's her hand on his dick. He puts a pair of her underwear on his dick to heighten the experience, thinking that he's gonna come back by himself when she's here alone and give her all this dick. Looking at the picture of her in the bikini, he imagines she's sucking his long, full dick. It fills her mouth, and she loves it.

He strokes harder now as he sees himself pushing all his dick in her tight pussy, then up her ass. He imagines her going crazy with pleasure as he fucks her for all he's worth. He feels himself getting ready to explode. He feels the cum start to ooze from his dick. He puts his dick in the drawer. He wants to explode all over her underwear. Rob couldn't help noticing that damn statue though as he strokes his dick, and that fuck'in thing pisses him off.

He pulls his dick harder and harder. It feels good. He's ready to explode. Looking at her picture, lusting for her body, he feels himself starting to cum, and the sensation is powerful. He looks at that statue again. It's spoiling his moment, so he aims the first wad of cum right on the head of the statue. He quickly puts his dick on the top of her panties. *It feels good,* he thinks, as he puts half his dick in the drawer. Covering it with her panties, he then shoots his whole load. The pleasure he feels is overwhelming. Then he hears a loud slamming, sound and his pleasure is replaced with a sharp, numbing pain unlike anything he's ever felt. His mind goes blank for a split second, and his whole body is numb. Then he screams.

Tears roll uncontrollably down his face. He screams louder as he pleads for someone to help him. He looks down at his dick. The drawer is closed to the seam with the dresser, and his dick is caught in the middle. He screams again. The pain is beyond excruciating. He can't move, he can't pull away, and he can't drop to his knees. He can see nothing through his tears. He can only stand there and watch what's left of his dick swell, and the pain is impossibly getting worse.

Coming back from the van, Tony thinks to himself, *It's time to get the fuck outta here. We have more than enough shit, especially now that we got the safe. Let me find those two stupid motherfuckas, drop them the fuck off at their houses, and as soon as I sell this shit, I'm gonna blow town with all the money. Fuck them. That's what they get for letting me fence this shit by myself. Anyway, this was my idea. I never liked their asses anyway.*

Tony calls out to both Rob and Chuck, "Yo fellas let's wrap this shit up and get the fuck outta here. The safe's loaded. Let's roll." From the basement area, Chuck said, "Alright. I'm coming. I got this 50-inch coming up right now."

Tony responded, "You need help, man."

"No, I got it," Chuck said.

Tony looks up toward the stairs and says, "Rob, let's role." Rob heard Tony calling for him, but he could barely talk through his pain. He could only mumble, and since the door was closed, Tony couldn't hear him begging weakly for someone to help him. "Please, somebody, help me, please." Rob looked at the part of his dick that was exposed, and it looked like a short, fat balloon ready to explode. His legs were numb, and his back and head felt as if they were on fire. He also noticed his cum on the head and face of that fuck'in' statue oozing down onto the dresser.

Waiting for the others, Tony noticed a door he hadn't checked out, so he figured while he waited for the others, he may as well have a look. He opened the door, stepped inside, and turned on the light. He thought it looked like a large utility room. Two more doors faced him, but the room was empty otherwise. *Fuck this,* he thought. *There's nothing here.* Just then, the door he came through closed behind him. He walked over to it and tried the knob, but it wouldn't turn.

Chuck thought to himself as he struggled with the 50-inch that he should have gotten one of the others to help him. *There's a lot of weird-looking shit down here, and I can't get the fuck outta there fast enough. Besides the 50-inch, there are a lot of really fucked-up looking statues and shit. Oh, well, fuck it,* he thought to himself. *I just need to get this damn TV upstairs.* He knew he couldn't lay the damn thing down because that would fuck the TV up. His short arms made carrying the TV awkward. He couldn't carry it with his arms stretched lengthwise, so he had to carry it to one side, with his arms stretched in a vertical position, and he had to be careful not to bump the damn thing against the walls. It wasn't heavy, thankfully, he thought to himself. Carrying it left him walking up the stairs in an awkward way, and all the fucking steps weren't helping, he thought to himself.

He had about one flight of stairs to negotiate after this last left turn, and then he was home free, he thought. Then he can get the fuck out of here and take his new TV home. He was claiming this one no matter what Tony said. Taking the stairs one at a time because he was a bit tired, he leaned against the wall for a quick second of rest, then said to himself, *Let's do this*.

As he made his way up the stairs, he fell into the light switch, turning it off, which startled him. He tried to regain his footing, but he couldn't get his right foot off the step for some reason. Then he realized his damn shoes. He stepped on his fucking laces, and seeing that head in a glass case mounted on the wall startled him again. He lost his balance for a split second, but that's all it took for him to stumble to his left, against the wall with the TV in his outstretched arms. He lost his grip and his footing, and both he and the TV came crashing back down the stairs.

As they fell down the stairs, Chuck's head was against the screen of the TV, and on impact with the stairs' railing, his head went completely through the TV screen, up to his shoulders. His scream only lasted a second as he and the TV came to rest between the stairs' first and second rail supports.

With glass everywhere, it looked as though someone had broken a large picture frame over Chuck's head. Glass was sticking out of both eyes, and a silvery liquid all over his face was burning his skin off. He tried to shout for help, but he couldn't talk or move. The pain he found himself in screamed volumes in his now paralyzed body. As he lay there dying, he could have sworn he heard Rob and Tony say, "The hell with Chuck. He's bullshittin' in the basement, man. We gonna leave his ass here." In his mind's eye, Chuck sees them both get in the van and leave him. His last thought before death takes him is, *Why wouldn't anyone help me?*

Rob couldn't stand the pain anymore. His whole body was in excruciating pain. His legs we're numb, the pain in his back and head was horrible, and every time he tried to use his free hand to open the drawer to free his dick, pain shot through his body at the slightest movement.

The tears wouldn't stop flowing, and now he sees blood seeping from the bottom of the drawer. His legs getting so weak he can no longer support himself, he feels himself fall backward, and as he does so, the pain of his dick tearing off his body is horrific. Blood spurting everywhere in huge quantities, he lands on his side, hands between his legs, covered in his own blood. Whimpering now because he has no energy to scream for help, he lies there totally helpless, slowly and painfully bleeding to death. He thinks he hears Chuck and Tony downstairs talking. "Man, look, fuck Rob's punk ass. We gotta roll outta this motherfucka now." In his mind's eye, he sees the van pull away and wonders why he had to die this way.

Tony turns the doorknob, but it won't budge. He pounds on the door and shouts for help. "Hey, Rob, Chuck, open this damn door. It's stuck and won't open."

He tries the other two doors, and they too are looked. He tries kicking on both, but all that accomplishes is pain in his legs. He looks around. There are no windows in this room, only a drain in the floor. And there's nothing to help smash the doors open, so he keeps pounding and shouting for help. Since no one comes to aid him, he starts thinking that maybe they left him.

That thought infuriates Tony, He thinks to himself, *I know those motherfucka's didn't leave me. This was my gig.* Angered now by the thought of his boys leaving him behind, he hits the door harder. He moves from one to the other in a mad fury, pounding the doors and screaming for one of them to get him the fuck out of here.

He bangs on the doors for what seems like hours. Both hands and feet hurting and sore from the pounding, he stops, looks at his watch, and realizes it's 5 PM. They have to get the fuck out of there, but he thinks, *How the fuck can I get out of here if I'm trapped in this damn room?* He screams in rage, "Let me out of here. Somebody open this goddamn door."

He rests against the wall for a while after his last futile attempt to break through the doors. Both hands are now sore and swollen. As he sits down on the floor enveloped in the silence of the room, he thinks he hears voices. They sound far away, but he can just barely make out what they're saying.

"Fuck Tony, bitch motherfucka. Let's leave his ass here."

"Yeah, we searched this motherfucka, and he's not here."

"The hell with him. Come on, let's get the fuck outta here."

His heart starts to pound in his chest. Rage fills him with new strength. He pounds harder on the door he came through and shouts,

"Open this fuck'in' door. You motherfuckas better not leave here. I'm gonna kill you motherfuckas. Get me the fuck outta here." His cries go unanswered. He thinks he hears the van start and pull away. They are gone.

Tony hears a hissing sound come from the vent in the floor. He turns to see what's happening. He doesn't see anything, but there is foul odor coming from somewhere. He thinks it smells like a dead fuckin' animal, no hundreds of dead fuckin' animals.

The smell assaults all his senses. Without conscious thought, he immediately covers his mouth and nose and holds his breath. That does him no good. The smell is overpowering. He gags and vomits. He vomits uncontrollably for what seems like hours. He knows his stomach contents are gone, but still he gags violently. Then he starts to vomit blood. It shoots out of his mouth like water through a hose. The smell of death in the room is so thick and powerful that his eyes burn. Then they start to bleed.

His eyes no longer work, and every breath is torture. He brings his hands up to his face, and touching his skin increases his agony. It feels as if his skin is melting off his face. He lies on the floor in a pool of blood and vomit, jerking and twitching like a fish out of water.

Incredibly, through all his suffering, he thinks about all the horrible things he's done in his useless life, all the crimes he's committed, the people he's hurt, all the women he's abused and raped, all the children he fathered but never attempted to take care of. He thinks of all of this, and in the instant before death takes him, he realizes what a fuckin' waste his life has been.

A white, unmarked van returns Saturday morning. The van is backed up into the empty garage bay, the door closes, and the van exits the property at precisely 6 PM.

Monday morning, the bank manager returns to work. All the employees acknowledge him as he passes by. He arrogantly nods his head in the direction of those greeting him as he heads to his office, carrying his briefcase and a rather large gift bag.

Carla notices that he almost looks happy today as he was not wearing his usual smirk that greets everyone on a daily basis every morning. Well whatever, she thinks. *I don't have to deal with him and as long as he leaves me the fuck alone,* I'm good.

Carla was about to go to lunch when she was summoned to the bank manager's office. She thought, *Goddamnit, I was having a good day. What does he want?* Carla had only been in his office on a few occasions. She made it a habit to avoid him and his office whenever possible. She was hungry, so she figured, *What the hell., Get it over with and go eat*.

Carla knocked on the door. "Please come in, Carla." She does so and is directed to take a seat on the other side of his desk. Carla sits down and sees a bowl of strawberries on the desk and three unusual-looking little statuettes, *ugly little motherfuckas* she thinks to herself.

"Carla, would you care for some strawberries?" He lifts the bowl and says, "Please, take as many as you like. I love strawberries, and these are a very special kind. They where treated with a very special kind of care just for me. So please enjoy them." Carla reaches out and takes three of the strawberries. She likes them, so maybe fat boy isn't all that bad, she thinks.

As she brings a large berry to her mouth, she stops just short of biting it when something peculiar catches her attention. She really takes notice of those ugly fuck'in statues. Something about one of them seems familiar. She knows she's never seen those motherfuckas before, but there is something familiar about them.

"Oh, I see you've noticed my figurines. I got these three while I was on vacation. I call them the three blind mice. Yes, these three cost me a bit and made quite a mess of my finances to acquire them, but they were worth every penny."

"Notice the one in the middle," the manager says. He didn't need to though. Carla saw why it was familiar to her. Just as she put the strawberry in her mouth and bit down, her heart started to race just a little.

The middle figure has on a little silver necklace with a ring at the end, an exact match for the necklace and ring she gave Tony. It was her class ring from high school. Her eyes zero in closer, as if they are magnifying glasses. As she chews the strawberry, she is almost mesmerized by the figurine. Its twisted face seems familiar. The taste of the strawberry is also familiar, and then something hits her with a clarity that seems totally impossible.

The thought comes to her with such clarity that it feels like someone hit her with a baseball bat, and her heart starts to pound in her chest. She thinks to herself, *Bullshit. This is impossible. That fuck'in thing looks like Tony, even with the face all fucked up*. Sitting at his desk with his hands clasped together on top of his desk and an almost evil looking smile on his face, the manager says, "Carla, let me tell you why I wanted to see you." Carla's begins to tremble as he speaks. "We need to discuss your future at this bank. Oh, by the way, did you enjoy your strawberries?"

Sometimes hate is a good thing. It helps you to overcome your fear and do what you know is right.

Infestation

Perhaps you worry every day of your life that you will slip up. You know you're an illegal in the U.S. and the authorities will catch you, that someone will challenge your status. It frightens you to your core, knowing you'll be caught one day and deported to your country of origin, never to see your new family again. You fear you'll be sent back to that filthy land you escaped from, back to a living hell you'd rather forget. Remember this: Anyone who has something to hide knows fear. Now you have something new to fear, and it's not the police.

There is an interesting letter circulating on the Internet, and it's gaining momentum and more readers everyday.

***

My fellow Americans, I have an urgent message that concerns all of you., What I have to tell you is frightening and disturbing, but this topic needs to be understood by all American citizens. I urge you to please listen to what I have to say, and then you decide.

America is being destroyed from within. Our society is being ravaged by illegal immigrants from all over the world that swarm over our borders by the thousands like insects each day. They burrow into our cities and towns like maggots feeding on a corpse and infest our nation like cockroaches, and the worst of this group and the first we'll deal with is the Mexicans.

We can no longer count on our government to protect us or defend our borders. Our politicians are too concerned with counting votes and being politically correct while at the same time stealing our hard-earned money and giving it away to deal with this issue.

We as American citizens, who have the right to protect our homes and communities, must now take a stand or our society is doomed, Illegal aliens come to this country and contribute absolutely nothing to our society. What they do bring is crime and poverty to our neighborhoods and overcrowding to our schools. They pack our jails and destroy our housing and economic markets. They don't pay taxes, and they put a strain on our economy.

Go into any hospital in America, and you will see dozens of illegal Mexican men and pregnant women with multiple babies in tow using our hospital emergency rooms as their own private clinics, with absolutely no way to pay for the services they demand. They don't care about the cost to American taxpayers. Go into any fast-food restaurant or convenience store, and the cashiers barely speak English. You place your order multiple times to the same idiot, and they look at you as if you lost your damn mind because you don't speak their fucking language. And on top of that, these illegal fuckers act as if you are the inconvenience to them, like it's an American's privilege to be served by ignorant illegal aliens!

We as Americans need to stand up and shout out loud, "We speak English in this country, not Spanish, not French, not Italian, not German, not African. You are now in America, legal or otherwise, and the least you can fucking do is learn the language."

This should not be tolerated in America. Those illegal fucking Mexicans come here over and under our borders and act like they are doing us a favor.

Mexicans have taken over our service industries. Africans control our airports and taxi services nationwide. Middle Eastern terrorists now infiltrate our society on every level. Europeans, Asians, and Canadians bleed our economy to the point that we can barely compete with the rest of the world, and the U.S. dollar is almost worthless.

My brothers and sisters, you have to understand there are many threats that we must deal with and many struggles from within that are destroying us. It makes no difference what the color of your skin is or where you live or your economic status. If your great-grandparents were born and raised in this country, you're an American, and this is your cause. We are being conquered from within, and we must develop contingency plans to deal with this on our own. The first group we must put down are those fucking lazy, uneducated Mexicans who come here and overtly, illegally, and proudly break our laws then want to demand rights they haven't fought for or earned. They don't care that we have American vets who have fought in wars to protect this nation living on the streets of every major city in this country. My grandfather fought in WWII, and I'm a Vietnam vet, and our own government and politicians turned their backs on us.

They don't care that we have American families who have fallen on hard times living on the streets who can't get help from their government. Our senior citizens who have lived and paid taxes here all their lives have to struggle and beg for the benefits they've earned. Our young people can't even find work in the goddamn fast-food industry anymore. In my day, teenagers were expected to work in fast-food and other convenience-type industries. These were the first real jobs many of us had when we were in junior high and high school. Now they are the domain of illegal Mexicans.

Our elected officials love to be seen making the sound bites on the evening news. Sure, they'll say our vets and young people in general are the future of our nation and how proud they are when they're in front of the cameras, but ask any injured vet of any conflict how hard it is to get any politician's or government's help-federal, state or local, it makes no difference-we know the reality is totally different when the cameras are turned off. Our own president has failed our vets, young people, and the country.

Those same politicians who can't help their own people would freely open our borders to illegals and welcome them with open arms into our nation, assisting them with financial aid, housing, and employment.

Our country is being overrun by Mexicans, Europeans, Asians, Middle Eastern fucking terrorists, Indians, Africans, and those disgusting marijuana-smoking Caribbeans, These fucking leeches come here and put honest, hard-working Americans out of work because our businesses can get away with paying these illegal fuckers pennies on the dollar.

I have witnessed firs hand American teenagers being turned away from employment in many fast-food restaurants because they're filled with old Asian men and women and Mexicans who can barely speak English, if at all.

You as an American need to witness first hand the hurt on a teen's face when they go to seek out that first job at a fast-food restaurant or convenience store and are turned away by an illegal fucking alien who's an employee and who tells our children, "We no hire now. Go way." And our children are ridiculed and called names in foreign languages because they want to work in their neighborhoods. You, as a parent, a citizen, an American, should be outraged by this. Our young people are being supplanted by illegals and are being made to feel useless in their own society, and we're allowing it to happen.

It's time for this bullshit to come to an end. I am not advocating the overthrowing of our government or civil disturbances of any kind. Our plan is to take back our communities from within one at a time. We will start with ridding our communities of the Mexican infestations.

As you are all aware of by now, many communities across the country have allowed illegal Mexicans to set up day-labor sites, where they can gather like packs of feral animals and wait for people to offer them work. It is at these sites where my plan is set into motion.

Read the story of how a small, northern Virginia community got rid of unwanted illegals and how our crusade to save America began.

***

Every morning at 8 AM, Enoch and Jose would join other men at the corner neighborhood 7-11 and wait for individual people or business owners who needed laborers for work. It didn't matter what the work was, from landscaping to painting to hauling trash, skilled or unskilled labor, as long as it paid in cash for that day's work.

Jose noticed that each week, there were fewer and fewer workers coming out. But that was no big deal. There'd be more work for the rest of them.

Jose didn't really enjoy doing this kind of work, but it was all he could find. He knew he didn't speak English very well, and he was in the country illegally, just like his friend Enoch, who he's known for more than a year. Even though he liked Enoch, he didn't completely trust him. Jose hoped for a better life in America, which is why he came here. He needed to make money to support his girlfriend and their child, so for now, he thought, *this is better than committing crimes to pay the rent*, which is what he did before he met Enoch. He didn't have many regrets for the crimes he committed against whites. He didn't like or trust them, but he had to work for them to support himself for the time being. But he knew one day that would change.

Jose's routine was the same every day. Go to the 7-11 every morning, buy a cup of coffee for one dollar using the five bucks he carried each morning which was for his lunch also, stand around for hours until someone came by offering work, and try to ignore the dirty looks people would give him and the ugly things they would say to all the men there who just wanted to work. This also included watching out for the police and government men who would come to the location sometimes with the police to drive them away. Well, today is Friday, he thought, so he could deal with it for another day since he took the weekend off.

As he waited for a work offer to come his way, he saw his buddy Enoch talking to a man in a pickup truck. The man he was talking to was white, and the guy in the driver's seat was black, and Enoch thought to himself, *this might be a job*. The thought excited him because usually white men in pickup trucks meant that a businessman wanted men for jobs that could pay up to one hundred dollars a day and could last for a few days. The thought cheered him up because if this was a good-paying job he could take his family to dinner tonight and maybe a movie.

Jose watched Enoch take something from the white man and leave. Then the truck pulled off. He thought to himself, *maybe that wasn't for work. Maybe Enoch is up to something illegal again*. Jose thought to himself that he was done with that life. He promised his girl, no more crimes or she would take their kid and leave him. It didn't matter though what Enoch was up to. If it wasn't real work, He wasn't going to get involved. He looked at his watch, and it was only 9 AM. He knew by 12 noon, all the men here would be on jobs somewhere, so he thought, *no big deal*, It was just a matter of time.

Enoch approached him, smiling, and said he had good news. Jose asked him in Spanish what was the news. Enoch told him that the guy he was just talking to in the pickup truck was looking for five men for some major landscaping work, and the job paid two hundred dollars a day and would last for at least a week. Two hundred dollars a day was good money, Jose said.

"When do we get started?"

"He wants us to be ready for pickup at 10 AM." Enoch explained to him that first he would have to pick three other men to go with them and explain what kind of work they would be doing, then he was to call the guy back on the phone he gave him.

Jose said, "That's what he gave you?"

"A phone?" "Yeah, I'm gonna be like the foreman for this crew." They both laughed, and Enoch said, "come on, bro. let's go find three more guys."

After recruiting three more workers—which wasn't very difficult considering the money they would be paid— Enoch called the man back for pickup. After Enoch got off the phone, Jose asked him if anyone would be checking for their legal status on this job. All the other workers gathered around to hear the answer.

Enoch told the men what was told to him. "No one cares where we're from. All they want is a few days of landscaping labor. Water and food will be provided each day, and we get paid in cash at the end of each day." That brought smiles to the faces of all the men. Since they were all here illegally but still needed to work to support themselves and their families, if they had families.

Enoch made the call, and their employer was there promptly at 10 AM. He arrived at the site in a white minivan. The five men got in the back, and they drove off for the work site. Inside the van, the passenger, William, in the front seat, explained to the men that they would be performing various landscaping duties. (Enoch translated in Spanish for those who didn't speak English very well.) There would be some planting, lawn work, hauling away of debris, and digging drainage trenches, and they'd be using several kinds of tools. Each man acknowledged they understood and smiled.

He also explained that the men would be provided water and food for the time they worked at the site at no cost to them. After the work was explained to them, William asked if anyone had any questions. The men all looked at each other smiling and shook their heads, all except Jose, who asked, "Where is the site, and when do we get off?"

William explained that the work site was an hour away, off Interstate 15, and that today's work would be completed by 4:30 PM. "Since it's Friday, we're gonna cut you guys loose early, and Monday morning we'll start at the same time and work till 5 PM."

William and the driver exchanged knowing looks with each other as they drove to the site. Thirty minutes into the drive, William offered the men a bottle of Gatorade from the cooler he had up front. Each man took a bottle. William also took a bottle, opened it, and said, "Drink up, men, We're gonna need our strength. It's gonna be hot today." Everyone downed there bottles contents.

Thirty minutes later, everyone in the back of the van was sound asleep. William looked in the back of the van and saw they were all knocked out. He then proceeded to check each man, shaking them to ensure they were asleep. "Scott, they're all knocked out."

"Good. Now tie there asses up good and tight with the flex cuffs and put the hoods over their heads."

"I'm on it", William said. As William tied the men up, he removed all the contents of their pants and jackets and placed the items in a canvas sack. He went through each wallet, removing any money he found, and discarded everything else into the sack. Any jewelry the men were wearing was also removed and placed in a separate small, metal box.

"William, you find anything interesting?"

"No. The usual shit, a few dollars on each guy, and they all wore a crucifix of some kind. How much longer till we get there?"

"About another twenty minutes."

"Good. I have other shit to do this evening after I dump their crap," William said. "Don't worry, my friend. We'll both be done before rush hour."

***

They pulled off the highway and continued into the woods for another few miles until they reached their destination. There was nothing around for miles in any direction of the location they had chosen for the dump site. The van came to stop in a heavily wooded area surrounded by tall trees and thick bushes.

Scott pulled the van alongside three other vehicles that were waiting at the location. He and William got out to greet the other men who had been waiting for them. After they all greeted each other Scott said, "let's get on with it and get the hell outta here. Is the perimeter secure?"

"Yeah" Harold said. "It's clear for two miles. John and Frank are leaving now to post as lookouts."

"Alright, then let's get our guests of honor outta the van," said Scott. William, Scott, and Harold went to the van, pulled each man out, carried them a few yards away down to a clearing, and laid them out in a straight line next to a large pit.

After the men were laid out, Scott and Harold each lit a cigarette while William drove the pickup down to the clearing and maneuvered the trailer so that it was positioned several feet away from the pit. As William exited the van, he said to both men, "Those stinking things are gonna kill your old asses." All three men laughed, and Scott said, "Hell, we all gotta go some day. Might as well enjoy some things while you can." Harold looked over to the bound and hooded men and noticed they were starting to move, "Hey, fellas, our boys are starting to wake up. William, start the motor," Harold said "okay, Scott, give me a hand with this," said William.

Returning to the bound men, Harold and William sat them up and placed them back to back in a circle facing the pit. The men started to curse and shout protests but were quickly silenced when they heard what sounded like shotguns being racked and each man felt a barrel against his head.

Scott began to speak. "Now that we have your attention, I want you illegal fuckers to know something. We don't want you here. We don't need you here. We're tired of you motherfuckers destroying what it's taken us Americans years to build, and now it's time for the Mexican invasion of our country to come to an end, at least for you four anyway. And there will be thousands joining you in the months to follow, until you fuckers realize we don't want you here. For years your people have flooded our cities and taken our jobs. No more. A new day for America is coming.

"Harold, remove the hoods. It doesn't matter now." Each tied man looked around to see the faces of their captors.

"We tried to be civil with you fuckers, but you wouldn't listen. If I thought letting you go with a promise to never come back to our town would work then we wouldn't be here. That's been tried, and it failed, because you people always come back, like roaches, and the best way to get rid of roaches is to exterminate them."

The men listened to Harold as he spoke, looking at him through tears of blind terror. Bound as they were, they knew what was to come. They were going to die here. They all shouted protests and pleaded for there lives to be spared, speaking in both Spanish and English and trying desperately to free themselves to no avail.

Harold told William to get things ready, and he continued to speak. "You see, that's part of the problem. I can't understand a damn thing you're saying. You see, I don't speak Spanish. "None of us do. And we sure as hell ain't gonna learn. But I know you fuckers understand every word I'm saying."

"You see, every man here has been a victim of one crime or another committed against us by one of you—maybe not you personally, but one of your people. It doesn't really matter now, but at the time, it was hard for us to understand why, for years, the crime rates were low and nothing really major occurred, then in the early 80's, when you people came swarming in, everything changed."

"Now we have to deal with gangs, home invasions, armed robberies, drug trafficking, and our children being afraid to go to school because of you fuckers. So we got together and came up with a solution to our problem. Since you people won't go away, we've decided to get rid of you permanently."

"You're all too spread out to get you all at once, but once you people are entrenched in a community, it's hard to get you out. So we decided that, before you have the chance to send for all your relatives and friends to join you here, we'd make it easy for the men to gather in one place to get work. And since you stupid fuckers are afraid of the police, if any or all of you turned up missing, you wouldn't report it. I'll let you in on a little secret. The police chief, members of the town council, and people in the mayor's office are with us too. So you people have good reason to be afraid of the police and everyone else here in authority."

The men trembled and continued crying as Scott spoke. "The beauty of the whole plan though is that just as you destroy our communities from the inside, we will solve our problem the same way. Come here, Enoch. We brought in one of your own to join us, our inside man," Scott said. Jose couldn't believe his eyes. His heart pounded in his chest, and now tears of anger and betrayal poured down his face. It was as if someone tore out his still-beating heart as he realized the person he called his friend was a part of this. Jose begged Enoch to let him go. He pleaded for his life, trying to remind Enoch of his child and girlfriend waiting at home for him. Enoch knelt down in front of Jose and told him, laughing, that there was nothing he could do for him. "you all gotta die, bro. You see, this is how I make my money. But don't worry about Rosa. I will personally take care of her. Yeah, man, I plan on fucking her every night." he tapped Jose's foot and walked away laughing.

"Enoch, come on, let's get rolling." The four men each went to the trailer. A large canvas tarp was removed from the large machine it covered. Meanwhile, William and Harold tied gags around the men's mouths. The captured men tried to resist, but they could do nothing as they each realized what was about to happen. Begging in muffled voices that could not be heard by anyone and crying like babies, their eyes bulged from their sockets and their terror intensified as Harold started the machine. The roar of the motor increased their horror tenfold. "William, do you smell something? "Yeah, man, they're shiting themselves", he said to Harold, laughing. "Happens all the time."

Enoch and Scott positioned the chute over a hole four feet wide and eight feet deep. When the captured men awoke, a large canvas tarp covered the hole. Now the cover was removed, and they knew they were staring at their grave. Scott told the others to bring one. "Let's get started." Enoch turned the huge, heavy-duty wood chipper to full power, increasing the roar of the machine. Scott and William lifted a very large piece of wood and fed it through the chipper. It was gone in seconds. "Okay, we're ready." said Scott.

The bound man could do nothing, even though he tried to resist with all his strength, all his will to survive. He was totally helpless as two of his captors violently snatched him to, then off his feet and carried him to the giant wood chipper.

He cried, kicking and screaming in a muffled voice as his head drew closer and closer to the giant spinning metal teeth of the machine. The terror on his face and in his eyes was unimaginable. As he realizes he is seconds away from meeting a horrible death, he hears a voice say, "Don't worry. You won't feel a thing." He was thrown into the chipper head first. The machine made quick work of his flesh and bone. The other captured men watched in abstract horror as his head was gone in seconds. They faced the front of the machine, so they were all able to watch his body thrashing horribly like a giant puppet who's strings had been cut. When the body stopped moving because the teeth of the chipper couldn't get a grip on the rest of it, they used a long two-by-four to push the lower half of the corpse to the teeth of the machine. It was gone in seconds.

What came out of the chute was a red liquid soup of muscle, flesh, bone, and shredded clothes. The sound of the now crushed body being ground up and mangled by the chipper was akin to water sputtering through a garden hose. The now totally crushed and mangled body lay at the bottom of an eight foot deep hole. The mass barely covered the bottom of the hole.

In went the next man, screaming muffled screams of terror and trying to plead for his life. Harold said to the condemned man as he was carried to his impending death, "Look here, boy. We're not cruel. That's why we put you in head first. If we wanted you to suffer, you'd go in feet first." "And besides, you fuckers brought this on yourselves. Maybe your next life will be better." They threw him in the machine forcefully, head first, laughing as his body was consumed in seconds and spit out the chute into his grave. The look on Jose's face was one of pure horror and disbelief, knowing he would soon be next.

William and Enoch came for the third man, who was so terrorized by what he'd seen, he'd passed out from shock. "Passing out is not going to save your ass," Enoch said as he snatched the man to his feet. As he did so shit slid down both pant legs, "Damn, this motherfucker shitted all over himself."

Enoch let his tied body fall to the ground. The man did not move. William looked at the fallen, helpless captive closely. He bent down to check the pulse at the neck, but there wasn't one.

"Scott, we lost our first one to a heart attack," William shouted. "Damn, that is a first," Scott said as he looked at the now dead Mexican. "Okay, throw his stinking ass in. What the hell, he's already dead."

Jose watched in horror as another body was sucked into the chipper. The sound of the body being destroyed left him trembling uncontrollably, knowing he was next. Enoch looked at Jose and said, "You're next to go, bro." As Enoch and William approached him, Jose tried to plead for his life, looking deeply into Enoch's eyes for some sign of compassion, but his words were stifled by the gag. He tried to struggle, but his efforts proved to be futile. With tears streaming down his face and piss freely flowing down his legs, his muffled screams became louder and louder as they brought him closer and closer to the death machine.

Enoch talked to Jose as they approached the chipper, telling him how much he was going to enjoy fucking Rosa and making her suck his dick with their small child watching. He told Jose he was going to make Rosa his bitch, and she was going to love it. This drove Jose into a mad frenzy. He tried to shake loose of their grip, pulling and kicking, trying to get away, but it was no use. All the while, Enoch taunted him.

"Scott, can we do him legs first? I want to hear him scream." William said, "Enoch you're one sick dude." William turned toward Scott after Enoch made that statement.

"We are not evil men. We don't do this for the joy of killing or making people suffer. There is a purpose in what we do here, and I won't have you turn this into some kind of game for your enjoyment. Hell no, he's not going in feet first. Put him in head first like the others," said Scott.

As they approached the machine, Jose's cries became louder and louder, just as he had heard from the other men. He now knew their terror, their horror, their sorrow, as he was lifted off his feet and tilted toward the opening. He could hear Enoch laughing and the count as he was swung back and forth. "One"... Jose thought of his baby son and how he'd never see him grow into a man and how sorry he was for that. He asks for his son's forgiveness. "two"... He sees Rosa in his mind's eye and how beautiful she is. He remembers her gentleness and how her smile always comforted him and how warm her body felt. Now he cries because he feels sorrow for the life she must live without him and sorrow for bringing her to this country. "Three"...In his mind, he says good-bye to everyone he has ever cared for. He knows it's time to die. he approaches death head first, and he feels the indescribable pain of the top of his skull being crushed, the flesh being torn from his face, then nothing.

Enoch used the two-by-four to feed Jose's lifeless body into the chipper, forcefully thrusting the wood into the now lifeless corpse as it is consumed and spat out into the pit.

"Ok, boys that'll do it for today. Let's get this shit cleaned up and get outta here." Enoch fed all the two-by-fours they used into the chipper, as well as several large pieces of wood. The others gathered up the canvas covers and threw them into the blood-and-flesh filled pit as Enoch continued to feed wood into the chipper.

Scott was backing up the F-150 that was carrying a fifty-gallon drum of cleaning solution, which Enoch would use to clean and wash the chipper. William, Harold, and Scott talked and smoked cigarettes while they watched the equipment being cleaned.

Scott brought out three shovels after they packed up all the other tools and the cleaning equipment, and he radioed for John and Frank to come in. The last task to be performed for the day was to fill in the pit. As the three men started to shovel dirt into the pit, John and Frank walked up. Enoch asked Scott how long it would take to get back to town. Enoch said, "Rosa's pussy is waiting for him" laughing, Enoch continued to shovel dirt into the pit.

"Well, you know, Enoch I don't think you're gonna make it back to town." Scott looked at Frank, and the next sound heard was a shotgun blast and Enoch screaming, holding what was left of his left leg. It was blown off below the knee. Screaming and gasping for air, Enoch said, "I'm one of you." Why? "You see, Enoch, Scott continued, you have to understand something. First off, you were never one of us. Second, fuckers like you are the reason we want all you illegal bastards out of our country. The sheriff gave us your name and the list of crimes you've committed, and after a little persuasion on my part, I convinced him to let us deal with you. We've been watching you and your boy Jose for weeks now. All we had to do was offer you a few dollars, and the thought of you having his women turned you into an animal. Look what you did. You turned on him faster than shit. How the fuck could you think you'd ever be one of us? You're not an American, motherfucker. You're barely fuck'in human. We hate everything you're about. And soon, all real Americans will join us in ridding our country of your kind."

Crying and holding his leg, Enoch knew he was soon to die. William said, "Do we let his ass bleed to death, or do we finish him off now?

"I'm tired of hearing him scream. Gag his ass and throw him in the pit with his friends." John twirled a towel and stuffed it in his mouth while William secured it with a flex cuff. Screaming and crying, Enoch tried to plead for them to not do this. The thought of being buried alive in human remains and in agony was driving him insane.

"Bye Enoch. You'll be dead soon."

He was pushed into the pit.

Enoch couldn't stand up. He found himself submerged and drowning in human remains. The gag in his mouth allowed the pit's contents to flow freely in his mouth and nose. The pain of his lost leg was unbearable but soon forgotten when the stench and the taste of the nearly liquefied bodies entered his mouth and nose. He tried to spit out his mouth's contents, but he couldn't. Then the dirt started to rain down on him and darkness soon followed. He cried tears of blood as the dirt mixed with the liquefied bodies of the dead and turned to quicksand. He soon sank to the bottom. He died knowing what no human should ever know in life—what it really means to go to hell.

When your heart is ripped out, what do you have left? The fear is gone

A Father's Sorrow

Donna was running late. It was 10 AM. She had quite a few things to get done today, and she didn't want to get backed up. She figured she'd stop by the cleaners before she went to the mall. She needed to pick up Michael's suits before he had a fit. He constantly reminded her of the fact that she didn't have to work and only had the baby to take care of, so there was no excuse for her not to get more done during the day.

Michael also never let her forget he had to work his ass off to support them. Donna got so tired of hearing how she does nothing except lie around the house all day getting fat, while he has to bust his ass at work. As if taking care of his fucking house isn't work.

When Donna thought about these things, it made her so mad, she could barely think straight. She decided to call her best friend Julie to vent while she drove to the cleaners.

"Hello, Julie. What's up girl?

"I'm fine, Donna. How are things with you and the new house?"

"I don't know. Okay I guess. Michael is driving me crazy. I hate it here, and I miss you," Donna tells her friend.

"I miss you too, girl. What's going on down there in Hicksville?" Julie asks.

"It's Michael and his attitude about shit since we've been here. He's driving me crazy. It was his fucking idea for me to quit my job and for us to move to this fucking town in the middle of nowhere North Carolina after the baby was born." Donna tells her friend.

"You know, my mom told me it might be a good idea for me to support his plans. It sounded good at the time, but, Julie, it's not working out," Donna says.

"Well, Donna, try to stick it out. He's probably having a hard time too. You know you will always have me to talk to," Julie tells her friend.

"But, Julie, my mom and Michael kept telling me I need to spend quality time with Heather. That wasn't a problem for me, but Michael's selfish ass got that new fucking job as a partner in that damn real estate development firm making all this money. So he decided how things were going to go, so for the first few years of the baby's life, I could take care of her and stay home," she tells Julie.

"But, Julie, the real reason Michael wanted to make this clean start was because he wouldn't hear of anyone else watching his kid—not our kid, his kid. Not even my mother could watch her. She volunteered to baby-sit if I returned to work."

"Well, Donna, you know how men are. They just do shit without thinking things through. That's why he needs you," Julie says.

"You're right about that. Hey Julie, I'm almost at his cleaners. Let me call you back when I get home."

"Okay Donna. You know I'm always here for you," Julie says.

"Okay girl, I'll call you later this evening."

Shaking her head in disgust, Donna turned her thoughts back to driving and all she had to get done today. Coming up on the cleaners, she wondered, *How the hell did he ever find this place?* There were three or four dry cleaners in the immediate area where they lived that were closer. This damn place was out in the goddamn boonies. *Talking to Julie felt good,* Donna thinks to herself. She really misses her best friend.

Donna pulled up into the parking area, put the car in park, and looked at the dashboard clock. It said 10:35 AM. She'd be okay time-wise, she thought. She turned to look at little Heather in the back car seat. she was wide eyed and smiling that big, toothless baby smile. Donna said, "Mommy will be right back, sweetie." Donna took the clothes that had to be put in for cleaning from the front and back seats and went inside.

Ten minutes later, she was back in the car. She hung up Michael's suits on the front hook above the front passenger's seat and headed home. As she drove, she couldn't help but think of all the shit she'd been through in the last nine months since Heather was born.

Michael had changed. He seemed so distant. *It's almost like he blames me for getting pregnant. I admit at twenty-four I didn't plan on having a kid. But during the pregnancy, he was so supportive, and I thought he was happy with the situation. Like him, I just graduated from college and was looking forward to starting my career too.*

I know a paralegal job doesn't pay the best, but it could have alleviated the pressure on him. But, no. Mister fucking macho decided he'd take care of us, so I can stay home with the baby.

Thinking about all this made Donna's head hurt. She decided to concentrate on driving and finishing her tasks for the day. After she dropped Michael's suits home, she had to hit the mall, then she and the baby would come back home, rest for a while, and then go grocery shopping. *And he says I don't get anything done,* she thought to herself.

Donna pulled into the driveway at 11:15 AM, grabbed Michael's suits and went around to the rear passenger-side door to get the baby. She opened the passenger-side door, and a panic she'd never experienced took hold of her entire body. Heather was gone.

Donna wanted to pass out, but she knew she couldn't. Her baby had been stolen from her. She took out her cell phone and called the police, then she called Michael. The only thought that crossed her mind was, *how do I tell Michael our child is missing*? Her heart almost stopped when he answered the phone.

"Hello, Michael speaking."

"Michael, you need to come home." "What's the problem?"

Crying and hysterical, Donna tried to explain what had happened, that someone had taken Heather out of the car while she was at the dry cleaners and that she didn't notice the baby was gone until she got home because she assumed she was in her seat asleep. She didn't notice until she got home. Michael couldn't believe what he was hearing. This had to be some twisted joke she was playing on him. He kept thinking, *This can't be happening*. "I'll be right home," he said.

Donna stood outside crying and looking at the now empty car seat, as if staring at it would bring her baby back home. She kept playing and replaying events in her mind. She was only in the cleaners a few minutes.

She thought she'd kept a close eye on the car the whole time. She wanted to die. The only thought that crossed her mind now was, where was her baby, her precious nine-month-old little girl? Donna leaned against the car and cried uncontrollably.

The police pulled up fifteen minutes after her call. Two officers approached her. She was still outside crying when they arrived. They identified themselves and explained to Donna that they received the call about a missing baby. Donna tried her best to explain through tears what had happened. One officer took notes while his partner talked on his radio. The officers then tried their best to calm her down. Once inside the house, Donna tried to compose herself, knowing she needed to have a calm mind to explain this all again to her husband.

As Michael pulled up to the house, he saw two police cruisers in the driveway. His heart was pounding in his chest. He didn't know what to think. All he could do was think about his little girl. He parked his car and ran for the house. Before he could get there, an officer who was dusting Donna's car for prints stops him and asked that he identify himself. Michael explained that he's the owner and is allowed to go in.

***

Todd called Kyle on his cell and told him he'd found them a new target and to bring his gun and plenty of ammo. When Kyle asked why, Todd told him he had a major surprise for him. Todd told Kyle to meet him at their usual location in the woods in thirty minutes.

Thirty minutes later Kyle arrives and asks Todd what's going on. Todd explains, "Remember how we always used to say we wish we had something other than birds and dogs to shoot at, something exciting that wouldn't die on us right away?" Kyle responds, and Todd says he has a target that can't fly, run, or tell on them.

Todd tells Kyle to look in the box on the stump. Kyle walks to the box, takes a look, and says, "Man, you're a genius." A baby girl. Where did you get it? This is the coolest idea you've ever had. This should last for hours, and you're right, no one will ever know. They looked at each other and started laughing.

What happened for the next few hours was beyond anything any sane person could ever possibly imagine. The boys undressed the baby and sat the child in a plastic crate, tying both of her hands to opposite sides of the crate to make sure that the baby couldn't sit for long. Sitting down the baby's head barely came over the edge of the crate. The boys then hoisted the crate about ten feet off the ground, securing it between two trees.

They unbagged their gas-powered pellet rifles and took out all the ammo they brought with them, loaded their weapons, and started off the atrocity. Todd said, "Watch me take that stupid smile off her little fat face with my first shot." And they began shooting the baby from opposite angles with pellets.

The look on the child's face was horrific and indescribable as the first pellet hit her. She cried out, tears pouring down her face. She looked around as if she were trying to find her protectors but couldn't.

Her little body jerked horribly from the pain that was being inflicted upon it with each shot.

Welts and open wounds were appearing all over her tiny body as the stinging pellets made contact with her fragile skin. The helpless baby could do nothing but shed tears and bleed, her little body shaking and contorting in a vain attempt to avoid the pain. Her tormentors watched and laughed at her in the crate as the stinging pain rained down on her. She tried to sit, but every time she tried. There was more stinging pain. Her little eyes filled with blood as the skin was slowly ripped from her head and face by the multiple hits of the pellets.

They prolonged the baby's torture for as long as they could. At first they would take one shot at a time, first one firing then the other. Then they would stop to smoke, re-load, take a piss, or do the drugs Todd had brought with him.

After two hours, the baby stopped moving, her blood dripping to the ground between the openings in the bottom of the crate until no more blood could be seen dripping to the ground. They decided she must be dead. To make sure, each boy aimed one shot at the now blood covered baby's eyes and fired. Mercifully, the baby didn't move.

The torture of the child in combination with the drugs they had taken left the boys feeling euphoric. They high-fived each other and swore that from here on out, this was the only kind of target they'd ever use and they began planning how they'd find and steal another baby. They both pissed in the small puddle of the babies blood that now lay on the ground. They bagged and slung their rifles and left her there hanging between the trees, a monument to cruelty beyond belief.

***

Shortly after Michael arrived at home the sheriff and a detective arrived. Both Michael and Donna were reassured by the sheriff's presence and the way in which he coordinated the work of his men. Donna, her eyes bloodshot from crying, could barely contain herself though. The tears and guilt of what she had allowed to happen wouldn't go away. Michael also tried to contain himself as the officers questioned them both.

The sheriff dispatched men to return to the cleaners to see what could be learned at that location and to canvas the area. After fingerprints had been taken from the car and the detectives had gathered all the information he would need, all the officers departed the home of the grieving parents and the sheriff again told the couple that they would do everything in their power to locate their baby girl.

Michael sat on the couch holding his crying wife. After the police left his house, anger started to rage within him for what happened and what might be happening to his daughter. He wanted to blame his wife. His daughter was with her. She should have been more careful. But just as quickly, it dawned on him that Donna would never knowingly allow anything to happen to their child. At that moment, feeling her tremble in his arms, he wanted— no he needed— to comfort her, to let her know that everything would work out. He also realized how much he truly loved her and how this had devastated her. His only thoughts were to assure her that he didn't blame her for what happened, which he did as he whispered softly in her ear that everything would be okay. Even though he tried to hold back his own tears, he couldn't.

***

Two days had gone by since the child went missing, and the police had no new leads. The prints taken from the car yielded no new leads. The police did visit the dry cleaners and talked to all the merchants in the area but no one saw anything out of the ordinary on the day in question. Evidence collected at the scene and on the mother's car was being processed, but so far it turned up nothing. On the third day of the investigation, the police got the break they needed.

A call came into the station about 1:30 PM that Saturday afternoon. A very frantic sounding man stated that he thought his son and his friends found something in the woods. The man stated he let his boy lead him to a location about half a mile from his home in a wooded area. As soon as he got there, he knew something was wrong and that's when he came home and called the police.

The call was transferred to Detective Harrison, who was handling the missing persons case. He took a ride to the caller's address. Arriving at the home of Steve Evans, he asked to be taken to the location in the woods. Upon arriving at the scene, the detective cautiously approached what appeared to be a crate of some kind tied between two small trees. Upon closer inspection of the area beneath the crate, he saw what appeared to be blood stains. He instructed Mr. Evans to return to his home exactly the way they had come and to call his office immediately and inform them that he was on scene and he needed crime scene support.

Detective Harrison got on his cell and called dispatch and asked to speak to the sheriff.

"Sheriff White, Sheriff, this is Harrison. Sir, I think you need to see this for yourself. That call that came in a few hours ago about something being found in the woods, well, I think I just found the missing Carrington baby. We're gonna need crime scene techs and homicide investigators out here."

"I'll make the notifications, you secure that scene," the sheriff replied.

"Yes, sir," said the detective.

Less than thirty minutes later, the first uniformed officers arrived on scene, soon followed by the sheriff and crime scene techs. A one hundred foot cordon was established around the area where the crate was discovered, and the scene was carefully and methodically photographed. Evidence markers were placed and photographed. and homicide detectives soon arrived on scene, taking notes and directing the crime scene techs, all under the watchful eye of the sheriff, who allowed his people to do their jobs while he and Detective Harrison watched as the investigation proceeded.

Three hours into the investigation, the homicide detectives were ready to lower the crate, having collected all the evidence they could on the ground. From the vantage point of the ground, what they could see in the crate was a bloody pulp that appeared only remotely human except for the little arms that were tied to the sides of the crate.

Homicide detectives Graham and Lee stood in front of the trees that the crate was tied to as it was lowered: What they and the crime scene techs saw when it was on the ground broke their hearts—the body of the missing baby. Its body was swollen, covered in dried blood, and much of the child's skin looked like it had been stripped away, bit by bit. There appeared to be dozens of small metal objects imbedded in the baby's skin.

The investigators discovered dozens, possibly hundreds, of rounds of small metal pellets littering the area around the scene. It was not hard to imagine what happened here, but it was truly horrifying to believe someone could do this. Every officer present had the same look of horror on their faces.

The sheriff watched as the crime scene techs fought to hold back the tears due to witnessing the aftermath of the atrocity that was committed on this child. Sheriff White knew his people and their level of professionalism, but he also knew that every man had a breaking point, and this was especially hard because most of these men had children.

Detective Harrison walked a short distance away from the scene after having viewed what was left of the child's body and lit a cigarette. The sheriff came over to where he was smoking.

"Sheriff, I've been a cop and a detective for twenty-five years. I've seen shit that would make most men blow there fucking brains out or send them over the edge, but I've never seen anything like this. Monster doesn't begin to describe the kind of mind it would take to even conceive of doing shit like this to a helpless baby."

"I know exactly how you feel, Sam," said the sheriff. "Like you, I've been in this business a lot of years, and I thought I'd seen it all—rapes, killings, gang violence, domestics, assaults—but this level of evil has me fucked up. So we can both imagine what seeing something like this is gonna do to the young officers here."

"Yeah, it'll make them wonder if this is really what they want to do with the rest of their lives," said Detective Harrison.

"Sheriff, how the fuck do we tell the Carringtons that we found their little girl in this condition?" Just as the question was being asked, the homicide team walked up.

"This kind of shit is never easy, especially when it's a young child, never mind a baby," said Detective Lee. "To answer your question, John, we'll find out together. You'll be with me when I tell them."

"What's the preliminary, Lee?" the Sheriff asked.

"From what we can gather, sir, at least two people stood at distances of between seven and fifteen yards and fired pellets at the baby in the crate. We've collected cigarette butts, discarded pellet cartridges, and several sets of footprints at the immediate scene. Our perps may have been here before. This area is secluded. The thing is, sir, I think we have all we need to catch these animals, if they haven't fled the area. It's almost as if they didn't care about covering their tracks. They left the baby in that crate and just walked away when they were done, like they didn't care. And in my opinion, anybody who could do this needs to be slaughtered," said the detective. The look in the sheriff's eyes told the detective that he concurred.

"Hopefully the evidence collected here will lead us right to these sick fuckers," said the sheriff.

"We're pretty much done here," said Detective Graham.

"Okay, then let's wrap it up, and get the victim to the medical examiner's office. Detective Harrison, I want you to talk to Mr. Evan's son again. He may remember something that could help us. Boys like playing in the woods, so his son may have seen something," said the sheriff.

As all the investigators prepared to wrap things up on the scene, two of the officers who were assisting volunteered to place the child's body in a small black body bag and carry her to the waiting medical examiner's vehicle. The sheriff watched as the two young officers, being as gentle as they could be with the child's body, lifted her out of the crate and placed her lifeless body in the bag. Each officer kneeling beside the body, head down and tears flowing, said a silent prayer for the child before they carried her away. Now it was the sheriff's turn to hold back tears.

***

The sheriff and Detective Harrison pulled up to the Carrington's home at 8 PM that Saturday evening. They both wore very somber expressions. The sheriff had worked out what he would say to the couple. He knew there was absolutely no way to break this kind of news to anyone gently. Experience had shown him that the best way to tell someone that a loved one had died or been killed was to come straight out and tell them the truth. There was no need to initially provide a lot of unnecessary details. As they knocked on the door, the sheriff wished he knew a better way.

Mr. Carrington answered the door. Looking at the sheriff and the detective immediately gave Michael a bad feeling. He invited the two officers in and offered them seats. Michael explained that his wife was asleep and that her mother was with her. The sheriff looked Michael in his eyes and told him that what he had to tell him was not good. Michael put his face in his hands as he listened to what the sheriff had to say.

"Mr. Carrington, it breaks my heart to tell you that we found your daughter's body in the woods about five miles from the cleaners. We received a call from a man who lives about half a mile from where your daughter was found. His son and his friends found something that didn't look right, and they called it in to us. Now I know this is hard for you to hear Mr. Carrington, but I wanted to be the one to tell you what happened, and that we have good leads to follow, and we're gonna catch those responsible."

Looking at the sheriff, all Michael could do was sit there paralyzed and listen as he gave him the news no parent ever wants to hear, that their baby is dead. Michael tried to be strong as he heard the news. He could tell this was just as hard on the officers. He could see it in their eyes, and he could also tell they weren't telling him everything.

Michael asked through tears if he could he see his baby girl. The sheriff explained that her body was at the medical examiner's office and that his office would make arrangements for them to identify her body tomorrow, if he was up to it. Michael insisted that he would be. As the officers left, the sheriff said he would send a car to pick them up tomorrow. Michael closed the door and sank to his knees, crying. Now he had to tell his wife.

The sheriff told Harrison he would have to have a talk with the medical examiner before the Carringtons got there. He wasn't sure just how much the doctor would tell them concerning the death of their baby since her death was so horrible. But they did have a right to know. He simply didn't want the family to be further traumatized, but he wasn't sure if there was anything he could do to prevent it.

***

The next day, a police car arrived at the Carringtons home to escort Michael, Donna, and her mother to the medical examiner's office. The officer assigned to take them there was Officer Ryan Tucker. He'd been on the force for two years, and he was one of the officers at the scene when the child was found. In fact, he and another officer carried the child's body to the M.E.'s vehicle. The officer was instructed by the sheriff to say absolutely nothing about the case to the family, just escort them to the medical examiner's office and return them home. Even though he had strong personal feelings about the case and it gave him nightmares after he witnessed what was done to the baby, he did not want to arrest those who were responsible. He wanted to murder them. He knew that was wrong, but he couldn't help the way he felt.

The cruiser pulled up to the building. The Carringtons got out and went inside. A receptionist guided them to the doctor's office. Dr. Wilson didn't keep them waiting. After he introduced himself, he informed the Carringtons that it wasn't necessary for them to see the child, that due to the nature of her injuries, he identified her body using the hospital records where she was born. He had them emailed to his office.

"Her injuries," Donna said crying.

"Yes", said the doctor. "I understand how upsetting this must be for you both, which is why you need only verify your signatures on her original birth record." The couple verified their signatures beneath the baby's footprints. Donna touched the card and began crying. Dr. Wilson told them to take their time and that someone would contact them when they could pick up the child's body. The doctor left the room.

Michael left Donna in the office with her mother and went to catch Dr. Wilson. He explained that he had to see his daughter one last time and that he could not live with himself if he didn't. No matter what was done to her, he had to see his baby one more time. The doctor agreed, but he warned Michael that this would be extremely hard on him and that he should seek counseling afterwards. Michael agreed and was escorted to where his daughter's body was. He followed the doctor into the room, trembling. The doctor opened a door on the refrigeration unit and pulled out the metal table on which his baby laid. The sheet was pulled back. When Michael saw his baby, he cried out, "Oh, God." His legs became so weak, he almost fell to the ground. The doctor had to help him steady himself. He stood there, barely able to contain his tears. Seeing now what was done to his baby, images flashed across his mind of what she must have endured, the unbearable pain she must have suffered. Tears freely flowing down his face, Michael told his baby girl he was sorry daddy wasn't there to protect her. Over and over, that thought repeated in his mind.

On the ride home, nobody spoke. Michael rode in the front seat of the cruiser while Donna's mother held her in the back seat. All Michael could think about is his little baby girl, that he'd never see alive again. He wouldn't be able to watch her grow and experience all the things a father should with his child because she was stolen from them and brutally murdered. Michael was numb with grief and felt there was absolutely nothing he could do except wait for the police to bring those fucking psychos to justice before they killed someone else's child.

Officer Tucker pulled up to the Carringtons home and said goodbye to the three as they got out of his cruiser. Donna's mother led her daughter to the door while Michael thanked the officer for bringing them home. As Michael walked away, Officer Tucker called him back. "Mr. Carrington," the officer continued. "Sir I just want to let you know how sorry I am for your loss. If there is anything I can do to help you, I will. I want you to know, sir, the whole force wants the animals who did this dead. I could lose my job for saying this, but I'd rather turn these fuckers over to you than arrest them."

Without thinking about his words, Michael said, "I'd love for that to happen." He thanked the officer again and went inside his home.

Three days had gone by since the Carringtons identified their baby, and there had been no word on the investigation. The Carrington's had made plans to bury there daughter on the last Saturday of the month, which was four days away. Michael and Donna weren't speaking much. it was still too painful. Even though Michael didn't blame her for what happened to Heather, Donna was destroying herself over it, and Michael honestly didn't know how to help her. He was just thankful her mother was there to help him care for her.

Michael sat in his study thinking why the hell God would allow something like this to happen to his baby. She was only nine months old. What could she, an innocent baby, have possibly done to deserve such a horrible death? These thoughts gave Michael no comfort at all. He knew in his heart that there was no God, and what happened to his daughter proved it. What kind of fucking God would allow a baby to be tortured to death? He could no longer cry. He'd cried all the tears he would ever cry. The only thing left in him now was hate for the monsters who killed his baby, hate for the parents who would bring such abominations into the world, and hate for himself because he couldn't protect his daughter.

Michael didn't want to sleep, and he didn't want to talk to anybody— not friends, not family. He only wanted to punish those who killed his child, and he thought to himself that he could if only he knew who they were.

He could call the sheriff's office to see if there was any news, but he knew they'd only go so far with what they'd tell him, and they damn sure wouldn't give him any information that would lead him to his child's murderers. Michael decided that he had to get out of the house, go for a walk. These thoughts were driving him mad. He had no outlet for his rage. He felt totally helpless, and there was nothing he could do about it.

A short while later, Michael let his mother-in-law know he was going for a walk, and she could reach him on his cell phone. As he left the house, he felt numb to everything and everyone. He was on indefinite leave from work due to the situation. His wife had not spoken in days, but that was okay. Her doctor had given her powerful medicine so she could sleep, and right now, he just wanted to get out of the house.

Michael had no destination in mind. He just wanted to walk until he fell off the face of the planet. He thought to himself if he couldn't avenge his daughter, then he could be with her in death. But even that thought gave him no comfort. He wanted his baby back home. Twenty minutes into his walk, Michael's cell phone rang. It was Officer Tucker.

"Mr. Carrington, your mother-in-law told me I could reach you at this number. I hope I'm not disturbing you, sir," said the officer.

"No, I'm just taking a walk. What can I do for you?" Michael said.

"Mr. Carrington, can we meet some place tonight that would be convenient for you? I need to speak with you." "Sure, what's this about?" Michael asked,

"Sir, I have information I think you'd find interesting. It's really important."

"Okay," Michael said. "Meet me at a bar on Seventh and Jay street called the Spot at 9 pm."

"I'll be there," the officer said.

***

When Michael arrived at the bar, he saw the officer dressed in civilian clothes, wearing a jacket, and sitting at the main bar. Michael walked over and sat next to him.

"Hello Mr. Carrington. Can I buy you a beer"

"Sure. And call me Michael"

"Okay and I'm Ryan." Michael asked Ryan why he wanted to see him again. Ryan suggested they take their beers to a booth where they could talk in private.

In a very low tone, Ryan tells Michael why he needed to see him. "Have you talked to anyone at the Sheriff's Office lately?"

"No", says Michael.

"Good. I want you to hear what I have to say before you do. Since I was at the scene when your daughter's body was found, I've been assigned to one of the detectives working the case, and we have a solid lead on one of the people responsible for your child's death. The young kids who found your daughter's body told one of the detectives they sometimes see older boys shooting guns not far from his home, and that these older boys would let them fire their guns as well. The boys told us their names. One of the boys is named Todd, and we found out Todd and his buddy Kyle were seen coming out of the woods on the day your daughter was killed. We got the same information from all the kids we talked to, and a right thumbprint matching Todd's was found on your wife's car. Once we got that, we had the fucker."

"I was able to read the case file, and I ran the fucker's name through the system. "Todd Byrd, age 16. He's been in trouble with the law and at school since he was born. He was kicked out of school last year for smoking drugs and bringing loaded weapons into the building. He has seventeen counts of cruelty to animals for shooting neighbors pets with pellet guns and two assault charges against female classmates. This kid is all-around bad news."

Michael was stunned to learn that a sixteen-year-old punk could be responsible for what was done to his daughter. The memory of seeing her little body riddled with scars, the flesh torn away from her body, and what they did to her eyes—even in his mind, he couldn't continue with the memory. But seeing his baby that way on that metal table and knowing what was done to her took all the strength Michael had to contain the rage that was building inside him.

The more the officer told him, the stronger his rage grew, until his mind became so focused, he knew without any doubt whatsoever that no matter what happened from here on, he knew he had to be the one to kill the piece of shit who murdered his baby. Ryan continued talking, but Michael barely heard a word he said. His thoughts focused now on avenging his daughter. Ryan also told Michael that Todd had a best friend, according to their information, and that he too has been in a great deal of trouble. That focused Michael's attention back to what Ryan was saying.

Ryan told Michael the other boy, Kyle Long, was going to be picked up tomorrow morning for questioning on his way to school.

"After he's questioned, they're going to pick up Todd. We need Kyle to give us everything he knows about what happened in those woods on the day your daughter was killed. The thing is, if he cooperates, who knows what the District Attorney may do? That little bastard may come away with a deal if he rats Todd out." The thought of either of them getting off lightly for what they did made Michael sick to his stomach, so much so he wanted to throw up.

Michael was not going to let that happen. He thought to himself, *It was Todd's fingerprint on my wife's car, so it was that motherfucker who took our baby.* He's the one Michael wanted. The police could have the other one, but Todd was going to die by his hand.

"Ryan, why are you telling me this. You have to know what's going through my mind," Michael said.

Ryan looked him in the eyes and answered Michael's question in a low but very intense voice. "Because I saw your daughter after they killed her. I saw how she was killed. they murdered her, and my heart shattered. At that moment, I felt like she was mine. I wasn't just talking the other day when I told you if I could, I'd turn the animals responsible for this over to you. It's within my power, and I'm asking you, what do you want me to do?"

It didn't take Michael long to decide. He told Ryan he wanted Todd, that he'd make him pay for Heather's death.

Ryan gave Michael a computer printout of Todd's address which also had a picture of him. Michael studied it, and his loathing grew stronger. Now he thought he could and would exact retribution for his baby daughter's death, and in that instant, he knew exactly what it would be. Michael asked Ryan if it wouldn't look odd to the police when this little fucker up and vanished during the investigation. Ryan told him it's not unusual for criminal suspects to disappear once they know their under investigation, especially when the charge is first-degree murder, and we can make sure he finds out he's a suspect. He'll be expected to run, and we'll guide him right to us.

During the next hour, Michael and Ryan outlined a plan that included luring Todd into a trap they would set for him. The first step would be for Michael to take a letter to the Byrd home addressed to Todd Byrd Jr. The letter would state that someone knew he and his friend killed a baby a few days ago, and if he wanted to save himself, he needed to meet the writer of the letter at a particular location at a specified time. There they would discuss what needed to be done. The letter also warned him not to call anyone or attempt to leave town because from the moment he got the letter, he was being watched.

The two men continued their talks for another hour, each assuring the other that what they discussed on this night would never be spoken of again and how they would each take steps to ensure that nothing they we're going to do could be traced back to either of them. Ryan offered Michael a ride home, but Michael told him he'd be fine walking. He had a lot to think about.

Ryan said he'd call Michael tomorrow concerning their plans, and the two men shook hands and parted. As Michael walked home, he experienced a curious sensation, knowing what he was planning in his mind to do to his Daughter's murderer. He at first thought he should feel some guilt over the deliberate planning of another person's death. But just as that thought came to him, another thought occurred to him, and it came to him with perfect clarity—the thought that killing your child's murderer is justified in the eyes of God. But then he thought to himself, *Fuck God*, and with that, his every thought was focused. His body felt strong again. He was filled with a renewed sense of purpose. It was as if a veil had been lifted from his eyes, and he promised his daughter he'd mercilessly make her killer pay.

***

Michael returned home at midnight. Everyone was asleep as he made his way to his study. He sat at his desk and wrote a very simple letter that would set their plan in motion. The letter read—

I know what you did to that baby in the woods a few days ago, If you want me to keep quiet meet me at the baseball field at the corner of 6th and Elm today. Come alone.

Michael sealed the letter in an envelope, addressed it to Todd Byrd Jr, and put it in his jacket. Shortly, he would drive to that animal's house and put it in his mailbox, but first he would check on his wife.

Michael went to their bedroom. The lights were on, and Donna was sleeping. *She looks so beautiful when she sleeps*, Michael thought to himself. He sat on the bed next to her, and as he did, he whispered to her, "Baby, I can't change what happened. I wish I could. But I will make it right for Heather. Rest well, baby."

Michael got up off the bed, turned out the lights and left the house to deliver the letter. He sent Ryan a text message when it was done.

***

The next morning, Michael woke up next to his wife, who was still asleep. He didn't want to disturb her, so he quietly got out of bed, went into the bathroom to clean himself up, got dressed, and went downstairs. His mother-in-law was in the kitchen fixing breakfast. He ate and told her he'd be out most of the day and probably wouldn't be back till late. She responded that it would be okay, she'd take care of things until he got back. He thanked her and left the house.

Officer Tucker was sitting in his personal vehicle on the street about twenty-five yards away, watching the mailbox in front of the Byrd residence. The house was at least fifty yards away from the mailbox at the end of the driveway, so keeping an eye on it discreetly wasn't a problem. He had called out sick today so that he and Michael could carry out their plan. He knew that after he did this he planned to resign from the force and head west, he wanted nothing more to do with being a police officer, but before he left the force, he wanted to do his part to make sure at least this one monster would never walk the streets again.

He waited patiently for someone to come to the mailbox. He'd been watching the mailbox for hours. It was now 1pm, and no one came out yet. The letter was there. He checked before he started watching the house. He knew Todd was inside because he called the house pretending to be a friend of his, and he was told Todd was asleep. Ryan thought to himself, *you sleep, fucker. After today, you'll be put to sleep per-*

manently. Twenty minutes later, Ryan saw Todd walking down the long dirt driveway. He starts his car and waits for him to check the mailbox. Todd walks past it without checking it. Ryan curses to himself and calls Michael. As Todd rounds the corner, Ryan pulls up to the mailbox and takes the letter out of the box.

Ryan stays at a discreet distance from Todd as he follows him down the street. Ryan also calls Michael to let him know there has been a slight change of plan since Todd didn't take the letter out of the mailbox. He tells Michael he will keep Todd in sight until he comes to a location where he can stop him on the street and arrest him. Ryan asks Michael if he is ready on his end. He tells Ryan he will be by the time he picks that little fucker up.

***

Donna woke up to find she had slept through the morning and Michael had already left. Her mother told her Michael would be back sometime tonight, but if they needed him to call his cell. Donna ate the meal her mother had prepared for her, but she found she couldn't enjoy the food or anything else, and she found she was glad Michael wasn't home now. She didn't want to face him now, and she didn't want to discuss the burial plans for Heather. She asked that her mother and Michael deal with that. It was too much for her to deal with now.

***

Donna got out of the shower and found she had no energy to do much of anything. She didn't want to be anywhere except with her baby. She found herself staring at Heather's crib and wondering where her baby was. She honestly didn't know where Heather was. For a split second, she started to panic, until the memory of her child came rushing back to her so hard it was almost as if a great force had thrown her to the ground and rattled her whole body.

Heather is dead, she thought. *My baby is dead*. Donna wanted to cry, but she couldn't. She found she couldn't feel anything, and she didn't know why that was. Looking at her baby's crib which was now empty, made her realize something she hadn't before.

Donna went over to the crib and picked up one of the blankets lying inside and brought it to her face. She could smell the scent of her baby on the blanket like only a mother could, and she realized that

Mama's baby is just asleep, that's all. And soon Mama will be asleep too.

Donna went downstairs to thank her mother for the meal and told her she was going to lay back down because she didn't feel too well. Her mother told her to get all the rest she needed, that Mama would take care of everything, and she gave her daughter a hug.

Donna thanked her mother and went upstairs. She got the bottle of sleeping pills the doctor had prescribed for her, and read the warning label that stated not to take more than one tablet in a twelve-hour period, Donna poured the contents of the bottle into her hand and counted twenty-two pills. She put half of them in her mouth and swallowed them with water, then swallowed the remaining pills. She took her baby's blanket, held it up to her face as she laid down on the bed, and thought. *Mama will take care of everything. That's right, baby. Mommy will be with you soon, baby.*

***

Ryan followed Todd for almost a mile. Until he realized where that little bastard was headed. The cleaners where Michael's baby was abducted was less than a hundred yards away. The thought infuriated Ryan. He sped up the truck to get ahead of Todd. He pulled over about ten yards ahead of him, got out of his vehicle with his badge in one hand and his service weapon in the other, and identified himself as a police officer.

Todd was so frightened, he couldn't move, his heart pounding as the officer walked toward him with his weapon pointed at him. Todd was told to put his hands on top of his head and walk toward the vehicle. Ryan got behind Todd and pushed him forward, telling him if he moved or talked he'd blow his fucking brains all over the street. Todd, frightened out of his mind, did what he was told.

Ryan put his weapon in the front of his pants and ordered Todd to put both hands behind his back and not to say a word. Ryan cuffed him and patted him down for weapons. Moving quickly Ryan pulled Todd to the rear passenger door of the SUV, shoved Todd inside, and climbed in behind him. Before Todd could fully understand what was happening, Ryan punched him in the face with everything he had, knocking Todd out cold.

Ryan quickly tied a gag around Todd's mouth and put a black hood over his head, pulled the strings around the opening and tied them tight. He then used flex cuffs to bind Todd's feet together. Then Ryan said out loud as he looked at Todd, "How's it feel you sick little fuck?" How's it feel, to be trapped like an animal?" Tonight you die for what you did."

Ryan called Michael to let him know he had Todd and he would bring him to Michael's location. Michael instructed Ryan to bring him to the old Miller farm on Jay Street. It was an old property that had been abandoned for years and was thirty miles outside of town. Michael instructed Ryan to pull up behind the main house and he'd see his vehicle on the side of the barn. Michael said he'd be ready by the time they got there.

Michael sat in the barn thinking about his baby who he would never see again, his wife, and how his life had been destroyed, all because some punk had kidnapped and killed his child. He didn't care about anything else except making the person responsible for his baby's death pay, and he knew it wouldn't be quick. He would show him the same mercy he showed Heather, he would make his daughter's killer feel every excruciating moment of the pain he was going to inflict upon him.

Michael thought to himself how much he was going to enjoy Todd's suffering, and that thought gave him a great deal of pleasure.

Forty minutes later, Michael heard a car pulling up beside the barn. He went out to meet Ryan. Ryan stepped out of the SUV and went to the passenger-side door as Michael came out of the barn. Ryan said, "I got the little fucker, and he's all yours." Ryan also gave Michael the letter that was placed in the mailbox. Ryan pulled Todd's bound-and-gagged body out of his vehicle and let him fall to the ground. Ryan asked Michael if he needed any help moving him. Michael told Ryan no, that this was as far as he needed to go and he would take it from there, Michael thanked Ryan, shook his hand, and drug Todd into the barn. The gag muffled his screams of protest.

Ryan got in his vehicle and left. Michael drug Todd into the barn by his feet as he was screaming through the gag. Todd was in mortal terror. He had no idea what was happening to him or why. He felt his skin burn from the friction of being dragged across the ground. Once in the barn, Michael used a cable he had prepared to bind Todd's legs together at the ankles. He then threw the loose end of the cable over one of the low hanging support beams in the barn and pulled with some effort until Todd was hoisted three feet off the ground. So that Todd's body couldn't swing, Michael used bolt cutters to cut away the cuffs and tied each of Todd's hands to hooks in the floor using nylon straps. Michael ripped off Todd's shirt and used scissors to cut away his jeans and underwear. Then Michael removed the hood that was covering his head. Michael saw that he was gagged and crying. The look of shear panic on his face was priceless to Michael.

Michael put a chair in front of Todd and sat down. He wanted to enjoy the look of horror on his face. He wanted to enjoy every tear that fell from his eyes. But he also wanted to see if he would feel any sorrow or compassion for the person he had planned to torture to death. His answer to himself was hell no. Todd was indeed crying. Hung up by his feet with his arms stretched out to his sides and tied down, trying to plead for his life through the gag, he wanted to know what was going on and why this man was doing this to him.

In his chair, Michael asked Todd how it felt to be tied up and helpless, as helpless as a baby. Being hung by his feet, Todd's head was pointing to the floor. He could look down and see he was hung over what looked like a deep hole in the ground. His only response to Michael's question were muffled words and tears of terror.

Michael said, "I see you've noticed the hole below you. When I'm done that's gonna be your grave. It's an abandoned well. You fuckers left my baby hanging in a tree, but I guarantee you no one will find your ass here." Michael left Todd's view while shouting at him from behind. "How the hell do you torture a helpless baby, you sorry piece of shit? "My baby!" he shouted, as he picked up a four-foot piece of steel rebar off a table and slammed the metal rod across Todd's back. Todd tried to scream with all his might, but any sound he made was stifled by the gag.

Michael hit him several more times across the back with the steel rod. After the fourth strike, Todd's back opened and blood spattered with every blow. As Michael struck him with the rebar, he saw in his mind's eye his baby being shot with pellets and crying for her daddy, wondering where her father was. He saw the pain inflicted on her, and it drove him wild now that he had the one responsible in front of him.

Todd continued to scream as the pain on his back grew impossibly worse. He lost control of his bladder and pissed himself as Michael continued to hit him with the metal rod. This time Michael hit him several times across his ass with the same result. After the fifth hit, large welts across his ass began to swell and his skin split open. Todd tried to move, but he only succeeded in causing his muscles to severely cramp, causing himself more pain.

Michael walked around to see the look in Todd's eyes, to see the pain on his face. Through the gag, Michael could tell he was crying to the top of his stifled voice, but Michael wanted him to scream louder, and before he was done, Todd would do just that. Breathing heavily, Michael sat in the chair to catch his breath. Todd's blood and other bodily fluids dripped into the well. He was in so much pain, he couldn't think straight. His eyes did focus on Michael when he spoke, but the words made no sense to him.

Michael had no feelings about what he was doing or to whom. He was totally numb to the pain he was inflicting on Todd. He only thought about his baby, who he would never see again, and the thing that took her away from him. Michael lit a cigarette. He'd just started back smoking after having quit for three years. He just wanted to sit there while he smoked and look into the eyes of his baby's killer. Michael wanted him to know that death was coming. But before he left this world, he wanted him to know what real pain was. Michael got up to get the baseball bat that was also on his table of torture. From his inverted point of view, Todd saw Michael's legs and waist first through his tears, then straining to look up, he saw the bat in his hands and resting on his shoulder. Todd's eyes grew larger still as he knew he would now be beaten with the bat and more tears came.

Michael put the bat on the chair and walked out of Todd's line of sight, he went to pick up a two-gallon bucket filled with salt water. The mixture was so thick with salt, it had the consistency of a syrup. Michael picked up the bucket and poured its contents on Todd's bleeding and swollen ass and back. Todd reacted as if a thousand volts of electricity had just been pumped through his body. His whole body spasmed with intense pain as the salt made contact with the open wounds on his back. The liquid slowly mixed with his blood as it oozed down his back and filled his every cut. He twisted and pulled involuntarily against his restraints in a desperate attempt to flee his pain and torturer, but he could go nowhere.

Michael picked up the bat, stood to Todd's left side, and swung the bat at Todd's face. the bat hit him square on the jaw, and blood splattered everywhere. The sickening sound of his jaw shattering on impact was satisfying to Michael, who then used scissors to cut away his gag. Todd couldn't fully open his mouth due to his shattered jaw, but blood, teeth, and vomit came pouring out of his mouth with every attempt to scream after Michael removed the gag.

Michael said to Todd, "I'm not gonna let you pass out on me. Don't worry about that, you're gonna feel the same pain you put my baby through." Michael lit another cigarette and watched as Todd bled into the well, his face quickly swelling and fluids pouring from his body. With his cigarette in his mouth, Michael swung the bat and made contact with Todd's stomach. The impact was a loud slapping sound. Todd released his stomach's contents along with a great deal of blood into the well below. After the third strike to his stomach, his skin started to split open.

Michael next used the bat to break his hips. To be sure the bones where shattered, he hit Todd twice on both sides, swinging the bat with all his might. The more Todd screamed, the more pleasure Michael got from beating him. Michael told Todd he was almost done with the bat. Michael swung at Todd exposed penis. When the bat made contact, his dick and balls went numb and started to swell grotesquely. The pain was so intense, Todd couldn't even scream.

Michael walked over to the table, picked up a pouch and sat back in the chair to finish another cigarette. He truly enjoyed watching his baby's killer hang there and bleed. Todd was barely breathing, and Michael started to wonder how much longer he'd last. Michael really didn't give a fuck. He was going to carry this thing out exactly as he had planned.

***

Ryan left the building thinking now he can start over. He found being a cop wasn't for him, even though at times it was rewarding in many ways to be of help to others, and there was satisfaction when he helped put criminals away for the crimes they'd committed against innocent people. But after having seen what was done to the Carrington baby, Ryan knew he no longer wanted any part of being a cop. that experience changed him, and he knew at the moment he saw her dead body that being a cop had lost all appeal for him.

Ryan knew it was no longer a matter of protecting people. After seeing that baby he wanted to punish the criminals, and that is not what police officers are supposed to do, but helping the father of that child exact revenge for her murder gave him the satisfaction of knowing that, while he was no longer a cop he could live a good life knowing at least in this one case the murderer got exactly what he deserved.

Ryan felt he could resign from the force and head west to pursue a career that would make him happy, like finally applying his communications degree doing something that didn't require him to confront the ugly things people do to each other on a daily basis. He also told himself again that he could live with the role he played in helping Michael because Todd deserved whatever Michael did to him. He just hoped this would bring some kind of closure to Michael's life and that, afterwards, he and his wife could move forward.

Ryan closed out his affairs at the station, turned in all his equipment, and signed all the required paperwork. He gave a forwarding address and was ready to leave this chapter of his life behind him. He told himself he'd head out in the morning and wouldn't look back. He had a new life to start.

***

Michael looked at Todd hanging above the well, his body covered in blood, bleeding from every orifice of his body. This gave Michael extreme pleasure, to know his baby's killer was soon to be dead and he was the one that sent him to hell. Michael unzipped the pouch he'd gotten off the table and pulled out a pistol. He screamed at Todd to look at the weapon. Looking at Michael through swollen eyes, hanging upside down, Todd tried to focus on what was in Michael's hands, but he couldn't. So great was his pain, he couldn't focus on anything. Michael shouted, looking at Todd, "You know all about these don't you, you sick piece of shit?" "Isn't this what you and your friend used to kill my baby?" "You had fun shooting at her with a fucking pellet gun just like this one. Well, before you die, motherfucker, you're gonna feel her pain".

Michael plucked the cigarette he was smoking and threw it at Todd's face. It made a hissing sound as the lit tobacco made contact with his blood and fell into the well. Michael didn't need to take aim. He was only six feet away from Todd when he began shooting him with the pellet gun. He was surprised that the pellets made a smacking sound as they hit Todd's body and splattered in his blood. Michael fired the first full cartridge at Todd's chest. His body flinched involuntarily as each pellet made contact with his swollen flesh.

Michael looked at Todd and asked him sitting in the chair. "How did it feel, for someone to do to you what you did to a helpless baby?" Again Todd said nothing. Michael reloaded the gun, and this time he fired the whole cartridge at Todd's swollen penis, every hit made his penis jerk from the impact. The shooting went on for what seemed like hours. Todd was in agony with every impact of the pellets. His moans of pain were loud and terrifying to listen to. The pellets split his penis and testicles open, and blood ran down his body in torrents with every beat of his heart.

Michael knelt down in front of Todd, lit another cigarette, and tried to figure out if Todd was still alive or not. He watched Todd's blood flow down his chest and into the well, but he stopped moaning a few minutes ago. Michael thought back to his baby girl on that metal table. He remembered what her eyes looked like, like someone had scooped them out, and now he knew why that was. With rage he couldn't contain any longer, he took two steps back from Todd, pointed and fired the gun at his left eye. The pellet made an almost splashing sound as it tore into Todd's eye, and even through his shattered jaw, Todd's scream filled the room. Michael fired ten shots at each eye. Todd screamed and his body jerked until he was physically unable to move any longer.

Todd hung there dead, blood and other fluids flowing out of his eye sockets into the well. Michael sat down, lit another cigarette, and stared at his baby's murderer, and he was satisfied with what he'd done. To Michael, the scales of justice had been balanced. Heather's murderer was killed just as she had been killed, slowly and painfully. Michael made sure he felt every agony-filled second of it, just as his helpless child did.

Michael thought, *this piece of shit will never harm anyones child again.* In his heart, he knew he'd done the right thing. He did what any father would have done if given the opportunity, and he was content.

Rest in peace, baby, Daddy made things right.

Michael's cell rang, He didn't answer it, even though it may have been Donna or her mother calling. He didn't want to be distracted because he still had to dump the body and get this place cleaned up. He threw the gun, bat, and rebar down the well. Next the dropcloths that he placed around the opening below the body were dropped. His cell rang again. This time he decided he'd answer it. It was Sheriff White. Michael's heart almost leapt from his chest as he turned away from Todd's dead body and froze while the sheriff talked.

Sheriff White told Michael they had both of his child's murderers in custody. Michael turned toward Todd's dead body and froze in place. The sheriff continued, "We had planned to pick up one of our main suspects on his way to school this morning. His name is Kyle Long. We wanted to see what he would tell us. We got another break in the case when we got a call early this morning from the brother of Todd Byrd, Tony Byrd. He called to let us know he was coming to the station."

Michael dropped to his knees as all the strength left his lower body. "Tony Byrd called the station late last night to tell us his brother came in high last night, and he overheard a phone conversation with his brother bragging to someone about having killed a baby girl in the woods a few days ago. Tony, it seems, is the exact opposite of his brother, and he doesn't live with Todd and their father. He knew his brother kept a diary of sorts, and he knew where it was, so when his brother went to sleep, he got it out and everything he'd done was written down. We were waiting for Tony to come in to the station this morning, but he never showed."

Michael lost all sense of time and space as the realization of what he'd done hit him with such force he almost passed out. The sheriff continued. "We picked up Kyle, and thirty minutes later he gave us everything we needed. Soon after we had his confession, it didn't take long before he turned on his friend. We picked up Todd at his house passed out on drugs. "We searched his house and found his guns and the diary".

Michael lost all strength in his hand as his phone fell to the ground and shattered. He looked at the broken and mutilated body hanging in front of him, and, trembling, he found the strength to utter only a few words. They came as whispers first and got progressively louder.

"Oh, God. Oh, Goddd! Oh, Godddd!, What have I done? DEAR GOD! WHAT HAVE I DONE? He stayed where he fell, begging for forgiveness. There is no one there to grant it.

Some physicians practice to save their patients. Others, though, who have faced their fear, practice to save us from their patients.

Dr. Feelgood

The doctor's first session of the day, 10 am

Before we begin, there's something you need to know about how I practice. I don't know who sent you to me, and frankly I don't give a damn. My style of practice deals with getting right to whatever's fucking with you, so please don't come in my office bullshiting and wasting my time. My calendar is full.

I want the hard truth, and I need you to be brutally honest with me, because I won't hold back on you or mince my words. My goal is getting to the heart of the matter as quickly as possible because I don't have all day to sit here bullshiting with you unbalanced motherfuckers.

Many people can't handle my style of practice, so if at any time you feel uncomfortable during the session, you can get your shit and leave. I was paid the minute you walked through my door.

There are a few rules we need to go over.

One. I ask the questions, you give me straight answers.

Two. I smoke during my sessions. Feel free to join me. If you're a non-smoker, I don't want to hear your complaints.

Three. If during the session you need a drink, go for it. You're grown. The cabinets over there, so knock yourself out. But you are not allowed to get fucked up.

Four. If you leave before our session is completed, that's on you. As I stated earlier, I get paid whether your problem is resolved or not.

Five. If you feel like your losing control and you think you might want to attack me, don't. I won't hesitate to fuck you up.

Six. Don't ask me to prescribe a damn thing for you. I rarely write prescriptions. If however, I deem you're in need of some shit, that's my call not yours.

Now shall we get started?

Patient: Yes, I understand.
Doctor: What brings you to me today?
Patient: I've been having a lot of strange feelings lately. I can't seem to concentrate on anything at home or work. I find I don't enjoy the activities I once did, and even my family has noticed I'm not the same, but I don't know what's going on.
Doctor: When did this shit start?
Patient: Maybe six months ago.
Doctor: Now didn't I tell you not to come in here trying to bullshit me? Everybody says six months. Whatever's got you all fucked up started before six months ago. Now go back beyond six months and tell me what happened to bring about this change in you.
Patient: I'm an airline pilot for a major carrier, and as you probably know, we're away from home quit a lot. On one particular trip a year ago, I had a lay over in New York, and I met this woman at the hotel bar where I was staying.
Doctor: What airline?
Patient: North American Air.
Doctor: Go on.
Patient: We ended up having sex, and she got pregnant, and everything started from there.
Doctor: First off, you didn't end up doing anything. What are you not saying to me? You meet women all the time. How did you come to fuck this particular women?
Patient: When I met her, I was instantly attracted to her. She's young and very pretty. She seemed interested in me, and when she asked me what I did for a living, I told her, and we talked for quit a while. Afterward, we had dinner together. After we ate, she invited me to her room.

The doctor lights a cigarette

Doctor: You didn't have to carry your ass to her room. So you knew you wanted to fuck this woman from the minute you saw her at the bar. She gave you the opportunity, and you went for it.
Patient: I was attracted to her, and, yes I wanted to be with her.
Doctor: Is this the first time you fucked around on your wife?

Patient: No.
Doctor: Is this the first time it's bitten you in the ass?
Patient: Yes.
Doctor: To your knowledge, has your wife ever fucked around on you?
Patient: No.
Doctor: How's your relationship with your wife?
Patient: Until my problem started, we were fine. Now things have changed.
Doctor: Are you still fucking your wife?
Patient: Now you wait just one damn minute…
Doctor: No, motherfucker, you answer my goddamn question. Are you still fucking your wife? it's a legitimate question, and you will answer me or get the fuck outta my office.
Patient: I've been unable to.
Doctor: Why the hell do you think that is?
Patient: These past few months have been hard on me.
Doctor: Bullshit. You know exactly why shit has been fucked up. You just want to live in denial, and I told you that's not the way I do shit, and if you continue on this course, you can get the fuck out of my office. Do you understand?
Patient: Yes, Doctor. This is just difficult for me.
Doctor: If the shit were easy, you wouldn't need me.
Patient: I've been diagnosed with herpes.
Doctor: How'd you find that out?
Patient: A friend of mine is a doctor, and when I explained to him what I'd done, he examined me and gave me the results. I got symptoms of herpes four months after the last time I slept with her.
Doctor: What's this doctor's name and where does he practice?
Patient: Anthony Dukes. He works out of Washington, D.C.
Doctor: Now we're getting somewhere. Does your New York girl know she's burning?
Patient: Yes. She told me after I found out I had it that she is a carrier.
Doctor: Did you have relations with your wife before you knew you were burned?
Patient: Yes.
Doctor: Have you since told your wife you're burning.
Patient: No, but to my knowledge she's never had an outbreak.
Doctor: We'll come back to that.
Patient: Fine.
Doctor: Continue with the story.

Patient: I told her I wanted to see her again, so we exchanged numbers and said we'd keep in contact. This was before I knew anything about the pregnancy or the herpes.

Doctor: You said to yourself, what the hell? I found me some young New York pussy that I can hit whenever I'm there.

Doctor: Smiles and asks, how old are you?

Patient: Fifty-one.

Doctor: Did it ever occur to you that she was playing you?

Patient: What do you mean?

Doctor: We'll get to that later. Continue with your story. Getting laid usually doesn't depress most men, especially when the women is young and fine, so please continue.

Patient: I didn't hear from her again until about two months after our first encounter. She asked me when was I going to be back in New York. I explained that I could get back anytime if she wanted to see me, so we made arrangements to stay at the same hotel. That's when she told me she was pregnant.

Doctor: Did you fuck her on that occasion?

Patient: Yes, we had sex.

Doctor: What did she run down on you?

Patient: I don't understand what you mean.

Doctor: What the fuck did you two talk about after you were done fucking her?

Patient: Doctor I'm becoming uncomfortable with the way you're talking to me.

Doctor: Did you hear a word I said to you before we started this? You came to me. I didn't ask you to come here. Now if you stop bullshiting and talk to me straight, we can get to why you're all fucked up. If not, there's the door. it's your call.

Patient: You're right, I need a drink.

Doctor: Go for it.

Patient pours himself a bourbon and continues.
Doctor lights another cigarette

Patient: When I suggested she get an abortion, she told me she couldn't do that and that she wanted to keep the baby. This was her first child. Doctor I have two grown children, and I sure as hell don't want another baby. She said she wouldn't interfere in my life, that she just wanted me to help her financially.

Doctor: How old is this women?

Patient: Twenty-five.

Doctor: Why are you so sure you're the father?

Patient: I paid for the DNA test after the baby was born. It confirmed I was the father.

Doctor: Did your doctor friend help you with this as well?

Patient: Yes.

Doctor: Has any of this shit gotten back home to your wife yet?

Patient: No, but it's only a matter of time before it does.

Doctor: What makes you believe that?

Patient: Over the last few months, she's called my company trying to find me posing as my daughter, even though I answer her calls and I've never tried to duck her calls. I send her money when she needs it, and now she's made even more demands since the child was born. She's sent letters to my home. I wish this had never happened. The thing is, I don't know how the hell she got my address. I never gave it to her.

Doctor: How the fuck do you think? At twenty-five she's pretty savvy and conniving, and she played you to the hilt. The internet is a motherfucker.

Doctor lights another cigarette

Doctor: Wishing for a thing to never have happened when you had complete control of the circumstances in which the incident occurred speaks not only to your character but to your judgment and impulse control.

Patient: I understand that, Doctor, but this thing has gotten to the point that I honestly don't know what I should do, and it's made me a nervous wreck. I can't tell anyone, and if she threatens my job, I don't know what I'll do. If I tell my wife what I've done, I know she's going to leave me.

Doctor: What the fuck did you think could happen when you go out and have unprotected sex with a woman you don't know?

Patient: I wasn't thinking. I looked at her and wanted her. I even feel like I could kill her for ruining my life.

Doctor: First of all, little Miss Hottie didn't ruin your life. You were thinking with your dick, and it caught up to you big time.

Second, how can you sit here and say you could kill the mother of your baby? That tells me quite a bit more about where your head is. You got yourself in this predicament, so you need to take responsibility for it. That's the first step in coping with the shit you've gotten yourself into.

Patient: You have to understand, Doctor, all that I have to lose because of this situation.

Doctor: What would that be?

Patient: Everything I've worked for—my job, my home, and my family.

Doctor: Tell me this, why wasn't all that shit on your mind when you fucked the woman you met in New York, and all the other times you fucked around on your wife.

The doctor works on his desktop while the patient talks.

Patient: I always told myself that what I did in the street didn't concern my wife, that it wasn't about her, I just wanted something extra.

Doctor: No, call it what it is. You wanted some strange pussy. With your job, you could play all you wanted, and not get caught as long as you didn't fuck up.

Patient: Something like that I suppose.

Doctor: You said earlier that her demands started to increase. What did you mean by that?

Patient: I send her five hundred dollars a month, and she wants more. She's threatened to take me to court, and she wants me to put her baby on my health insurance.

Doctor: Shouldn't that have been-our-baby? after all, you did fuck her, and it took two of you to make that baby.

Patient: My wife handles all the bills because I'm gone so much. If I were to put the baby on my health insurance policy, she'd find out.

Doctor: What would you say your net worth is? I'm trying to see from your perspective everything it is you have to lose because you fucked up, had a baby outside your marriage, and now can't do right by your new baby.

Patient: My home is valued at 650,000 dollars; cars and possessions around 150,000; savings, money market, and retirement accounts, I'd say around 475,000. Those are my combined assets with my wife.

Doctor: So just under a million three.

Patient: Yes, I suppose.

Doctor: That's not a bad piece of change your sitting on. Now how the hell could you not have realized that every time you fucked any women other than your wife, you were ejaculating all your hard earned money into their pussy?

Patient: says nothing.

Doctor: I need an answer.

Patient: I just never thought this kind of thing would happen to me, and now my head is messed up. I really don't know whether I'm coming or going, and the stress is killing me.

The Doctor is finished working on his computer and turns back toward the patient.

Doctor: Let me do a quick recap before we move on. You're a fifty-one-year-old airline pilot for a major carrier who fucks around on his wife and can do it with impunity due to the nature of the job. Your last encounter with a women you met in New York produced a baby, and the bitch gave you herpes and she knew she was burning.

Since you had sex with her unprotected on another occasion prior to finding out her health status, you subsequently passed a very nasty disease to the women you've been married to for more then twenty years, and you haven't found the balls to tell her that she now has herpes. You've also jeopardized the medical practice of your doctor friend because he didn't report your infection status to any agency that is required by law to have that information, nor has that DNA result been filed. You also said you've had thoughts about killing the mother of your baby and that you have a great fear of losing your job and everything you've worked for.

Did I miss anything.

Patient: No, that about sums it up.

Doctor: What do you have to say about the choices you've made?

Patient: I never intended for any of this to happen.

Doctor: Who gives a fuck about what you intended? The fact remains this shit has happened because you allowed it to. You got played by an attractive women who set your ass up twice in a major way.

Patient: How do I fix this?

Doctor: You tell me? How can you make this shit right?

Patient: I don't know. I'm so filled with worry, I can barely function, and I'm scared.

Doctor: You should be. You have to understand, you have gotten away with doing whatever it is you do for so long it's all been a big game to you—until now.

Patient: I don't know what to do, Doc, and I need help to fix this.

Doctor: I can't help you fix your past fuck-ups. I can help you to see how those fuck-ups are going to effect the lives of the people you've involved in your shit though.

Patient: What do you mean?

Doctor: I've given you every opportunity to take responsibility for the shit you've gotten yourself into, and you refuse, so here's how this shit plays out.

You're a fifty-one-year-old pilot who flies large jets around the country, carrying hundreds of passengers a day. One of those passengers could be me, and at this moment, your personal life is so fucked up, you can't concentrate on anything, nor by your own admission, can you focus on your job and performing the duties of an airline pilot. You shouldn't be flying anyone anywhere, and your airline and your chief pilot will be informed of your current unstable condition.

We don't need another 9-11 incident, and people who are unstable have been known to take out everyone around them.

Now, I'm not here to judge you or how you live your life, but the fact remains, a man of your years should be smart enough to override the impulse to fuck a strange women unprotected. Nowhere in our conversations did you speak of using protection. They're called condoms. While they're not one hundred percent effective they offer a lot of protection when compared to your dumbass using nothing at all because you weren't concerned about damaging your health or your spouse's. You can no longer control your impulses, which makes you a dangerous person now. Your health care provider will be informed, also, of your current health condition.

You got some young skank you met in New York pregnant, and make no mistake about it, she's encroaching on your life and your wallet and that scares you to death. She gave you herpes and a baby, and you in turn gave that shit to your wife. You spoke of killing the mother of your baby when compared to the cost of you losing everything you've worked for. People who have something to hide know fear, and fear can make you do really dumb shit. The New York City police and the local police departments in your area will be notified about the threats you've made against the mother of your baby.

You allowed your wife to contract the herpes virus from you, her husband, the motherfucker she's lived with for more than twenty years, and the man she trusted, and you're so fucking worried about a baby you've never seen and losing all your shit that you haven't even told this women what you've done to her. That makes you the lowest piece of shit on this fucking planet. Since you can't find the balls to tell her, I will make sure she is made aware of your current health status.

Your boy Dr. Dukes will be in hot water as well. He violated a number of regulations to help you hide the fact that you carry herpes and you infected your wife. The DNA test he helped you acquire should have also been filed with the proper agencies. You see, the courts, ethics boards, and other entities need to know certain shit we doctors do for a reason. In helping you, he violated those regulations, and I'll inform the medical review board in DC.

Patient looks at the doctor and can't believe what he was just told.

Patient: Why would you do this to me?

Doctor: You did this shit to yourself. This is what happens when you act impulsively and recklessly. And it's not just your life you've fucked up. You've involved everyone around you, and you can do a lot more damage to others. I'm not gonna let that happen.

Patient: What about your obligation to me? What gives you the right to disclose to others what I tell you in confidence?

Doctor: You're correct in that I have an obligation to you as a patient, but I have a larger obligation to public safety, which outweighs your right to privacy. I deem you to be a menace to public safety, therefore I can and will disclose to the proper entities what I know about you.

Patient: Do you know that will ruin me?

Doctor: I don't give a fuck about how your life turns out. You set all this shit in motion, not me. Now you have to face the consequences of your actions.

Patient: I don't know what to say. I came here thinking you would help me.

Doctor: What the fuck would you have me do?

Patient: What about me?

Doctor: I can't make this shit any clearer. There is nothing else we need to talk about. I can't fix what you've gotten yourself into. All I can do is try to make you see that all your problems are of your own making. You need to carry your ass home and talk to your wife. Now if there's nothing more, I have other patients to see, so please get the fuck out of my office.

The patient leaves the doctors office.

He sits in his car overlooking the city from Haynes Point Park. He thinks to himself how beautiful the city looks from there, how peaceful things seem from that point of view. His cell phone has been ringing for hours. He sets it to vibrate and throws it on the passenger seat of his car. From here, he can see the airport, and he watches as the airplanes land and take off.

He knows he'll probably lose his job, which means he'll never fly again, and that thought saddens him. What he most regrets is not being able to face his wife and tell her what he's done. It's been hours now since he left that fucking doctor's office, and true to his word, he must have talked to his wife because she's been calling for hours.

As he ponders what he's about to do, he realizes there are a great many things he now regrets, but there is no way humanly possible to fix them now, and he can't face what he's done. He walks back to his car and takes the gun out of the glove box, says a silent good-bye to his family, puts the barrel of the gun against the roof of his mouth, and pulls the trigger.

***

The doctor's second session of the day, 1300

His administrative assistant lets the doctor know his next patient is waiting. He tells her to send the patient in.

The patient takes a seat, and the doctor goes over the ground rules for the session.

Doctor: Now, what the fuck can I do for you today?

Patient: Is that how you talk to your patients?

Doctor: Is there a problem with your hearing?

Patient: No. I wasn't expecting that kind of language from a therapist.

Doctor: We're not all alike. I don't believe in wasting my time or yours. I prefer to keep things simple, and I see no reason to complicate shit with twenty-dollar words that I'd have to explain to you anyway. I'm not here to treat you like a child or to insult your intelligence, so give me the same courtesy. Now that we're past that, I ask again, what the fuck can I do for you?

Patient: It's cool. I'm a cop, so I can take it. My supervisors told me that in order for me to return to work, I needed to have a psychological evaluation.

Doctor: Evaluation for what?

Patient: I have a few issues.

Doctor: What the fuck are these issues your referring to? Obviously your aware of why your people sent you to me. I told you before we started this, I don't have time to waste bullshiting with you.

Patient: I have anger issues. And certain sexual fantasies and urges I am having a hard time controlling.

Doctor: I'll make this easy. Can you please tell me what you've done for your department to be on the verge of firing your ass?

Patient starts to get angry with the way the doctor's speaking to him.

Patient: (Raising his voice) Hey, Doc, you need to tone down your language. I'm not gonna allow you to continue to curse at me.

The doctor is working on his desktop as the patient speaks. When the doctor is finished with the computer, he returns his attention to the patient.

Doctor: Fuck you, you are not in charge here. Furthermore, motherfucker, this is my house. Let me break it down to you. First of all, I don't owe you shit, not respect, courtesy or any other social nicety. Your police conduct record tells me everything I need to know about you on the job.

So I don't give a fuck if they fire your ass today or tomorrow. And it's plainly obvious to me that if we don't get to what's got you all fucked up by week's end, you can kiss your law enforcement career good-bye. Have I made myself clear?

Patient: Yeah, Doc. Crystal

Doctor: Now why is your department ready to fire your ass?

Patient: I work in the southeast section of the city. Crime in those neighborhoods is rampant—drugs, prostitution, murder, gang violence, you name it. I deal with this shit every day, so if I sometimes get a little overzealous when I make an arrest, then fuck it. I get those pieces of shit who commit crimes off the street.

Doctor: How many times has doing your job as you see it gotten you jammed up?

Patient: Many times.

Doctor: How many excessive force and misconduct complaints have been filed against you? Let's deal with the excessive force complaints first.

Both the doctor and the patient light cigarettes.

Patient: At least thirty excessive force complaints in a sixteen-year career.

Doctor: And you don't think you have a problem? Why so many? That's almost two a year. Aren't you trained to make an arrest without beating the shit out of people?

Patient: What we learn in the academy and what happens in the street are fucking worlds apart. Sometimes the only way to get those fuckers to talk is to kick'em around a little.

Doctor: But you got caught more than thirty times kicking the asses of those who you perceive as the bad guys.

Patient: I have a damn good arrest record, and my work on the street has put a lot of bad people in jail.

Doctor: I wasn't speaking about your arrest record, but all the assault charges filed against your ass.

Patient: You learn it goes with the territory.

Doctor: According to some of the information sent to me, you were involved in an incident that sent a male suspect to the hospital last month. What happened there?

Patient: We had an all-points bulletin for this drug-dealing scumbag who was wanted for questioning in a homicide case. I work the midnight shift, I recognized one of his crew on the streets, so I asked the motherfucker hard where his boy was, and told him if he didn't tell, he'd end up in a box. I got what I needed, and I went to go find the motherfucker.

Doctor: What happened when you found him?

Patient: My partner and I caught that piece of shit selling drugs to kids not two blocks from an elementary school. He saw us coming and took off. We called it in and began a foot chase.

Doctor: What happened when you caught his ass?

Patient: We arrested the motherfucker.

Doctor: What the fuck did you do to your suspect when you caught him that was so fucked up charges of police brutality were filed against you again?

Patient: I had to tackle him to bring him down. His goddamn head was slammed to the pavement. He received a minor skull fracture.

Doctor: So you had nothing to do with the broken arm and ruptured spleen? and where was you partner?

Patient: (getting excited) He may have been a little bruised up. So fucking what? This motherfucker is a goddamn scumbag drug dealer. I'm not the one selling that shit to kids on the streets. I took him down. Who gives a shit how I did it.

Doctor: I don't give a shit how you talk in here, goddamnit, but when you get excited like you're ready to pounce, I suggest you calm the fuck down. The fact that you get emotional when you talk about your issues shows me exactly the kind of out-of-control cop you are. In the pursuit and apprehension of a suspect, your fucking emotions take over and you're liable to do anything, which makes you a serious liability to your department.

Now where the fuck was your partner when you beat the shit out of your suspect?

Patient: He was right there. He only helped me when we cuffed the motherfucker.

Doctor: Did he try to stop you from beating the suspect?

Patient: Yeah, after I got him down.

Doctor: Is it your job to exact retribution?

Patient: That's not what I do.

Doctor: What do you call kicking the shit out of suspects?

Patient: Part of the job.

Doctor: Is that supposed to be fucking funny?

Patient: No, it's reality.

Doctor: Who the fuck appointed you judge and jury? So it's your job to catch and punish suspects, the hell with the courts?

Patient: You don't see the shit I have to deal with on a daily basis.

Doctor: You don't have a fucking clue about what I see. I see motherfuckers like you every day, I see the end result of what people like you do when you go on rampages. I see the worst in human behavior every day, so don't tell me what the fuck I have or haven't seen, and let's concentrate on your shit.

What did your partner do when you got back to the station?

Patient: He put in a request for another partner.

Doctor: How'd that make you feel?

Patient: I didn't give a shit.

Doctor: Why?

Patient: Because I've had other partners before, some good, some pussies. I prefer to work alone anyway.

Doctor: Is the real reason so that you can do what the fuck you want in the street and not have another officer around to report it?

Patient: That has nothing to do with it. My methods are a little unorthodox, and some rookie cops can't handle it.

Doctor: Unorthodox or illegal?

Patient: What's your point?

Doctor: If you can't see where I'm going with this, it's because you don't want to see the point.

Patient: I see you accusing me of shit like everybody else.

Doctor: I haven't accused you of shit. I'm trying to get you to talk to me about what's going on.

Patient: I'm trying. This shit isn't easy.

Doctor: It should be if you've done nothing wrong, nor should you be defensive if you have nothing to hide, but we both know that's bullshit, don't we?

Patient: Hey, I do my fucking job. There are other pussy cops on the force who would shit themselves if they worked my beat. And I don't run from problems, I deal with the shit.

Doctor: And you have no problem with your methods?

Patient: If it works, I don't.

Doctor: What is the racial makeup of the area you patrol?

Patient: It's predominately black.

Doctor: What percentage of the suspects you arrest would you say are black?

Patient: Eighty percent.

Doctor: Are you a racist?

Patient: I do my job. I don't give a fuck what color they are.

Doctor: You didn't answer my question. Are you a racist.

Patient: No. I work in a predominately black area. Of course most of my collars are gonna be black.

Doctor: According to reports I've had sent to me by your department and the arrest record you're so proud of, you could have arrested dozens of whites but you chose not to, mostly white women and young white males you observed coming into high crime areas to buy drugs, yet you let them go and busted the dealers.

Patient: I'm after the people who sell that shit on the streets.

Doctor: What about the motherfuckers who buy that shit on the streets? Are they in any way guilty of perpetuating the very thing you hope to eliminate?

Patient: I guess you have a point, but that's not my focus.

Doctor: Please explain that asinine statement.

Patient: I see the dealers as the problem.

Doctor: No, motherfucker, you see a bunch of useless, no good niggers on the street selling that shit to good, upstanding white citizens, and you want to punish them for it, isn't that the case?

Based on your own department's internal affairs reports, for the last four years, you requested to work drug unit details in parts of the city with the highest concentrations of open-air drug activity so that you can target the dealers. You've never wanted to be part of the sting unit that arrests the buyers. In fact, your record shows you've flat out refused that detail.

Patient: That's bullshit. That's not the way it is.

Doctor: Well, tell me how it is. Tell me what happened to you, officer badass, that turned you into a motherfucker your department now wants to get rid of.

Patient: I don't know.

Doctor: I told you, I don't have time to waste bullshiting with you. Either tell me what I need to know or get the fuck out of my office and kiss your career good-bye. It's your choice. Either way, I don't give a fuck..

Patient: I've always been aggressive on the streets as a cop. Like you, I don't have time to be bullshiting or wasting time playing games with scum. About four years ago, my daughter was in the ninth grade, she experimented with crack at a friend's house and it damn near killed her. She can barely function now.

Her mother blamed me because, in her eyes, my job was more important than our family, but that was never the case. I was a good father. Yeah, I worked long hours, but I had a family to support.

She told me that if I were home more, maybe this wouldn't have happened. She blamed everything on me. We didn't last much longer after that, and we divorced less than a year later. My daughter lives with my ex, and I only see her maybe once a month.

Doctor: When you see your daughter, what goes through your mind?

Patient: All the things she could have been, all the things she could have accomplished if it weren't for that shit that poisoned her.

Doctor: Who do you blame for what happened to your daughter?

Patient: Who the fuck do you think? The motherfuckers that sold that shit to her and her friends.

Doctor: Think before you answer this next question. Was your daughter in any way responsible for what happened to her? After all, teens think it's a right of passage to experiment with drugs and other shit they know could hurt them.

Patient: In a small way, maybe, but she was my baby, and she was so young. If she couldn't have gotten any of that shit, she'd be fine.

Doctor: You said she and a friend tried the drug. Was the friend that gave her that shit not partly to blame for what happened to your daughter?

Patient: Yeah, she provided the shit, but she was just a kid too. Look Doc, the people who sell that shit are the people I blame, not the kids who get caught up. If it wasn't available, they couldn't use.

Doctor: You really believe that shit?

Patient: Yeah, I do, and I'm gonna do whatever I have to when it comes to taking down the fuckers who sell that shit, and I don't give a fuck what their goddamn color or ethnic background is, and if that means killing every fucking one of them, I'll do just that, and you can write that down and send it to whoever the fuck you want.

Doctor smiles

Doctor: I see you've had a few complaints filed against you by women who work as prostitutes.

Patient: That's all bullshit. I was cleared of all that shit.

Doctor: Why don't you tell me about one of those incidents?

Patient: As on any typical night, I'm on patrol on my beat, and I'll see a known prostitute get in a car or van with a trick. I follow them till they stop, and I bust both of them.

Doctor: Had they done anything?

Patient: When I walked up to the car, she'd usually have his dick in her mouth.

Doctor: If it went down like that, why did you get a complaint?

Patient: Look, all those skanks lie and will do whatever they have to to avoid getting arrested or to get the arresting officer jammed up.

Doctor: Have you ever fucked a prostitute in exchange for not arresting her?

Patient: What?

Doctor: You heard what the fuck I said. How many of those skanks have you fucked in exchange for not hauling their ass off to jail?

Patient: A few.

Doctor: You've been accused of doing more than just having sex with prostitutes. What else have you been into on the streets? Tell me about the sexual urges you find hard to control.

Patient: Look, this is something I'm not proud of. The shit just happened, and I couldn't stop.

Doctor: You want to tell me what you're talking about?

Patient: There was this one hooker who I had a few times. One night, she was giving me head in my patrol car. After she finished, she told me she could turn me on to something that would blow my mind. I asked her what it was, and she told me to come by her place the next week.

Doctor: What was it she turned you on to?

Patient: Her daughter.

Doctor: How old was the daughter?

Patient: Ten.

Doctor: What did you do with a ten-year-old girl?

Patient: When I got to the hooker's place, she took me into a room, and the girl was sitting on the edge of the bed. She looked a lot older than ten. I didn't fucking know she was that young until her mother told me. Her mother led me over to her, and she sat in a chair across from us to watch. The next thing I know, the girl is in my pants and she's sucking my dick.

Doctor: How long did this go on?

Patient: With her daughter, about once a week for about four months. Sometimes her mother would join us.

Doctor: How did it make you feel, knowing a child was performing oral sex on you?

Patient: Like I said, this is some shit I'm not proud of, but the two of them were the best head I ever had in my life, and before I knew what was happening, I only wanted her daughter.

Doctor: How long did you have that child sucking your dick?

Patient: Less than a year.

The doctor tries to maintain a neutral expression as he talks to the patient.

Doctor: What other shit did you do?

Patient: Hey, like I said, I'm not proud of what happened, but I found that I enjoyed it and couldn't stop.

Doctor: Did you want to stop?

Patient: Not at first.

Doctor: Why, if you knew what you were doing was wrong? Why didn't you stop?

Patient: Because the more I did it, the more I liked being with young girls. The bitch that turned me on to that shit would line up other neighborhood girls for me about once a week. It was addictive.

Doctor: As a police officer, what you were doing didn't bother you?

Patient: No.

Doctor: Why do you think that was the case?

Patient: I don't fucking know. I didn't give a shit.

Doctor: Don't hand me that bullshit. You know exactly why. You see them as throw-away people. You see them as less than human, as objects you can use as you see fit. And because you're a cop working rough areas, who's gonna know and who gives a fuck?

How many children have you been involved with?

Patient: Since this started, a lot. I didn't fucking keep count.

Doctor: When is the last time you were with a child?

Patient: A few weeks ago.

Doctor: How is it you were able to get away with this for so long without any of the children talking?

Patient: Look, they were paid or threatened, I don't fucking know. All I know is, I would be told when and where to be. If I agreed, I'd be there.

Doctor: Were you ever involved with young boys?

Patient: Fuck no.

Doctor: Motherfucker, don't come off on me like you're above being with little boys. If it doesn't bother you to be with ten-year-old little girls, there's no telling what you'd do. You get off on little girls sucking your dick, so why not a little boy?

Patient: I'm not a fucking faggot.

Doctor: That's what most pedophiles claim, and I wish the fuck you would sit here looking me in my eyes and say you're not a pedophile.

Patient: I've never had a boy.

Doctor: Think about what you just said. "I've never had a boy." Not that you're not interested, not that the thought disgusts you "I've never had a boy." you haven't been offered any one's little boy yet.

You'd jump all over that, because in your sick, twisted, fucking mind, you've turned the hood you work in into your own private sexual playground. Your as much a predator as any other child molester.

Patient: I'm not a fucking child molester. Their parents make them do that shit.
Doctor: It's just another fringe benefit, is that it?
Patient: That's the way I saw it.
Doctor: What would you do if you couldn't get a little girl once you found that's what you were interested in?
Patient: I'd get pissed and threaten to lock somebody's ass up.
Doctor: So you lock up only the ones you couldn't extort for sexual favors, including their children.

How many little girls do you think you turned out, girls whose innocence you've stolen?
Patient: I don't know. They're all ani...
Doctor: Was animals the word you were looking for?
Patient: Hey, the way I see it, if I can get a little head for free, why the fuck not? They're on the streets trying to make a living. A lot of them do that shit to take care of their kids. Most of the time, I let that shit go unless it's obviously in my face. I'm helping them.
Doctor: So it's fine for women to sell themselves on the streets to make a living as long as you can get a free piece of pussy or some head from either them or their children now and then, is that it?
Patient: Call it a fringe benefit.
Doctor: No, I call it fucked up. How are prostitutes any less a menace to society than drug dealers? What they do can have just as many negative consequences to society and to the neighborhoods they work in. It's not like the shit they do is legal. And you take shit to the next level. You're abusing children of prostitutes, and you call it a fucking fringe benefit.
Patient: Yeah, well, in our eyes, selling pussy isn't the same as selling drugs.
Doctor: Who are you referring to when you say "our."
Patient: Most of the officers who see what I see every night.
Doctor: Is your only sexual outlet prostitutes you bust on the streets and their children, How is your personal life?
Patient: Fucked up.
Doctor: Can you explain that?
Patient: My personal life is in the toilet. My last girlfriend and I felt that it was best if we parted company.
Doctor: What were the issues there?

Patient: I fucked up. I would get angry about shit that would happen on the job, and I would bring that shit home. We'd argue a lot, and one time I hit her. She said she had grown afraid of my moods.

Doctor: How long were you two together?

Patient: Less than a year. The bitch didn't give me a chance.

Doctor: So all women are bitches now?

Patient: I didn't say that.

Doctor: You didn't have to. It's evident in the way you treat women, who, as you say, sell themselves on the streets to take care of their children, not because they want to. You see an opportunity to exploit them and their children, not to be the guardian of women that you should be. You see, it's in your power to at least help some of them, yet you exploit their situation just so you can get a quick nut and go home.

Why should your ex-girlfriend have stayed with a motherfucker that was beating on her?

Patient: I never said I beat her. I got angry and hit her one time.

Doctor: Why should she put up with you hitting her? You're a cop with a gun, which must have frightened her.

Patient: She wasn't scared of me. She was a disloyal bitch.

Doctor: How the hell can you be loyal to someone you don't trust and who beats on you?

Patient: She wanted out of the relationship anyway.

Doctor: How was the sex between you two?

Patient: It was okay at first, and after a while it went downhill.

Doctor: Why do you think that was the case?

Patient: No matter what I did, I couldn't please her, it wasn't enough.

Doctor: Bullshit. You got used to being with children and women you didn't have to give a fuck about.

Patient: So what?

Doctor: So what? Now you know what your problem is motherfucker. You want children sexually.

Patient: I didn't ask for this shit to happen to me.

Doctor: No, the bitch that gave and then sold you her ten-year-old daughter made you do it.

Patient: That's the way it happened.

Doctor: Let's get back to your last girlfriend.

Patient: What about her?

Doctor: Were you able to satisfy her in bed?

Patient: She complained that I didn't care about her needs, that once I got my nut I was done.
Doctor: So you're saying you're a minute man. You'd cum quick, and she couldn't get hers.
Patient: Something like that.
Doctor: Was sex with your wife like that?
Patient: No, We had a great sex life until my daughter's accident, and then it all went to shit.
Doctor: Let's talk about that.
Were you fucking prostitutes when you were married?
Patient: Hell no.
Doctor: Why not? They were around then.
Patient: That shit never occurred to me.
Doctor: Did you fantasize about being with children?
Patient: No.
Doctor: Had you ever thought about fucking any of your daughter's friends before her accident?
Patient: Of course not. Hell no.
Doctor: You ever fantasize about fucking your daughter?

Patient quickly jumps out of his chair and starts to approach the doctor with a look of rage on his face.
Doctor also jumps out of his seat to meet the patient.

Doctor: You had better sit your punk ass back in that seat. I told you, motherfucker, I have no problem fucking you up. I'm not a small child you can intimidate or a crackhead junkie who's afraid to go to jail. I hold the cards here, bitch. Now sit your ass back in that seat.

Patient sits down and says nothing, seething with anger.

Doctor: How is sex with the street women?
Patient: I don't have to waste time being nice or friendly with those bitches. I don't have to spend a dime or give a shit how they feel. I get my dick sucked or I fuck one of them, and it's done.
Doctor: Have you had any real women in your life since your last girlfriend?
Patient: Not really.
Doctor: Why not? Afraid you can't handle a real woman?
Patient: Look, I don't want to answer any more of these fucking questions, and I'm tired of this psychobabble bullshit.
Doctor: Fine with me: There's the door, you're free to walk out that motherfucker any time you want. But know this: You'll be one

unemployed piece-of-shit cop by the time you get your sorry ass home.

Patient: I don't give a shit.

Doctor: Yes, you do, but you have to live with the choices you make and the consequences that follow, not me.

Patient: So how long do I have to keep coming here until you decide I can go back to work?

Doctor lights a cigarette.

Doctor: You don't understand how this shit works. It's not a matter of you going back to work. Working as what is the question.

Patient: What the fuck are you talking about?

Doctor: You forget why you're here.

Patient: Look, all you have to do is tell the department brass that all I need is some rest and I'll be fine.

Doctor: You must be out of your motherfucking mind if you think I'm going to tell anyone you're fit for duty as a cop, because your definitely not.

Patient: Well, how long will I have to keep coming here to see you then?

Doctor: Never again. Once the force releases your ass, you couldn't afford my fee.

Patient: What? You're gonna recommend I be terminated from my job?

Doctor: No, my recommendation will be that you are psychologically and emotionally unstable and under no circumstances should you be allowed to carry a weapon.

Patient: What? You asshole. They'll terminate me if you give them that recommendation.

Doctor: That's not my problem, and I don't give a fuck. You see all those degrees on the wall behind me? I didn't order those motherfuckers from Ebay. They say I am vastly qualified to determine the mental status of anyone I talk to, and you are indeed a time bomb waiting to explode.

Patient: You'd ruin my life.

Doctor: I'm not ruining your life. Maybe they'll assign you a desk job, I don't know. In any event, that's out of my control.

Patient: I don't wanna sit on some fucking desk. I can't do it.

Doctor: Does wearing that gun on your hip make you feel more manly? So much so that you two can't bear to be without each other?

Patient: Fuck you.

Doctor: No, I'm afraid not. Now your session is over. Please get the fuck out of my office. And rest assured, your department will have my report today by close of business.

Patient leaves the doctor's office in a rage and slams the door on his way out. He gets to his car and sits inside for a short while, trying to decide what he should do.

He thinks to himself that if the fucking doctor recommends that he not carry a weapon, he's gonna be fired from the force, and he could face charges for having sex with minors if that motherfucker reports him.

He realizes there is a confidentiality between doctor and patient, he knows the doctor can't reveal anything to the authorities that they discussed. *So fuck that goddamn doctor. If he does tell anyone what I told him, I'll sue his ass off.*

He decides to go home and sleep his anger off, and later he'll go see his favorite little dick sucker. He gets home thirty minutes later to his shity apartment, lays on his bed, and goes to sleep.

A knock on his door wakes him at 6 pm. He looks through the peephole and sees a pizza deliveryman at the door. He opens the door and tells the delivery guy he didn't order a pizza.

Before he can react, the deliveryman pulls out a canister of mace from inside his pizza bag and sprays him in the face. The delivery man quickly forces his way into the officer's apartment, followed by three other men.

They rush in and close the door. The officer then feels himself being punched in the face hard by one of the assailants. His eyes still burning from the mace, he feels each of his arms being held by two of the intruders as one mercilessly punches him in the face.

After the fifth blow to the right side of his face, he feels his jaw shatter, and blood pours out of his mouth. He wants to fall down, but they hold him up. The forth intruder now takes over the punishment to his face. All his blows make contact with the left side of the officer's face. Teeth come flying out of his mouth with each blow.

The intruders sit him in a chair, tying his hands behind his back and his legs to the chair. Each man now takes turns punching the officer in the face and kicking him in his stomach and chest.

The officer's pain is excruciating. He finds it hard to breathe, and he starts wishing for death. But the intruders don't grant his wish as the beating to his body continues. He passes out from the pain.

The deliveryman halts the beating and tells the others it's not time for this piece of shit to die. One man grabs the officer's hair and holds his head up while the delivery man pours water over his bloody face to try to wake him.

The officer comes to, but just barely. His face is so swollen, he can't talk. His eyes are almost swollen shut. He tries to think, but his pain is too intense. He can't swallow, so blood and saliva pour from his mouth. One word does come to him though, "why." Just as that thought came to him, one of the men begins to speak.

"Hey mothafucka, can you hear me? You're probably wondering why this shit is happening to you. I'll tell you, bitch. We know who you are. You're a piece of shit cop who thinks he can do whatever the fuck he wants. We hear you like fucking little girls and making them suck on your dick— little girls from our hood, mothafucka! We hear you been doin this shit for a while now. We have news for you, bitch. Your days of abusing our women is over. You see, bitch, the boys here wanted to just come by and smoke your bitch ass, but I wanted to make sure you felt a lot of pain first, and then I had an even better idea. Check this out and tell me what you think."

"We know you have a daughter. We hear the bitch is crippled. I figured if you can make our little sisters suck your dick, we should make your daughter do the same shit to us."

The officer tries to react to that, but all he can do is moan in protest and try to shake loose, but being tied to a chair, he can do nothing.

"We have your wife's address, and when we get finished with you, we're gonna pay that bitch a visit. I want you to die knowing we had fun with your daughter and your wife. I want you to imagine my dick in that crippled bitch's mouth, and me nuttin' down her throat. And while I make her suck my dick, my boys are gonna be gang fuckin' your wife, and we're gonna make the shit last for days."

He hears what was said, and he knows in his heart they mean every word, and there is absolutely nothing he can do about it. Tears of sorrow and pain pour from his eyes. He can, even through all his pain, imagine the scenario just laid before him, and he prays for God to help him and his family. He also realizes at that instant he thought of his ex-wife and child as his family and how much he really loved them.

The deliveryman takes out a semi-automatic pistol from under his jacket and attaches a silencer to the barrel. He looks at the bound officer and asks him is he ready to die as he points the gun to his head. The officer can only cry as the deliveryman pulls the trigger. The bullet soundlessly exits the gun and enters the officers head.

***

The doctor's third session of the day, 1:00 pm

The doctor's administrative assistant calls on the intercom to let him know his next patient is in the office and ready to be seen. She is sent into the doctor's office. She comes in and takes a seat.

The doctor goes over the rules and asks the patient if she is ready to begin.

The patient laughs and asks the doctor if he is joking.

Doctor: Do you see me laughing?

Patient: We do need to get a few things straight. You are not going to be cursing when you talk to me. I did not come here to be verbally abused by you. I don't smoke or drink, and I would appreciate it if you didn't do either while I'm here. You need to know that there is nothing unbalanced about me and I don't care who you are. You will address me with the same respect you yourself expect. You being a psychiatrist doesn't mean you're God to me, and your implied threat to harm me was totally unprofessional and uncalled for. Have I made myself clear?

While the patient was talking the doctor was working on his computer. She asks him again did he hear what she just said.

Doctor: I heard every word you said.

Patient: Good. Now can we get started? I have other business to attend to today.

Doctor: In the last year, how many patients suddenly got ill when they where recovering or mysteriously died while in your care?

Patient: What are you talking about?

Doctor: Let me try this one more time. First of all, I'm not one of your helpless, crippled, or sick ass patients. You are not in charge here. You don't dictate terms in my office.

This is my practice. I will speak however I deem necessary. I will conduct my fucking office affairs as I see fit. It is your license and possibly your freedom at stake, not mine.

You are free to get the fuck out of my office whenever you wish, but if you wish to continue to practice medicine I suggest you come down off that fucking high horse you're on and cooperate with me. Have I made myself clear?

Patient gives the doctor a nasty look, gets up, and heads for the door.

The doctor hits the intercom switch and asks his assistant to contact Doctor Wheeler at Mercy General Hospital. Patient stops at the door and turns to face the doctor.

Doctor: I told you, you are free to carry your ass out that door whenever you wish. I will not sit here playing fucking games with you.

Patient comes back to the chair and sits down.
Doctor lights a cigarette.

Doctor: Now, for the last time, are you ready to get started?

Patient: You know, I heard you are one of the best practicing psychiatrists in the state. I guess I'll have to make that judgment for myself. And please address me as Nurse Rashanaria, Doctor Feelgood, if that's a real name.

Doctor: I'm not going to address you by any title at all. Titles are meaningless in here.

Patient: Then how should I address you? Because based on what I've seen so far, you don't live up to your name, Dr. Feelgood. Nothing you've said so far has made me feel good.

Doctor: That's not what I'm here to do, I'm totally indifferent to how you feel. You might have major issues that need to be dealt with. The first being, what was your mother smoking when she named you Rashanaria?

Patient: Excuse me?

Doctor: If you want to sit here and play fucking games, I'll indulge that shit until Doctor Wheeler calls back. I have other patients today, and I want you the fuck out of my office.

Patient: All right, doctor. I don't want to be here anymore than you want me here, but we both know I was ordered to come here.

Doctor: You are wasting my goddamn time and my time is precious to me and my patients. If you wish to continue this antagonistic behavior please do it at your place of employment, not here.

Patient: Can we get started, doctor?

Doctor: Yes, if you're ready to stop bull shitting. Why the fuck are you here?

Patient sighs as she looks at the doctor.

Doctor: Don't come in here an act brand new on me. Doctors and especially nurses are some of the most foul-mouthed motherfuckers you can talk to, and that's on the job. I have an active practice at two area hospitals. I know how you motherfuckers speak about each other and your patients, so get over it and answer my questions.

Patient: I was ordered by my hospital administrator to come see you.

Doctor: Why?

Patient: As a condition of employment.

Doctor: Stop wasting my motherfucking time and talk to me straight. You know full well why. I need to hear it from you.

Patient: They suspect patients in my ward are being harmed by one of the nurses.

Doctor: You are the Charge Nurse. You have access to every patient in your ward. Have you harmed any of your patients?

Patient: I supervise a staff of nurses, but when I do care for patients, I've always administered the care prescribed by the doctors for their patients.

Doctor: That was not my question.

Patient: No, I have no reason to hurt the people I'm supposed to be caring for, and even if I did, I wouldn't be stupid enough to admit it to you or anyone else.

Doctor: Then if that's the case, why do your people suspect you?

Patient: There are other nurses who work my ward. No one suspects me of anything. We are all being ordered to undergo an evaluation, that means every nurse who works in the ward.

Doctor: What ward would that be?

Patient: Intensive care. I work the evening shift at my hospital.

Doctor: What has happened at your hospital to make your people think patients were being mistreated or harmed?

Patient: Patients come in to intensive care suffering all kinds of injuries. Sometimes if they are lucky, they get better. We do lose patients, but every hospital does.

Doctor: How many patients have died in the last year while in your ward?

Patient: Six.

Doctor: What type of injuries did these patients present with?

Patient: I can't remember them all.

Doctor: Give me the ones you do remember. You are the Charge Nurse for your ward, that's some shit you need to know.

Patient: One was a motorcycle accident, another was a stabbing, a shooting, and one guy fell from a ladder.

The doctor works on his computer as the patient recalls what she can.

Doctor: Do you remember the race of any of these individuals?

Patient: Their race? What difference does that make?
Doctor: I just want to know what you recall about these patients.
Patient: I can't remember, but I'm sure I can find the information for you.
Doctor: We'll come back to that.
Patient: Fine.
Doctor: How long have you been a nurse?
Patient: Ten years. I finished college in 1994 and all my nursing training in 1998.
Doctor: According to my records, you're thirty-six.
Patient: Correct.
Doctor: How is your life outside the walls of the hospital?
Patient: If your trying to ask about my personal life, it's fine.
Doctor: Are you seeing anyone.
Patient: That's none of your business.
Doctor: Everything that concerns you, your medical career, your past, present, and future is my business as long as you sit your ass in that chair.
Patient: Yes, I've been involved with the same guy for four years now.
Doctor: What does he do for a living?
Patient: He's a sportscaster for channel thirteen news— Jimmy Hale. You've probably seen him on TV.
Doctor: No, I don't waste my time watching TV.

Patient rolls her eyes at the doctor's statement.

Doctor: What justifies that air of arrogance you project.
Patient: Because I'm confident I'm arrogant? Because I'm sure of myself I'm arrogant? Because I'm educated, I'm arrogant? Is that the way you see me doctor?
Doctor: No. Normally, confidence, self-assuredness, and intelligence are all admirable qualities, so much so that those that possess them do not have to flaunt them to be noticed by others. You, however, need to feel as though you're superior to everyone around you. That's a problem.
Patient: That's your opinion.
Doctor: No, that's a simple observation based solely on your responses to me. I would say that someone like you has a very small circle of friends and confidants. Many people would be turned off by your smug attitude.
Patient: I have all the friends I need.
Doctor: How many of your close friends are black?
Patient: A few females. Not many.

Doctor: Why is that?

Patient: Who I choose to be friends with is my business, and I don't see how this is relevant to why I'm here.

Doctor: You wouldn't. That's why I'm the psychiatrist.

Doctor smiles as he lights another cigarette and makes note of the patient's behavior.

Doctor: Have you always been attracted to white men?

Patient: I prefer to be with white men.

Doctor: That wasn't my question.

Patient: No, I was not always attracted to white men. I started dating white guys in college.

Doctor: Why?

Patient: Why are you so concerned about my dating habits?

Doctor: Who you're fucking doesn't concern me.

Patient: Then why ask about my preference in men?

Doctor: Do you date black men?

Patient: No.

Doctor: Why not?

Patient: I have, in high school, but I came to the conclusion long ago that the vast majority of black men are pieces of shit, and, as I said, I prefer white men.

Doctor: Did you have a bad experience in your past that causes you to avoid dating black men?

Patient: It has been my experience that black men bring too much baggage and drama to a relationship, and I choose not to deal with that.

Doctor: Explain what you mean when you say "baggage" and "drama."

Patient: Most black men are intimidated by successful, educated black women. I don't have time for that. I don't need a man I have to financially support, and I don't need the emotional baggage that comes with them.

Doctor: What baggage would that be? Please go into detail.

Patient: Most black men are lazy and don't want anymore out of life than to work menial jobs, stay drunk, lay up with as many women as they can, and have babies everywhere that they can't afford and have no interest in taking care of. They believe all a woman needs is his dick, and that's the extent of his contribution to a relationship.

Black men have no concept of what loyalty is, and their only goal in life is to fuck as many women as they can. The vast majority of black men are incarcerated for all kinds of crimes, and the children they father often end up in jail like there daddies.

I worked hard to get where I am. I don't need a hustler in my life. I will not date a man who has been in jail for anything, has babies, has no education, who doesn't work and has no plan for the future. I don't associate with a lot of black women because I get so sick and tired of hearing them complain about the sorry-ass men in their lives.

Most of the women I know who choose to be with black men are women who are educated and have good careers, yet they choose to waste their lives on sorry-ass niggers who won't amount to a damn thing.

Doctor: This topic makes you angry.

Patient: Yes.

Doctor: Why? If you don't deal with black men what do you care?

Patient: Because I have had friends who found themselves in terrible relationships, always with black men, and it hurt to see them destroy their lives over a piece of shit man who wasn't worth a damn.

Doctor: Do you now have white friends who date black men?

Patient: Yes.

Doctor: What do you think about those situations?

Patient: I don't offer any opinion, and I avoid being with both of them at the same time. But when it ends in a disaster, as a few have, I tell them I don't want to hear about it.

Doctor: So are you telling me you have no contact with black men at all, not even the men in your family?

Patient: On a personal level, no, I don't have much contact with my family. I prefer to have as little social contact with black men as possible. That's my choice, and it's not a problem for me.

Doctor: Does the way you feel about black men affect the way you perform your duties as a nurse?

Patient: No.

Doctor: We'll come back to that.

Patient: Fine.

Doctor: Can you describe for me a little of your experiences with the man you're currently dating?

The doctor's intercom beeps. He is told Doctor Wheeler is returning his call. He tells his assistant to inform Doctor Wheeler he is with a patient, and he'll call him back.

Patient: What do you want to know?

Doctor: How is your relationship?
Patient: Fulfilling and wonderful.
Doctor: Describe your relationship for me.
Patient: Jimmy is a great guy. He graduated college the same year I did. He is not intimidated by my profession. He is supportive of my needs and goals in life. He has a great career and a bright future. He comes home to me every night and I've never doubted his faithfulness to me. We just bought a home together last year, and we plan on having a baby and getting married this year. We truly love each other.
Doctor: Prior to meeting Jimmy, how would you describe your other relationships with white men?
Patient: About the same as what I have with Jimmy, except we were not talking marriage or anything. My experiences with white men have always been positive and drama free, because at least they were going somewhere and had more on their minds than drinking and partying.
Doctor: So all black men, in your opinion, are pieces of shit who only want to get high, party, and fuck everything they see?
Patient: The vast majority, yes. We both know that's what youth is about, but at some point, that changes. And when it comes to men, especially black men, that part doesn't sink in, and I don't have time for that.
Doctor: Are you aware of how your use of language changes when you talk about black compared to white men?
Patient: What are you talking about doctor?
Doctor: Playing stupid on me again.
Patient: I am far from stupid, and I resent being called that.
Doctor: Then stop acting like it. Whenever you described any experiences with black men, your language became laced with very colorful expletives, nurse talk 101. How was your relationship with your father?
Patient: I have always had a good relationship with my father. He is a strong and gentle man. My mother adores him still to this day, and so do I.
Doctor: How does he feel about your choice in men?
Patient: My parents accept the choices I make for myself and the direction my life is taking.
Doctor: You say they accept the choices you make. Accepting a choice and parental approval are two totally different things. Your par-

ents love and support you, but do you know what their opinions are on your choice to date white men?

Patient: My father told me long ago, that he couldn't choose my partner for me. He said, "Just make sure whoever you do choose is good to you." That's approval enough for me.

Doctor: Have you always introduced your men to your father?

Patient: Not always. Only the ones I was serious with, and they were few.

Doctor: Have your parents met Jimmy?

Patient: Yes.

Doctor: What did your father think of him?

Patient: As far as I know, he was fine with it. My father wanted me to marry a brother, I know that deep down, but that's never going to happen. My mother liked him, but she probably feels the same way as my father. As long as my parents love me, they'll accept my choices in men. But even if they didn't, this is my life, and I will live it to make myself happy, not my parents.

Doctor: That doesn't sound like the kind of approval you were looking for.

Patient: Well, I am an adult. My parent's opinions mean a lot to me, but I won't live my life based on their views of the men I choose to be with.

Doctor: Do you have relationships with any of the men in your family besides your father?

Patient: I have no siblings, and I choose not to deal with many of my relatives.

Doctor: Why?

Patient: I've never really been close to any of my aunts or uncles, and growing up, I didn't spend a lot of time with my cousins.

Doctor: There must have been times when you were a young child at family functions, surrounded by children of other family members all playing together.

Patient: Yes, there was. Now can we move on?

Doctor: Is there a reason why you don't want to talk about your early family relationships?

Patient: I told you, I don't have any fucking relationships with any family members outside of my parents, and I don't see them often either.

Doctor: You're a goddamn liar. Something extremely significant happened to you as a young child, something within your family that altered who you were to a significant degree.

Patient: What do you want from me?

Doctor: The truth. Something has you fucked up inside, something you've been holding in for years, probably since you were a very young child. We need to find out what the fuck is going on.

Patient: You're a fucking bastard.

Doctor: Are you ready to talk about what it is you've kept buried inside you all these years?

Patient: No.

Doctor: Fine with me. You can let whatever it is you're keeping bottled up inside you destroy your life or you can face it head on. Either way, it's your call. You need to decide quickly because I don't have time to waste with you. As you said earlier, You're grown and quite capable of making your own decisions.

Be prepared to live with the consequences of those decisions when the anger inside you erupts and destroys everyone around you and all that you've worked for. No matter how it plays out, I don't give a fuck so, decide now.

Patient stares at the doctor as he lights another cigarette. The anger she feels is becoming more intense as she lets her thoughts go back to a time she has tried all her life to forget. She tells the doctor her story.

I was twelve years old. I went to stay with my uncle and his wife on my father's side of the family for a weekend while my parents went out of town for the weekend.

It was during the summer months, so I was out of school. I enjoyed spending time with my aunt and uncle. They were always so good to me. They had two sons. Michael was my age, and Reggie was eighteen. Reggie had taken Michael and me to the movies early one Saturday afternoon while my aunt and uncle went shopping. I remember us having a really good time that day. When we returned home from the movie, I remember Michael and I went bike riding for most of the afternoon.

I got tired of riding and wanted to go home, so I left Michael with his friends and went home. My aunt and uncle hadn't returned home, but Reggie was there. We watched TV for a while, and I remember him asking me if I wanted to play a game with him.

He said we had to play the game in his room. He sat me on his bed and told me how pretty I was and touched my face. He sat next to me and said that when people like each other, they play the touching game.

He put his arm around me and asked me to kiss him on his cheek. Being twelve years old, I didn't see a problem with kissing him on the cheek. Then he asked me if he could show me how adults kissed, and I let him show me.

He started touching my legs and my breasts and said it was part of the game. He put my hands on his waist and asked me to hold him as he kissed me. I remember not being nervous or frightened because this was my cousin. He was older than me, and I had no reason to believe he would hurt me.

He started taking his clothes off and asked me to take off my blouse and pants. He said it was part of the game. We got undressed, and then he said he wanted to show me something as part of the game. He pulled off his underwear, stood in front of me, and asked me to hold his dick with both hands. He said it would get bigger in my hands like magic.

He poured something on his dick and said I would like it, that it tasted sweet. He asked me to put it in my mouth and pretend it was a lollipop. He took off my bra and started feeling my breast. He got on top of me and started putting his fingers between my legs. He kept telling me how pretty I was, that this was part of the fucking game he wanted to play.

I remember that bastard's finger going in me and it hurt like hell. I think it was at that second I realized without knowing he was going to put his even bigger dick inside me, and I didn't want to play anymore.

When I told him I didn't want to play anymore, he said it was going to be okay, that I would like it. I felt the head of his dick go inside me, and it was the worst pain I could have imagined. I remember crying and asking him to stop, that I didn't want to play this game anymore, but he wouldn't stop.

Patient puts her hands to her face and starts to cry as she recalls this memory.

The doctor instructs her to take her time, to go slowly, to recall the entire memory just as it happened and to tell him all that she can remember.

He put one hand on my stomach to hold me down, and he used the other hand to spread my vagina open as he forced his dick in me. He didn't give a damn about the pain he caused me. When he finally got it all in me, he laid his body on me and fucked me like I was an animal. He used his body to muffle the sound of my crying. I don't know how long it lasted, but I was grateful his mother walked in to stop him.

I remember seeing a trail of blood shoot through the air when he yanked his dick out of me. He rushed to cover himself when my aunt walked in. The look on her face was horrific. I don't think she made a sound for the first few seconds. She just stood in the doorway, looking down on me.

I remember her closing the door and telling Reggie to get his god-damned clothes on and get out of the room. She came to me and held me in her arms, crying, repeating over and over that she was sorry.

She put me in the bathtub, cleaned me up, and then put me to bed. It took a while for the bleeding to stop. I remember her staying in the room with me the whole night. The next day, she begged me not to tell my parents what had happened. She told me that they would punish Reggie for what he'd done.

The minute my parents came to get me and I ran to hug my mother, without saying a word she knew something was wrong. When we got home, she asked me what was wrong, and I told her what Reggie had done to me, that auntie knew because she walked in the room while he was on top of me.

She held me and we both cried. Like my aunt she said over and over how sorry she was that happened to me. She also said if we told my father that more then likely he would kill Reggie. I remember telling my mother I didn't want my daddy in jail. She said, "Me neither, baby," as we both sat there crying. I remember my mother taking me to the doctor to be checked out the following Monday. I never knew what story she told the doctor about what happened to me, but I wasn't impregnated by that piece of shit and, thankfully, I didn't contract any diseases.

My mother made me promise to never tell my father what happened to me, and she promised I would never have to see any of those people again or anyone else in my family. She held me as I fell asleep in her arms, and I remember her saying, "Niggers aren't worth a fucking thing to do this to my precious baby."

The next time I would see that piece of shit would be two years later in the hospital. He was in a car wreck while coming home from work one day. He wasn't expected to survive, so the whole family was there.

I remember not wanting to go near that bastard, but my mother told me that in this instance, it was okay, because he might die, and that he deserved to die for what he did to me, and if it happened today, she'd like to be there to watch the motherfucker die.

I remember when we walked in the room, there was no one there but his mother. She could barely look at us. He was hooked up to oxygen masks and IVs. I remember thinking, *I wish I could hurt him the way he hurt me.*

My mother held my hand as we looked down on his helpless body, his mother holding his hand on the other side of the bed and crying. My mother looked at him and said, "Maybe this is payback for what you did to my baby. I hope you die, you sorry piece of shit. I hope you die and rot in hell for what you did." His mother said nothing. She sat there holding his hand and crying, not even looking up at us.

I guess he heard my mother wish death on him because he opened his eyes and turned toward us. He looked at me, tears coming down his face. He looked like a monster with all the tubes and bandages on his body. He looked at me and said, "I'm sorry." That was all he could say, those two words, as if saying that would somehow make up for what he did to me. My mother said, "Fuck you." Then she spat at him, and we turned away. I remember smiling when she said that. We left the room and went home. That bastard died a week later from his injuries. I think it was at that point when I knew I wanted to be a nurse. My mother somehow got us out of attending that motherfucker's funeral, and my father never knew what he'd done to me.

Doctor: Did your mother ever seek counseling for you?

Patient: No. We talked about what happened, and I knew it wasn't my fault that piece of shit raped me.

Doctor: Do you think it was a wise decision to keep what happened to you from your father?

Patient: Yes. There was no telling what my father would have done to that motherfucker, and like I said, I didn't want my father to go to prison for possibly killing him.

Doctor: He may have sought prison as punishment after he went to that ass with a baseball bat.

Patient: It doesn't fucking matter. That bastard died, and he died in pain, and I'm happy he's dead, and my father never had to lay a hand on him and he doesn't need to know what happened.

Doctor: Do you think your uncle ever found out from his wife what his son had done?

Patient: I would say no, because he and my father are very close, and I don't think that would be the case if he knew.

Doctor: Do you think what happened to you as a young child has anything to do with the way you feel about black men?

Patient: I'm sure it probably does. How the fuck could I not have been affected by being raped by my own cousin?

Doctor: Do you see all black men as rapist as?

Patient: I see all black men as pieces of shit. I think I said that earlier.

Doctor: Does that include your father?

Patient: Of course not.

Doctor: Then all black men are not worthless pieces of shit?

Patient: I've never felt that way about my father.

Doctor: Your father is not the only good black man in America, but if you can find one exception to your rule that all brothers are pieces of shit, then it stands to reason there are many more exceptions out there.

Patient: I feel the way I feel. I don't give a damn about any of you niggers.

Doctor: Yet you sit here and tell me the way you feel about all black men in general does not affect the way you interact with your male patients that happen to be black.

Patient: That's what I said.

Doctor: Tell me how that's possible, knowing how you feel about black men?

Patient: I don't let my personal feelings interfere with my professional duties. It's called detachment. You remember what that is, don't you? You went to medical school.

Doctor: Yes, I do, but I don't practice with the baggage you obviously carry, and have been carrying for years.

Patient: I have resolved my issues.

Doctor: Please tell me how the hell you accomplished that.

Patient: I worked it out.

Doctor: And what the fuck does that mean?

Patient: By not putting myself in situations where I have to deal with you people.

Doctor: When you say "you people," who the hell are you referring to?

Patient: Niggers. If you've listened to anything I've said, I don't deal with niggers: black men, women, or children— you people.

Doctor: If that's the case, then why the fuck are you sitting your ass in here with me now?

Patient: Because I don't have a choice.
Doctor: Didn't you know I was a black man before you came to see me?
Patient: Of course I did.
Doctor: Knowing how you feel about black men in general, why didn't you request to see another doctor?
Patient: I wasn't given a choice. Otherwise I wouldn't be here.
Doctor: The way you feel about black men extends to children as well.
Patient: To a certain degree.
Doctor: What fucking degree would that be?
Patient: To the degree that they grow into men.
Doctor: Please explain what the hell you mean by that.
Patient: I don't have any malice toward children, but when I see a little black boy, I'm taken back to what happened to me as a child, and I see that young child grow into a man who will be capable of doing what every other black man is capable of, and it frightens me.
Doctor: You hate your own people to the extent that you believe innocent children cannot grow into anything but rapists, thugs, and criminals. What happened to you was tragic. No child should ever experience the pain and horror you did. I can understand your feelings when your cousin died. But by keeping what happened to you between your aunt, your mother, and yourself, even with his death, you still haven't gotten closure.
Patient: I've moved on with my life and accomplished the goals I set for myself.
Doctor: So you believe that because you shun black people of all ages that you've solved your problem.
Patient: Works for me.
Doctor: What is your opinion on the issues that affect black Americans in this country?

Patient looks at the doctor and laughs.
Doctor lights a cigarette.

Doctor: What do you find funny?
Patient: Your question.
Doctor: Why do you find that question humorous?
Patient: Do you really think after all we've talked about here today that I give a flying fuck about the state of black affairs in this country?
Doctor: No. I wanted to hear what your response would be.
Patient: Why?

Doctor: Then it's fair to say you wouldn't lift a finger to help another black person in any way.

Patient: Pretty much. I barely want to deal with those fuckers at....

Doctor: Please finish your statement.

Patient: Why do we have to keep going over this. What do you want from me?

Doctor: I want you to finish your last statement. "You barely want to deal with those fuckers where..." Finish the fucking statement.

Patient: At work was what I was going to say, alright? Are you satisfied now?

Doctor: So why didn't you finish the statement originally? Something you need to tell me, or is there a great deal you aren't telling me?

Patient: Where the hell are you going with this?

Doctor: I'll tell you where. Right to the heart of what's truly fucked up about people like you.

Patient displays anger at that statement.
Doctor lights another cigarette.

Patient: People like me. What do mean, "people like me?"

Doctor: As I said earlier, what happened to you was tragic. But instead of truly dealing with that pain, you've allowed it to turn you into a truly selfish, self-centered and possibly very evil, fucked-up individual.

Patient: Oh, is that correct? Please explain, Doctor Feelgood. I can't wait to hear this.

Doctor: You say you don't have anything to do with black people outside of your work environment, that you avoid contact with blacks to the extent that you can, socially or otherwise, and to a certain extent this includes your immediate family.

Your hatred for your own kind runs so deep that it includes even small children who couldn't possibly harm you in the way that you, yourself, were harmed.

By your own admission, you adore your father, who happens to be a black, man but he isn't placed into the same category of hate you feel for all other black men, and you even keep your associations with black women to a minimum, even professional black women who you barely acknowledge as peers.

The fact that you adore your father, who is black, but hate all other black men is a disturbing contradiction. You love your father, but all other black men are pieces of shit. What sets your father apart from the rest of the race is the fact that he raised and protected you.

Protected you— no. That's not totally true. You see, your father wasn't always there to protect you. He allowed his little girl to be brutally assaulted by a family member, and he did nothing about it. He wasn't given the opportunity to seek justice for his little girl because your mother decided it would be best if he never found out what happened to you.

You've lived your whole life seeing your father as a man you love but a man who couldn't protect his baby girl. That has always been with you, just under the surface of your thoughts, which is why you don't have a great deal of contact with your family and why you only bring certain men around your parents, those that, in your opinion, can protect you and are better than your father.

Patient (Shouting): My father would have protected me if he'd known what was going to happen. He wouldn't have let that bastard harm me. I can take care of myself now, and I can make damn sure those bastards don't hurt anyone again.

Doctor: But your father couldn't have known what was going to happen to you. You weren't in his direct care at the time of the incident. Now what bastards are you referring to?

Patient stands up and says, "Fuck this. I don't need to hear anymore of this shit."

Doctor: The minute you step your ass out that door, your career is over.

Patient sits back down.

Doctor: Now answer my last question. What bastards were you referring to?

Patient says nothing. The doctor continues.

Not to worry. We'll come back to that last remark. I see black people like you every waking minute of every day. Motherfuckers like you enjoy looking down on others because it gives you a sense of superiority, a sense of accomplishment to look at those you deem as less accomplished and saying to yourself, "I'm better than you." Again, by your own admission, as educated as you, you said you wouldn't lift a finger to help another black person. You know what's so surprising? When you judge others at a glance, you don't have a fucking clue if the assumption you made is true or not, but because you are who you are and think the way you do, the cycle will continue.

Being a black man I know what that feels like, to be looked at like you're less than nothing by your own people— not by the white community, but by my own kind. We judge our own people as being worthy or unworthy based on outward appearance: the clothes we wear, the car we drive, the type of work we do, where we live or don't live, the hell with character.

We as blacks in America judge each other on skin color, eye color, and hair texture. I've always found that to be the highest order of insult one black could express to another. Not only is it asinine, but it shows how very little we as a people have changed in our thinking from the days when we were forced to walk around in chains.

You pride yourself on your education and your profession, and you should. But education alone doesn't always raise one's awareness, or heighten one's sense of community. We as blacks in this country go out of our way to hurt each other in every way possible— professionally, economically, and socially. We generate billions of dollars in the U.S. economy, yet we control not one single institution.

Hell, a well-educated and highly qualified black man runs for this nation's highest office, and his own people support the white women running against him. And you know what's shocking about that scenario? Blacks say he's not ready. I say, if we aren't ready to take the lead running this motherfucking country now, we never will be.

People like you hold the rest of us back, motherfuckers who wouldn't give another black person the time of day or a kind word, all because you see yourself as better than they are. When shit gets tight, what's the first thing motherfuckers like you say? "The white man is out to fuck me," or in your case, the administrator.

You need to realize we as black people treat each other like shit. White America doesn't have to do a damn thing to us except sit back and laugh at our asses. Many of us are incarcerated, and crime in our communities is rampant, but maybe it wouldn't be so if more of us came together to reach out to our youth. But someone like you would never be a part of that process.

We do more than enough harm to each other simply by failing to help each other, so much so that white America can pretty much ignore our dumb asses and let us continue to inflict the pain on ourselves that came at the hands of slave owners hundreds of years ago.

We fight amongst ourselves over petty issues. We see a brother or a sister trying to improve themselves, and we ridicule them as trying in some way to be white or cross over into white America. We see one of our own, through hard work, make it, and they become the enemy. We hate them for leaving our lazy asses behind, then we do all in our limited power to bring them down.

Educated blacks see themselves as the saviors of our culture and heritage. Then at the end of their academic training, they perpetuate our cultural stagnation by doing just what it is you're doing now, shutting your eyes to the plight of our young people and those that could benefit from what you've learned.

When the doctor finished talking, he turns to his computer and begins typing. The patient says nothing for a few minutes.

Patient: Doctor, in your words, what the fuck has any of that got to do with me? Exactly what was that diatribe supposed to accomplish?

Doctor: Exactly what I thought it would.

Patient: And that would be?

Doctor: That your hatred for blacks runs so deep that you justify the shit you've done based on what was done to you as a child.

Patient: What have I done doctor? Are you trying to accuse me of something?

Doctor: Earlier you said you were able to see to it that those bastards never hurt anyone again. I'm gonna ask you again. Who the hell were you referring to? The six people you killed?

Patient: I haven't killed anyone.

Doctor: Who the hell were you talking about then?

Patient: I was referring to the fact that I'm old enough to take care of myself, and I wouldn't allow any man to hurt me.

Doctor: You're lying to me.

Patient: I don't have to lie to you about anything.

Doctor: You said six patients have died while being cared for in your ward. Is that correct?

Patient: Yes.

Doctor: You said you could only remember four clearly.

Patient: Yes, that's what I said.

Doctor: According to my records, the last three patients were children, all male, black, and under thirteen years old. One child presented with severe asthma, one with a broken leg, and the last with third degree-burns over twenty percent of his lower body. Does this ring any bells?

Patient starts to shift in her seat and looks uncomfortable when these particular cases are brought up.

Patient: Yes, I recall the cases now.

Doctor: Let's talk about the young man who was burned and survived. According to his chart, the ER doctor ordered isolation in the intensive care ward and a 20 mg Demerol drip to control the pain until he could be seen by the burn doc. Somehow, five times that amount was found in his saline drip. In this particular case, you were the attending nurse for this patient. You want to explain how the fuck a lethal dosage of Demerol was injected into his IV?

Patient: I don't know.

Doctor: What the fuck do you mean you don't know? Was he or was he not your patient?

Patient (Shouting): "Yes, he was my fucking patient, but other nurses have access to the goddamn drug cart.

Doctor: Did you administer the Demerol to the patient?

Patient: Yes, but I didn't administer a lethal dosage.

Doctor: If you were his nurse, you and you alone were responsible for this patient's medication.

Patient cuts the doctor off and loudly says she had two other patients on the ward she was responsible for that evening, and that someone else could have administered the injection.

Doctor: Only one patient was prescribed Demerol, and that was your burn patient. How did such a high dose get into his IV drip? And don't sit here and tell me you don't know, because the patient sure as hell could not have done it himself.

Patient says nothing. She sits in her seat with her arms folded.

Doctor: According to the pharmacy records, you signed out seven, 20 mg bottles of Demerol at the beginning of your shift for the drug cart. What was all that medication for. It's highly unusual for that much Demerol to be signed out at once and in those doses.

Patient: In intensive care, Demerol is used a lot to control pain. You'd know that if you worked in that section of the hospital.

Doctor smiles and looks at the patient.

Doctor: Do you want to know how they caught on to what you were doing? It was actually quite brilliant— dangerous and stupid, but brilliant.

Patient looks worried after the doctor's statement.

Doctor: According to my information, you did sign out 140 mgs of Demerol, or at least that's what you thought you were signing out.

What they gave you at the pharmacy at the beginning of your shift was seven vials filled with sterile water, containing a harmless marker.

You were recorded injecting the patient's IV with what you thought was a lethal dose of Demerol. You then left to get rid of the vials.

Another doctor came in behind you, switched IV bags, and injected the 10 mgs of Demerol into the patients IV. Another intensive-care nurse witnessed the injection and stayed in the patient's room until you returned. A concealed video device was taken from the patient's room after the second team left, shortly after you were called away to finish some paperwork

The IV bag they retrieved from the patient's room was sent to the lab. Now, smart ass, what do you think the lab found in that one-liter bag of saline solution? One hundred fucking mgs of sterile water and the marker.

Patient sits in her chair and starts to cry.

Doctor: What the fuck do you have to say now? Do you have any fucking idea of what that much Demerol would have done to someone that young and in that condition? But of course you do. You're a highly educated, well-trained fucking professional killer, aren't you?

Patient says nothing. She wipes the tears from her face and looks at the doctor.

Doctor: Want to talk about the other patients who weren't so lucky?

Patient: You can go straight to hell.

Doctor: I won't be going to hell, but I can sure as fuck tell you where you're going.

Patient: Where would that be, Dr. Feelgood? I haven't told you anything. And if what you say is true, why am I not there now?

Doctor: I'd have to conclude that your people are not ready to go public with this shit yet. You know, lawsuits and shit.

Patient: I don't believe a thing you just said. If I was recorded doing anything, why haven't I seen this video?

Doctor: Would you like to?

The doctor taps commands onto his keyboard and a video starts to play. He turns the monitor toward the patient.

Patient watches the video and says nothing until the recording stops.

Doctor: Satisfied? Now do you want to tell me about the others?

Patient: Sure, why the fuck not? They where all going to fucking die anyway. It could have been soon after they were brought in, or years later. Who gives a fuck? I just helped them get there quicker.

Doctor: So you were killing patients.

Patient: I killed no good, rotten bastards that deserved to fucking die. I put those filthy niggers out of there misery to make sure they wouldn't hurt anyone again.

Doctor: How did you kill the others?

Patient: You really expect me to tell you that?

Doctor: Why the hell not? Your ass is going to jail anyway: Your life is ruined. Don't you think their families deserve to know how and why they died?

Patient: Fuck them and their families. My family was almost destroyed by fuckers just like them. I don't owe them shit.

Doctor: What about the two children? They were just kids. Did they have to die?

Patient: Did I ask to be raped at twelve years old?

Doctor: No, you didn't, but those children didn't deserve to die because of what happened to you.

Patient: How do you know they wouldn't have grown up to be rapists, murderers or something worse?

Doctor: Who the fuck gave you a license to decide who lives and who dies? Who decided that you have the authority to be anyone's executioner?

Patient: The State of Maryland.

Doctor: Was that supposed to be fucking funny?

Patient: I thought so.

Doctor: I am going to see to it that you never practice medicine anywhere, and that your ass is put in jail.

Patient: You can't do a damn thing to me, Dr. Feelgood. You're a psychiatrist. Anything we discuss is covered by a little thing called doctor-patient privilege.

You can't disclose a goddamn thing I've said to anyone. If that video was all they needed, I'd be in jail now. If you tell anyone anything we discussed, your ass is gonna be hauled before the state licensing board, and you'll be stripped of your license to practice in your field of psychobabble bullshit.

Doctor (Smiling): You have it all figured out don't you?

Patient: Actually, yes, I do.

Doctor: Why did you start to cry when I told you what was found in the saline bag?

Patient: It took me a minute to realize that if they gave me saline and not Demerol, then I couldn't have killed anyone. They can't prove shit, and what you know can't be used against me.

Doctor: You're absolutely right. Your session is over. I'd like you to now get the fuck out of my office.

Patient: With pleasure, doctor. Will we be seeing each other again?

Doctor: Probably not, but I'd keep my eye on the news in the next few days. Breaking stories happen all the time.

Patient gets up to leave, stops at the door, turns, and faces the doctor.

Patient: Should I be worried about that breaking news comment you made?

Doctor: I sure as fuck would be if I were in your shoes. It's amazing how news stations and reporters come by the stories they report. Sometimes it happens by chance. Other times, they receive anonymous tips here and there, and the beauty of that is, they don't have to reveal their sources. That's a protection they have, and it often holds up in court.

Patient: Fuck you.

Doctor: Your session is over. Get the fuck out of my office. Please give my regards to Mr. Hale at— what station was that again? Channel 13?

Patient: Motherfucker, are you threatening me? I'll have your black ass in front of a judge so fast, it'll make your fucking head spin.

Doctor: I'm only going to tell you to leave my office one more time.

Patient leaves, slamming the door behind her. The doctor smiles, turns toward his computer, and starts to type.

***

Rashanaria leaves the doctors office and decides she'll go shopping for the afternoon. There are a few items she saw in a boutique she wants to pick up. Then she'll head home so she can fix Jimmy a romantic dinner and they'll spend the rest of the evening making love.

As she drives to the mall, she finds herself going over her session with that jackass doctor. She decides not to give it too much unnecessary thought. He can't do a damn thing about anything they talked about and her career is safe. They have nothing on her they can use.

She decides for now that she will have to simply control her impulses to seek her brand of justice until this shit cools down. If she has to transfer to another hospital, so be it. But once all this shit goes away, she will make even more of those sorry bastards pay with their lives. To hell with them.

***

Later that same evening, a certified letter arrives by courier at the home of Eric and Maria Williams, Rashanaria Williams' parents. The letter is addressed to Eric Williams.

Mr. Williams signs for the letter and goes into his study. He sits down and opens the letter.

Dear Mr. Williams:

My name is Doctor Feelgood. I'm a psychiatrist in private practice. The reason I'm writing to you is that I've been in therapy with your daughter Rashanaria at the request of her hospital administrator.

The hospital's senior staff suspects your daughter is responsible for killing numerous patients in the intensive care unit she works in. During our session, she admitted to me that she has in fact killed at least six patients. Two were only children. Your daughter has a deep-seated hatred toward black men, as all her victims have been black males.

Mr. Williams, I have also learned that your daughter was raped as a child by your brother's son Reggie when she was twelve. I know Reggie passed away due to a car accident when your daughter was fourteen, but this has had a profound effect on your daughter's psyche.

During our session, your daughter informed me that you were never told of this incident. Your wife Maria and your sister-in-law decided it would be best if you never knew what occurred with your daughter. Your wife's fear was that you'd probably kill Reggie for what he'd done.

Mr. Williams, I know this is shocking news, and it must be difficult for you to learn that your daughter was sexually abused as a child, but your daughter needs help. She is a danger to everyone she comes in contact with.

Tears start to flow down Eric's face as he finishes the letter. He tries to control his hands shaking, but finds it difficult to do. At that moment, his wife walks into the study.

She asks him a question as she walks into the study. "Baby, are you ready to eat? Who was that at the door?" Then she notices her husbands face and that he appears to be extremely disturbed.

He holds up the letter and asks his wife in a very shaky voice, why she never told him what Reggie had done to his baby. She looks at her husband, and she starts to cry.

***

Also that same afternoon, a package arrives at Channel 13 news addressed to anchor Virginia Summers. She takes the package and sits it on top of her desk. She is due on air in fifteen minutes for the afternoon report and asks her staffer to open the package.

After her report, Virginia returns to her desk and is asked by her staffer to review the notes and video that were in the package she just received.

"This is hot," her staffer says. "If this is true, we have a cover-up at Mercy General Hospital. " A fucking nurse killing patients and the hospital knows," says the staffer.

"Check this out," the staffer continues. "The nurse the hospital suspects is Jimmy Hale's girlfriend."

"I know her," says Virginia. "And I can't stand that arrogant bitch."

"What are we gonna do with the story?" the staffer asks.

"I need to check something out, and we're gonna run this tonight. This is huge," Virginia says.

Calls are made, anonymous information is confirmed, what information the reporter can gather is quickly made ready to be presented to the public, and the story of the cover-up at Mercy General is given the green light for broadcast on the evening news report.

***

Jimmy Hale is headed home when he gets a call on his cell phone. He is told by a friend at the station that a story concerning his fiancé, murders, and a cover-up at Mercy General Hospital is going to run on the evening broadcast.

Jimmy can't believe what he was told, that his women is involved with deliberate patient deaths at the hospital where she works. He tells himself he won't believe it, they must have the wrong person.

He pulls into his driveway and heads inside. Rashanaria is home. Her car is in the driveway when he pulls in. He opens the door and is almost overwhelmed with the smells of a delicious meal waiting for him.

He goes into the kitchen and sees the love of his life preparing dinner.

"Hey, baby, how was your day? I missed your afternoon sports report. How did things go?" she asks.

"Everything went well. Babe, I have to ask you something. Is everything okay at the hospital? The station is gonna run a story about some kind of cover-up, "something about a nurse killing patients. Have you heard anything at the hospital?" he asks.

Rashanaria's heart starts to beat a little faster when he asks that question. She tries her hardest to control the panic that wants to overwhelm her. She thinks to herself, *No that motherfucker didn't tell anyone what I said to him. I'll kill that bastard.*

"Well there's always something going on at the hospital, but I don't know anything about a cover-up," she lies.

"Baby, from what I'm told, the story involves you," Jimmy tells her.

Rashanaria freezes, then just as quickly recovers.

"I don't have a clue, baby. I don't know anything about that."

Jimmy kisses her on the forehead and lets her finish preparing their meal. He goes into the living room, turns on the TV, and sets the station at channel thirteen.

They sit down in the living room to enjoy the meal Rashanaria prepared, and she put's in a movie for them to watch. Shortly before they finish dinner, Jimmy gets a call and is told to cut to channel thirteen.

Rashanaria watches as he picks up the remote, turns off the movie, and turns to his station. Rashanaria looks on in silent disbelief as reporter Virginia Summers comes on and gives a preview of tonight's breaking news story.

"This is Virginia Summers. Tonight at 8PM, we will bring you an exclusive breaking news story involving patient murders and cover-up at Mercy General Hospital."

"We will also show you a video of a highly shocking nature, therefore parents are cautioned that this may not be suitable for younger viewers. Please join us at 8 PM for this very shocking and disturbing story."

Jimmy looks at Rashanaria. No words pass between them. She gets the dishes and takes them into the kitchen. Her house phone rings. She sees it's her parent's number. She doesn't answer the phone.

***

The doctor's last patient of the day 4 PM.

The doctor's assistant informs him that his last patient of the day is ready to be seen. He comes in and takes a seat. The rules for the session are explained, and the doctor begins.

Doctor: Now, what the fuck do you want?

Patient: Doctor, can I have a drink?

Doctor: Yes, you can, just remember what I said about getting fucked up.

Patient pours himself a double Grey Goose on the rocks, and the doctor lights a cigarette.

Patient: No problem, Doctor. Can I ask you a question?

Doctor: Yes.

Patient: Do your patients respond well to you when you talk to them the way you do?

Doctor: I get the information I need to help them solve their fucking problems. My methods work well for me. Now, are you going to tell me what the fuck you want, or are you gonna sit here and drink all my damn vodka?

Patient: I don't know where to start.

Doctor: Try at the beginning. That usually works well.

Patient: Is it crazy to want to die?

Doctor: Motherfuckers who come in here talking about wanting to die are usually full of shit. Usually they want drugs. If that's your angle, you can get the fuck out of here now.

Patient: No sir, that's not my angle.

Doctor: Do you really want to die?

Patient: Sometimes I feel that way.

Doctor: Why? What the fuck is going on in your life that makes you feel that way?

Patient: I feel lonely and sad all the time. I'm up one minute, down the next, and I don't know why. I feel like my life is going nowhere.

Doctor: Are you on any medication or are you fucking with illegal drugs?

Patient: I'm not on any meds but I did experiment with drugs in high school and college.

Doctor: What drugs?

Patient: Weed mostly.

Doctor: Exactly how long have you been smoking that shit?

Patient: On and off for about seven years.

Doctor turns to his computer and pulls up information on the patient.

Doctor: You're twenty-five, and you've been smoking that shit for seven years? What did your grades look like in high school and college?

Patient: Not good.

Doctor: What the fuck does "not good" mean?

Patient: My grades really fell off in my last year of high school, from As to Ds and Fs. College wasn't much better. I just couldn't stay focused.

Doctor: Do you think your drug use had anything to do with that?

Patient: I'm not sure, but it probably did.

Patient finishes his drink.

Doctor: You're not sure? Where did you go to high school and college.

Patient: The Gordon Academy for high school and Bailey University.

Doctor: Those are two very prestigious schools. Students of those institutions usually do very well, and they are very expensive, so whose money did you fuck up?

Patient: My parents' money. My father is Senator Charles Kirkland, and my mother is a lawyer.

Doctor: They must have been pissed at you.

Patient: They were, and my dad kicked me out the fucking mansion when I dropped out of Bailey during my second year. The fucking Senator's son out on the streets.

Doctor: I bet that must have fucked your head up.

Patient: Yeah it did. I tried to explain to him that college wasn't for me, that I wanted something different for my life. And my bitch of a mother, who I can't stand, took his side.

Doctor: Do you work? How do you pay your bills?

Patient: I'm covered under their health plan for now, and they let me keep what was left of my trust fund. I have to find a job soon though.

Doctor: What the fuck is your problem? You're a grown ass man. Should your parents support you your whole life? According to what you've told me and what the record shows, you've been given opportunities that many kids would die for, and you fucked it up.

Patient: Now you sound just like my father. I try to talk to him, but he won't listen. I never wanted to go into politics or study the same shit my parents did. I know they think I'm a failure and a big disappointment, but I'm still their kid.

Doctor: You're a grown fucking man, and your wasting my mother-fucking time. If you can't see that your failings are of your own making and you can't accept responsibility for your fuck-ups, no amount of talking in the world is going to fix it.

Patient: I never said I'm not taking responsibility for my life, but I need help.

Doctor: If that's the case, why did you come in here talking about wanting to die?

Patient: Because that's how I feel. I've had these thoughts for a long time now. I'm tired of feeling this way.

Doctor: Have you seen any other therapist for this shit before?

Patient: No.

Doctor: Have you talked to anyone about how you feel?

Patient: I don't have anyone to talk to that would understand.

Doctor: Do you have a woman in your life now?

Patient: I did a while back.

Doctor: Where is she now?

Patient: That's a long story.

Doctor: Give me the short version.

Patient: When I was in college, I met a girl named Angela. She was born in South Korea. Her parents came here when she was five. We were really good together during my first year of college. That's where we met. We even took classes together. When I took her to meet my parents, that's when it all fell apart.

Doctor: What happened?

Patient: My fucking mother didn't approve of me being with an Asian woman or any women that wasn't white. She wasn't good enough for the son of a fucking U.S. Senator whose wife is also a lawyer, and she let Angela know it.

Doctor: What did your mother do?

Patient: My parents had a dinner party at the house a while back and my mother told me not to bring Angela. When I told her if that was the case I wouldn't be there either.

She insisted that I be there. This was a big fucking affair for my father, and it was important the family be together to support him.

When the party started and all the guests had arrived, I came in with Angela. No one took notice of her but my parents and a few of their snotty fucking guests.

If looks could kill, Angela would have been dead. My mother made sure we sat across from my father and her at our table. As dinner was served, she started asking Angela questions about her family background and shit, talked about her lack of a family business, her working-class status, and their life in Korea before they came to the states. She made Angela feel like she was trailer trash.

Angela tried her best to be cordial, but my mother made her feel like shit. After dinner, I saw my mother talking to Angela. I went to get us a drink, and when I returned, I saw Angela heading to the front of the house to leave.

When I caught up to her, she was crying and said she never wanted to come there again. She said my mother told her she didn't have a chance in hell of being a part of our family and that we didn't need any slant-eyed, half-breed, yellow babies in our home. I left with Angela, and I don't even speak to my mother anymore, especially after what happened between us. She didn't give a damn that I loved Angela or that soon after that fucking party we broke up.

As the patient looks at the doctor, he wipes tears from his eyes.

Doctor: Don't start that crying shit in here. The sight of a man crying is disgusting, besides it shows weakness.

Patient: Sorry. It's just that I miss Angela.

Doctor: What happened between you and your mother?

Patient: I don't want to talk about that.

Doctor: What the fuck did I say to you earlier? You answer my questions or get the fuck out my office.

Patient: Yes, sir, you're right.

Doctor: We'll come back to that.

Doctor: If you miss Angela so much, why did you allow that dumb shit your mother said to come between you two?

Patient: I tried to fix things between us, but she wouldn't talk to me, and after a while I let it go.

Doctor: Then you fucked up again.

Patient: I know.

Doctor: Did your drug use escalate after you and Angela broke it off?

Patient: Yeah, and I found myself in some real bad shit, and I did some really ugly things.

Doctor: What do you mean by that?
Patient: I really don't want to talk about that now.
Doctor: Then why the fuck did you bring it up? If you're not gonna get this shit off your chest, then your wasting my motherfucking time and I'm of no use to you.
Patient: This is something I'm trying really hard to forget.
Doctor: Those are the memories you need to come to terms with. Suppressing painful memories, no matter how bad they are, will come back to fuck you over later in life.

Patient gets up to get another drink.

Doctor: What is it that's got your head all fucked up now?
Patient: About a year ago, I went to a bar after having gotten into an argument with my fucking mother on the phone. I can't talk to that bitch without arguing. She makes me feel like I'm nothing. Our relationship has been bad for as long as I can remember.

Doctor interrupts the patient.

Doctor: Are you aware that whenever you bring your mother up in conversation, you use extremely foul language to describe her.

Patient says nothing.

Doctor: We'll come back to that. Continue your story.
Patient: Like I said, I went to a bar and got pretty wasted. I wanted to go out to meet women and have a good time. As the night went on, I got pretty fucked up, and the ladies weren't biting, so I decided to go home.

I went to the men's room to take a piss and this guy was in there. After I was done, I went to the sink to wash my hands and he started talking to me.

I went back to the bar, and he sat next to me and asked if I knew another place he could check out. I told him how to get to another more popular bar, and then he invited me to come along with him.

I said no at first, and then decided, What *the hell? Maybe I'll get lucky someplace else*. Since I live in walking distance from the bar I was at, I rode with him.

We got in his car and talked more about nothing. We smoked a joint, and then this guy tells me how handsome I am and that he'd like to suck my dick. I was really fucked up. At first I thought I misunderstood what he said.

He put his hand on my leg, and I moved it off and laughed and told him I'm not gay and that I need a woman to suck my dick. He kept insisting that I let him do it.

He pulled off on the side of the road and asked if he could feel my dick. He touched me, and I got hard. It was probably the booze and the weed. I mean, I wanted some action that night but not with another guy. But the next thing I knew, he had my dick in his hand, stroking me until I got hard.

Patient seems uneasy as he tells his story. The doctor notices his hands start to tremble.

Doctor lights another cigarette as he listens to the patient.

He goes down on me, and I'm ashamed to admit it, but it was good. He sucked my dick for about twenty minutes until I came in his mouth. Then he put my hand on him and asked me if I would like to try doing the same to him.

I was nervous and high, but I did it. I went down on another guy. I sucked another man's dick. I even liked the taste of his cum. I would have thought I would have been disgusted by that, and I'm ashamed to say I wasn't.

Then, to make matters worse, just before we were finished, a cop pulls behind us. I have no idea how long he was there. He orders us out the car. We get arrested for lewd and lascivious acts in a public place.

I had to call our family lawyer to bail me out. I don't know if my father found out, but my mother did because she had to authorize the money to get me out of jail. She was beyond furious from what our lawyer told me. And shit has gone down hill from there. I feel as if my whole life is fucked up.

Doctor: So do you think you're gay?

Patient: No.

Doctor: You suck another man's dick, and you're not gay?

Patient: I was wasted.

Doctor: If you need me to help you find an explanation for why you did what you did, I can't. The drugs and alcohol simply broke down your inhibitions. You are gay, and if that's unpalatable to you there's nothing I can do. You sucked that dick, and you said you liked it. So come to terms with what you've done.

Patient: Even if I've never been with another man since, I'm still considered gay?

Doctor: You can consider yourself whatever the fuck you want. I'm telling you you're a fucking fag. Men who don't have it in them would not do what you did.

Patient stares into nothingness. The look on his face is one of sadness and confusion.

Patient: I don't know what to say, I don't want to be gay.

Doctor: The first step in coming to terms with the things you've done is to acknowledge them and accept responsibility for your choices.

Patient: It's hard sometimes. I've done things I can't take back, and as you say, the choices I've made have put my life in serious jeopardy.

Doctor: What do you mean by that?

Patient: I found out that I'm HIV positive just over six months ago. The cost for the medications is draining my trust fund and when that runs out, I'll have to figure some other way to pay for my drug regiment.

Doctor: You don't think your parents would be willing to help you, and you lied.

Patient: I'm sorry, my parents won't help.

Doctor: Are you currently having sex with anyone, man or woman?

Patient: No, I honestly find myself not wanting to have sex. I don't want to give this shit to anyone else. I probably jerk off three times a day.

Doctor: Well, at least you're decent enough to not want to give that shit to others.

Patient: But, Doctor, I honestly thought about it. That fucking bastard who gave me this shit knew he was HIV positive.

Doctor: But you haven't acted on that impulse, which would have been tragic. Your life is a little fucked up now, but with today's treatments, it doesn't have to be an immediate death sentence.

Patient: I know I will eventually die from this shit, but sometimes I do think, *why not take as many motherfuckers with me as I can?*

Doctor: Because the innocent people you want to hurt haven't done shit to you. And who would your victims be? Teenage girls and boys? Unsuspecting women you meet in bars?

All these people have lives and families that care about them. Why would you want to harm people who haven't done a damn thing to you?

Patient: Because I can't get to that piece of shit who gave me this fucking disease.

Doctor: That's the chance you take when you have unprotected sex, straight or otherwise.

Patient: Doctor, I understand what you said earlier but I don't consider myself gay. What happened occurred because I was fucked up. And, yes, I know I can't take it back, but I'm not gay.

Doctor: Denial is a dangerous thing, but we'll address that again later. You said earlier you don't have friends you could talk to. Why is that?

Patient: They don't know about the encounter I had. If I told any of my friends, I'd lose them for good. All my friends hate gays.

Doctor: Are you acknowledging you're gay?

Patient (Shouting): I had one fucking gay encounter. I do not consider myself gay!

Doctor: Motherfucker, I suggest you lower your goddamn voice. The anger inside you needs a release, but I'll be goddamned if it's me. Do you fucking understand me?

Patient: Yes.

Doctor: Pour yourself another drink and we'll continue.

Patient does so as the doctor lights another cigarette.

Doctor: How is your relationship with your father?

Patient: I don't have one anymore. I'm an embarrassment to him. I've always been told that everything I do reflects on him and could have very negative consequences for his career.

I had to be the perfect son, the perfect student, the perfect child. I got tired of my parent's shit, and since I'm out of their lives, I don't have to worry about my shit affecting them.

Doctor: That's not totally true. You are still their son. And if the media ever got a hold of your HIV status, for example, and how you contracted the disease, sucking a stranger's dick on the side of the highway, I can see that hurting your fathers bid for re-election and or continuing in office. When you're a senator's son, the shit you get caught doing does reflect on that office.

Patient: Well, I didn't ask to be a fucking senator's son.

Doctor: That's a very childish attitude.

Patient: The story of my life.

Doctor: How is your relationship with your mother?

Patient: You don't want to know.

Doctor: If I didn't want to know, I wouldn't have asked the fucking question.

Patient: It's beyond horrible, and as far as I'm concerned, I never had a mother.

Doctor: Why.?

Patient: Growing up, my mother wasn't the most affectionate women in the world, and I never really felt the love for her that a son should feel for his mother.

I was raised primarily by our goddamn housekeepers, which is why I could speak fluent Spanish by the time I was in sixth grade. My mother never even noticed I spoke another language. My mother was always too fucking busy studying, going to class, or doing whatever it was she needed to do to advance her fucking career.

I got to a point where I didn't really care whether she was around or not. I didn't see her a lot, and I always had the sense that she wished I wasn't around, so to hell with her.

Doctor: Was your relationship with your mother always so distant?

Patient: As far back as I can remember, it's always been that way.

Doctor: Do you love your mother?

Patient: No.

Doctor: Did you ever try talking to your father about your relationship with your mother?

Patient: No, he wasn't much better than her when it came to raising me and spending time with me. Like I said, the housekeepers were my parents growing up.

Doctor: Growing up, do you remember doing things, good or bad, to get your parents' attention.

Patient: The rule in my house was do nothing to get noticed. My parents are busy important people who do not have time for the foolishness of a child. The housekeepers made sure that was drilled in my head.

Doctor: How would you describe your childhood?

Patient: Other than my parents not being in my life much, growing up, I'd say it was okay. I had all the shit I needed, except for parents that cared about me.

Doctor: Talk to me about these feelings you've been having concerning dying.

Patient: I feel like my life is just not worth living anymore. I've made one major fuck-up after another, and I just don't know how much longer I can go on like this.

Doctor: Do you see yourself as a failure?

Patient: Yes, all the time, especially after what happened between my mother and me.

Doctor: What happened between you two? And I don't give a fuck whether you want to talk about it or not. What the fuck happened?

Patient stares into space when the doctor asks the question, as if he's searching for a way to bring the information to the surface of his thoughts.

Patient: Something really awful.

Doctor: Take your fucking time and tell me in detail what happened between you two.

The patient's eyes become glossy as he faces the doctor.

Doctor: I told you goddamnit, don't start that crying shit in here. Take a deep damn breath, calm the fuck down, and tell me what happened between you and your mother.

I went by the house two months ago. I called my father at his office and asked could he and I talk. He told me to come by the house on a Wednesday morning at 10 AM.

I showed up on time, and like usual, he'd forgotten I was coming by. When I got there, he'd already left for his office. My mother was there, so I figured maybe I'd visit with her.

The housekeeper let me in, and I asked her if she could let my mother know I was here. The first thing my mother said when she saw me was "I hope you're not here to borrow any more money." I told her no. "I just wanted to come by to see Dad." The rest of the conversation went to shit from there.

My mother could barely stand to look at me. She poured herself a cup of coffee and asked me again, what did I want. I told her I was here to see Dad, but since he was gone, could we talk?

"I don't want to look at you, Charles, so why should we talk about anything?"

"Mom, why do things have to be this way between us? Can't we talk for just a few minutes? I'll leave afterwards," I told her.

My mother walked away from me with a very disgusted look on her face. She sent the housekeeper to the grocery store and returned to the kitchen.

"All right, Charles, what would you like to discuss? I know. How about your little boyfriend you got arrested with? Want to tell me about that." (The look on his face is one of extreme embarrassment.) "What, did you think I wouldn't find out you were arrested for having sex with another fucking man."

I sat there not knowing what to say. I wish I had just gotten up and walked out of her life for good, but I tried to talk to her. I felt at that time that I just wanted a mother to talk to. I truly wished I had one.

"Mom it wasn't like that. What happened was a mistake."

"Don't call me" mom. I'm disgusted by you," she said.

"I never wanted any of that to happen," I said. "I know it was my fault, but I was high and didn't intend for any of that to happen," I tried to explain.

"Do you think anyone would have cared what your excuse was for getting caught in a car with another man, doing what you were doing, whatever the hell it was? And I sure as hell don't want to know." Her voice got louder as she continued.

"Do you have any idea of the scandal your disgusting little escapade would have caused us? Your father is a goddamn U.S. Senator for Christ sake. Do you know what that kind of scandal would do to his career? The only reason I bailed your sorry ass out of jail and called in favors was to keep that shit quite so your father wouldn't have to find out," she shouted.

"Mom, please listen to me. I'm not gay, and what happened was because I was drunk and high and I made a very stupid mistake.

"I know I've caused you and Dad a lot of trouble, and I understand how disappointed you both are in me, but I'm just here to say I'm sorry and you don't have to worry any more. I'm gonna get help for my problems."

"Believe me, Charles, I'm not worried about you. I don't give a damn about you," she said.

"Charles, you do whatever you think you have to, but we are through paying your goddamn bills. When your little trust runs out, you're on your own. You were given every fucking opportunity in the world we could give you, and how did you repay us? With goddamn failure after failure.

"We are through wasting time and money on you. You are nothing but a goddamn loser and a junky. It hurts me as a mother to say this, but I wish you were never born, and I don't care if I never see you again. Now please, get the hell out of my house."

I felt great anger build in me as I heard her speak to me that way. I mean, this was supposed to be my mother. She was supposed to love me no matter what. Her words hurt me so bad, I wanted to die, but then I realized I wanted to hurt her too.

As he speaks, his tone becomes more intense and filled with anger.

"As a mother?" I shouted. Is that what you just said? When were you ever a mother to me? I don't recall you ever being a mother to me. You were never around.

"I considered our goddamn housekeeper my mother. At least she cared about me. All you ever fucking cared about was your goddamn career and fucking everyone over to get ahead. Who knows how many people you fucked to get to the top?"

She slapped me so hard, I saw stars and my face went numb. That's when I lost it. I slapped her back as hard as I could. She fell to the floor, and a trail of blood flowed from the corner of her mouth.

She got up holding her face. She tried to say something to me, but before she could, I slapped her again on the other side of her face. It felt good to hit that bitch. I know that's wrong, but it felt good to pay that bitch back for all she'd done to me all my life.

I went toward her. I picked her up off the floor by her shoulders. The look in her eyes was so hate filled, I couldn't stand it, so I threw her against the kitchen wall and she fell to the ground.

She got to her knees, her forehead bleeding, gasping, and she said, "So this is the faggot son my housekeeper raised. She did a hell of a job." Then she started laughing at me. I went over to her, and I didn't see my mother. I saw someone I hated.

She tried to get up, but I used my foot and pushed her down on her back. She tried to crawl away, but I grabbed her around her waist from behind and pulled her toward me. I said to myself, *I'll show this bitch who's a goddamn faggot.*

I threw her bathrobe over her back and ripped her panties off. She fought like a wild animal, kicking at me and screaming, calling me names. I came down hard on her back with my fist, and she stopped kicking.

Holding her from behind and around her waist with one arm and straddling her legs with mine, I took my dick out, stroked it until I got hard and shoved it as hard as I could in her ass.

I wanted to hurt that bitch, and this was the most brutal thing I could think of at the time. I had never had a woman that way before, and she screamed and cursed me every time I pushed my dick in her ass.

It was music to my ears to hear that bitch scream, to pay her back for all those years she hurt me. I don't remember how long I fucked her, but I did until I came in her ass. I wanted to share something with her, and I couldn't think of a better person to share my HIV with.

I looked down on her from behind. My dick was still in her ass, draining. She was gasping for air, her arms straight out on the floor, her face wet from crying. She turned her head to the side and said in a defiant voice that sounded almost evil, "You want some pussy too? You feel better now, you miserable piece of shit?"

I pulled my dick out of her ass and left that bitch on the floor and got out of her house. I went home and sat there for two days, waiting for the police to come or for my father to come blow me away. Either way, I wasn't gonna go out easy. I wanted to die, and I was going to force someone to kill me. It was at that moment I knew I wanted to die.

The patient sits in the chair, almost as if he's in a trance, until he hears the doctor's voice.

Doctor: You have got to be bullshiting me. Did you just sit here and tell me you beat and raped your mother, the woman who gave birth to you? You brutally fucked your own mother in the ass?

Patient: Yes.

Doctor: I need a goddamn drink.

The doctor gets up from his desk and pours himself a cognac. He returns to his desk and lights a cigarette.

Patient: I told you what I did was ugly.

Doctor: How did raping your mother make you feel?

Patient: I felt at the time that I just wanted to hurt her. After I left and had time to think about what I'd done, I was so ashamed I wanted to kill myself.

Doctor: Why didn't you? You had the courage to fuck your own mother but couldn't find the courage to take your own life?

Patient: I don't know. Maybe I thought I could find something to live for, or maybe I'm afraid to die. I don't know.

Doctor: What the fuck could you possibly have to live for after what you did to your mother?

Patient: At this point, I don't know.

Doctor: Why do you think your mother didn't call the police on your sorry ass?

Patient: I don't know, I guess I'll never know.

Doctor: Yes, you do, motherfucker.

The doctor shakes his head as soon as that word leaves his mouth.

Doctor: That term fits you as well as any I could imagine. You did actually fuck your mother. She didn't report what you did to her for the same reason she covered up your shit when you got arrested— to avoid a goddamn scandal.

Patient: It sure as hell wasn't to protect me.

Doctor: In not reporting her rape to the police, that's exactly what she's done. To avoid the shame and disgrace that would have befallen her husband and their careers, she believes she's protecting herself and her husband. Your sorry ass benefits from her silence as well.

Patient: I don't care anymore. They can do what they want.

Doctor: Then it's a safe bet she doesn't know your HIV status.

Patient: I didn't tell her, and I hope it kills her slowly and painfully.

Doctor: Do you really believe she deserved what you did to her?

Patient: At the time I did.

Doctor: What about now?

Patient: I hate her, so I don't really care.

Doctor: You showed remorse when you were telling me that shit. Your punk ass was almost in tears. You know what you did is probably the worst thing you can do to a woman and the fact that it was your own mother would make people want to rip your fucking head off.

Patient: My only regret is that I don't know if she's HIV positive yet.

Doctor: Why is that a regret?

Patient: Because I'll probably be dead soon and I want her to suffer and live with what I did to her.

Doctor: You are a sick motherfucker.

Patient: I know that. That's why I need help.

Doctor: What about your father? Does he deserve a slow, painful death as well?

Patient: Fuck him too.

Doctor: That's very bold talk coming from someone as cowardly as you.

Patient: I'm no goddamn coward.

Doctor: No? What would you call someone who runs away from their problems, someone who drowns his sorrows in booze and drugs, someone who can't stand the pressures of being the son of successful people, someone who blames others for their failures, someone who willingly sucks another mans dick and brutally fucks his own mother?

Patient: Someone who needs help.

Doctor: No, that description fits someone who deserves death, or at the very least an extremely long prison sentence.

Patient: I can't do prison.

Doctor: Someone like you wouldn't last a day in prison, especially after the other inmates learned what you did to your mother.

Patient becomes increasingly nervous.

Patient: If she didn't tell anyone after all this time, I don't have to worry about going to prison.

Doctor: That's where you may be mistaken.

Patient: What are you talking about?

Doctor: The story you just shared with me involves you committing a very serious felony offense, one that I'm obligated by law to share with the police, the rape of a woman. In your case, you brutally fucked your own mother.

Patient: Doctor, you can't tell anyone what we talked about.

Doctor: Don't tell me what the fuck I can and can't do. I know what my responsibilities are.

Patient: Are you saying you have to report certain crimes patients tell you they committed?

Doctor: Yes, but if I think I can help them through psychiatric counseling and drug therapy so that they're no longer a threat, I don't have to report their crimes to the authorities.

Patient: Do you think I can be helped?

Doctor: You're a suicidal rapist with HIV. That makes you a danger to anyone you come in contact with.

Patient: Yes, but do you think I can be helped?

Doctor: There's always that possibility. In your case however, I'd have to say no.

Patient: Why?

Doctor: Because anyone who could do what you did to your own mother, no matter how bad a mother you perceive her to be, is capable of committing other heinous crimes.

The fact that your mother called in favors to cover up your gay encounter and subsequent arrest to avoid a scandal says to me you know you can fuck up and not worry about it.

Then you get away with the rape of your mother because she is trying to protect her husband's career— stupid but true— says to you that you can get away with doing whatever you want. That's not the way shit works.

Do you think you should be punished for what you did?

Patient: I guess so.

Doctor: You guess so. What would you demand be done to a man who raped your girl Angela?

Patient: I'd want him dead.

Doctor: Would you care how the fucker died?

Patient: No.

Doctor: Why the fuck shouldn't you be punished for doing what you did to your mother?

Patient: That bitch deserved to be fucked.

Doctor: I've been in practice for more than twenty years now, and I've heard people say shit that would make the average person's skin melt away. But due to my training and experience, I'm not bothered by the dumb shit people say and do.

In your case, however, it's taking everything in me not to jump across this desk and throw your punk ass out the window behind me. How the fuck can you say your mother deserved to be actually fucked in the ass by her own son?

Patient: Because that's how I feel.

Doctor: You are gonna be extremely popular where you're headed.

Patient: Where would that be, Doctor?

Doctor (in a loud voice): Prison, motherfucker!

Patient starts to get agitated and nervous. He starts to tremble at the thought of going to prison.
Doctor lights a cigarette.

Patient: I can't go to prison.

Doctor: Then tell me, how should you be punished for what you did?

Patient: I don't know.

Doctor: You've gotten away with shit your whole life— fucking up in school, doing drugs, getting arrested, assaulting your mother in the worst way imaginable and possibly giving her HIV— and you don't know if you deserve to be punished?

Patient says nothing.

Doctor: Do you know what happens to people like you in prison?

Patient: My father won't allow me to go to prison. He's a U.S. Senator. He'll get me out of it.

Doctor: I don't think you'll be able to count on that when he finds out what you did to his wife.

Patient: If you say anything about my session here, you'll put your practice on the line. And my father has influence.

Doctor: Believe me, motherfucker, I'm not worried about my practice or your daddy's fucking influence, but I do see how you regard your father when he can come to your sorry ass rescue.

He's a piece of shit until your ass needs to be bailed out of some shit or the power of his office works in your favor.

Well, those days are soon to be over for your ass. I asked you how you should be punished, and you didn't have an answer. You asked me if you could be helped, and I told you no.

You have no regret or remorse for what you did to your mother. You hate her. That's fine, if that's how you feel. But to escalate your hate to the point of raping her is beyond atrocious.

You don't see yourself as the bad guy. It's other people's fault, never your own. You get caught sucking another man's dick, but it's not your fault.

Your mother bails you out of jail and gets the shit buried. Are you grateful? No you still hate her. You easily detach yourself from the shit you do. That is probably due to your privileged upbringing, that's why therapy won't work for you, but prison will do nicely.

Patient again says nothing, he sits in his chair staring into nothingness.

Doctor: I'll clue you in on what goes on in prison so you'll have an idea of what to look forward to. I did an internship with one of the best criminal psychiatrists in the country many years ago. in one of the most notorious prisons in the country.

The doctor begins his story.

First of all you, have to understand the guards are not your friends. They don't give a fuck about you. It's the prisoners that run the prisons. The guards are just there to get a paycheck and get the fuck out of there alive each day.

The most hardened prisoners in any institution— I'm talking about motherfuckers who have committed multiple murders, gang members, armed robbers, arsonists, psychopaths of all varieties, and terrorists— make it a point to torture other types of inmates, people like you, rapists, and the ever-popular child molesters.

The doctor smiles as he talks to the patient.

You see even prisoners have their own code of criminal conduct, what is acceptable and what can and can't be tolerated, and one thing they don't tolerate is child molesters and rapists.

They have children and female family members, and the rape of a woman or child on the outside is the most vile conduct imaginable to inmates. So they punish people like you. Before they eventually kill you they make you suffer the torment rapists like you inflict on their victims.

Remember how you said you wanted to hurt your mother and the most vile thing you could think to do was to go up her ass? Well, you'll get plenty of that, and Daddy won't be able to do a damn thing about it.

It's not clear how the type of crime one committed on the outside gets around the prison, I suspect they have their own system of communications. But rest assured, by the first night, everyone will know why you're there.

You'll be the bleeding fish in the water and real soon. You'll be surrounded by hungry sharks, and no one will want anything to do with you, not even the most hardened prisoner. Everyone you come in contact with will simply wait for an opportunity to pounce on your ass, whether it be walking to and from your cell, in the yard or in the shower, even the food you get at chow will have human piss and shit mixed in it.

You might request solitary for your own protection, but it won't be granted because the guards will lose the request, and you'll be put in general population.

The guards will know why you're there. They'll feed you to the prisoners. You see, the guards love their mothers, and the criminals do too, because no matter what those motherfuckers have done, Mom sticks by them. Then they'll learn what you did to your mother.

Tears start to fall from the patient's eyes.

The doctor continues his tale.

They'll feed your handsome, tight, white ass to a prisoner known for raping his cell mates. Chances are, he'll be a black man. Your mother would appreciate that irony. He'll probably be a murderer sentenced to multiple life sentences and infected with all types of diseases, a motherfucker who doesn't have a damn thing to lose and has fucked so many men, he's forgotten what pussy feels like.

He'll let you come into his house and tell you what his rules are, what you can and can't do. You will have gotten to prison in the morning, and they'll process you in during the whole afternoon. You'll be hungry but the guards don't give a fuck that you haven't eaten.

When you meet your cell mate, he'll smell the fear that'll permeate from every pore of your body. You see, lifers develop a sense for another's fear and weakness, and they are masters at exploiting those weaknesses.

Your hungry as hell, but your cell mate tells you not to leave the cell for evening chow. He explains that the guys know why you're here, and it's not safe, so he'll bring you your chow back to the cell. You'll do what you're told.

Patient starts to tremble uncontrollably

The doctor continues his tale.

He'll intimidate you with his size and apparent strength. You'll know in your heart that you're no match for him, and it wouldn't do you any good to put up a fight. Then the first night, the lights go out.

That first night, after lights out, your cell mate will make you take the bottom bunk because he wants to stand over you and keep watch while he pulls his dick out and makes you suck it. He tells you this is your dinner for the next few nights. He makes you suck his dick for hours and dares you to spit out his cum. You swallow every drop.

He tells you the next morning that you are now his bitch and now you belong to him. If you keep your mouth shut, he'll protect you. Then on the second night, the process repeats with you sucking his dick, only this time, while you're sucking his dick, he stops you, then he gets in bed with you.

He makes you take off your clothes, and he fucks you for what seems to you like hours, tearing your asshole to shreds. You do try to scream for help as he fucks you, but he has your head buried in a pillow and a powerful forearm at the back of your neck as he takes his time fucking you, cuming in your ass multiple times.

Even if he didn't smother your screams, no one would come to help you, not the guards and certainly not the inmates. He whispers a question in your ear as he buries his dick deeper in your ass.

"Was it fun fucking your mother, you low-life, filthy piece of shit?" He tells you how he's going to torture your asshole every night, how you'll be sucking his dick whenever he wants you to, and how he's gonna make prison money pimping you to other inmates.

After he finishes fucking you, he makes you wash his dick and clean his body using the sink in the cell, then he beats you for bleeding all over his sheets.

The only thing you can do is lay there and let him fuck you, night after torturous night, and cry like a baby, wishing like hell you had killed yourself when you had the chance.

The patient sits trembling in his seat as the doctor finishes his tale of prison life. Charles actually pictured himself in prison with the inmate as the doctor told the tale, and he makes a decision that will spare him that fate.

He tries to fight back the tears from falling down his face, but he finds he doesn't care. He comes to realize that he'll die before he ends up in prison. He'll die first.

Doctor: I'll make an exception about you crying in here, but could you please wipe your damn face before we continue?

Patient: I'll die before I go to prison.
Doctor: Do you really want to die, goddamnit?
Patient: Yes.
Doctor: Is that easier then facing what you've done?
Patient: I realize I don't want to face anything. I just don't want to be here anymore. I'm tired, and I want to die.
Doctor: Who gives a fuck what the reason is your having these thoughts? The fact remains that you do and the shit is real to you. Living or dying is your choice in any event.

The doctor continues.

I'm not going to try to talk you out of your decision, but here's some shit you might want to consider to help you focus your reasoning.

One second after you kill yourself thinking your death is going to change anything, the world will continue. No one will give a damn that your dead, and you will have died never having faced your problems or made reparations for the shit you did.

You obviously no longer want to be here, and that is your right, so I submit to you that you stop thinking about it and do it.

Stop fucking whining about how fucked up your life is and how you have nothing to live for and all that shit. Do us all a favor and do it. As I said earlier, any man who could do what you did to your own mother is living on borrowed time anyway. Once that gets out, you're a dead man.

You're a weak motherfucker the world can do without anyway, so go ahead and fucking kill yourself. Just don't be one of those attention-seeking losers, because if you fuck it up and are rescued or some shit, they'll have a straight jacket and a white-padded room waiting for you, and rightfully so.

You were always fucked up to begin with, and people will talk about your ass forever if you don't succeed. They'll say shit like, "The dumb-ass couldn't even kill himself. How do you fuck that up?"

Believe it or not, unsuccessful suicides happen quite often. Since you're already a loser at everything else, don't fuck this up. This is your one chance to show everybody you could do one thing right for a change.

Fuck leaving a suicide note behind. I've studied hundreds of these notes left behind by people and, honestly, no one wants to read that shit. It looks good on TV and in the movies, but the reality is, no one gives a fuck.

Everyone close to you already knows you're fucked up, and they wish they didn't have to deal with your ass anymore, so you wouldn't be telling them anything they already don't know. Hell, they want to be rid of you too.

Kill yourself because you're tired of being here. The world won't give a fuck about you dying, trust me. Look at how fucked up your life is now? No one cares about you.

School was fucked up, your parents didn't give a fuck about you, you have no friends and no job, booze and weed had you sucking dick and getting arrested, then you took your frustrations out on your mother's ass.

When you're dead, time won't stand still. The earth will continue its journey around the sun, and people will go on with their daily activities. No one will even notice you're gone, Charles, because you don't matter. No one cares about you. You're totally alone, and to be honest with you, humanity is better off with you dead.

If you want to die, go for it. Your death won't mean shit, so stop giving it needless thought. It's no longer required. You've made up your mind, so don't be a pussy and back out. The only thing left to decide now is how.

Do you go out quietly like a pussy, or do you go out strong? I say, if you have to go, go out strong. Pills and guns are not always successful, and those are among the pussy choices. But it's your call.

I suggest you do a little research, but be creative. For example, if you're into pain, fire is a good choice. If you do it right, you'll go out in a beautiful blaze of glory, and even if you fuck it up, you'll still die in excruciating pain.

Another tried-and-true method is to jump the fuck off the tallest building you have access to. It'll be exciting, and your mind will play back your entire life in a matter of micro seconds. You won't even know you're dead. Your life's movie and all sensations will simply stop, a painless death.

If you took that route, for example, don't wait for a crowd to gather. Don't give those fuckers a show. People are nothing but voyeuristic, pleasure-seeking scum that enjoy seeing others suffer to make themselves feel alive. They would cheer you on to jump and laugh at you.

If you took the jump route, for example, just go to the top of that motherfucker and walk the fuck off the roof. I guarantee you'll succeed, and no one will call you a loser ever again.

Along those same lines, a high bridge would do just as well, especially falling into traffic. If your gonna kill yourself, what do you care if you fuck somebody else's day up? They don't give a fuck about you.

Bottom line, do the right thing by you. You already know what the alternative is.

He sits in his seat no longer trembling. The thought of his being in prison and living the nightmare that was described to him has his whole body in a paralyzed state. He knows he can't allow that to happen.

Doctor: Do we have anything further to discuss?

The doctor's question brings him back to reality.

Patient: I have one question. Are you really going to report what I did to my mother to the police?

Doctor: You can count on it. Now please get your ass out of my office.

Patient says nothing. The look on his face is one of total bewilderment. He has never experienced the feeling that comes to him now. He knows what needs to be done. He gets up with his head hanging down and leaves the doctor's office.

***

The time is 9 PM. It's been hours since he left the doctor's office. He has wandered the city aimlessly on foot with no destination in mind. He thinks only of his death. Thinking about his worthless life and how big a failure he really turned out to be, he threw his cell phone and all his ID in a dumpster hours ago. He knows he has no intention of ever returning home or talking to anyone.

The session with that asshole doctor had a profound effect on him, he thinks. Everything the doctor said to him was correct. The decision to end his life is the correct one. Charles realizes his life is not worth living, but before he dies, he decides he might as well enjoy a few more drinks.

He finds a bar and goes in. He orders his favorite drink, a double Grey Goose on the rocks. He tells himself he'll have about three drinks, and then he'll do what he has to.

As he drinks his second Grey Goose, he tries hard to think of someone he'll miss. He searches his thoughts and can only come up with one name: Angela. She was the only person that ever really loved him.

He wonders what his life would have been like if she was still in his life. He curses himself for letting his mother's words come between them. He wonders if his love for her could have changed the course his life took.

Ultimately, he decides it really doesn't matter. He wasn't strong enough to hold her, he wasn't strong enough to be his own man, he's never been strong enough to chart his own course in life successfully, and he wasn't strong enough to conquer his own fears.

He asks the bartender, "Is there a bridge around here anywhere?" He's told the closest one is about two miles down Allentown Road, the new Wilson Bridge. He pictures the bridge's location in his mind, finishes his last drink, leaves the bar, and walks toward the bridge.

It's strange, he thinks to himself, *I'm walking to a bridge to end my own life, and I'm not afraid, not afraid of dying, of pain or of anything else.* He feels content and at peace with what he's about to do.

He knows this is the right decision. He takes in the beauty of the stars in the heavens as the bridge comes into view. The air is calm and warm. *A perfect night to die*, he thinks to himself. The bridge really is beautiful. Its construction simple but elegant, and the bridges lights are pretty. He wonders why he couldn't have been the one to design and build such a structure.

Again he is content. *It's okay that you are not the builder of bridges. Such tasks were always for men greater than you*, he thinks to himself. Again his feeling of peace comes over him. He thinks, *I may not have built this beautiful bridge, but my death on her will be something people will talk about for as long as it exists*, and that thought makes him smile.

He approaches the bridge from the southbound lanes that cross into Virginia. He sees his goal, the first tower of the southbound lanes. He has to just make it to that tower and climb to the top. The cars that pass him pay him no attention. Everyone is too busy to get where they're going. He figures it should take him less than ten minutes to reach his goal.

As he gets closer, he sees the rungs on the tower that will take him to the top and to his destiny. Destiny. That word makes all the sense in the world to him now. This is what he was destined to do. This is why he exists. This is the moment his whole life has lead up to. He starts to climb the tower.

Charles finds that his hands are not shaking as they usually have in the past when he was nervous or afraid. There is no trembling in his body as the warm summer air caresses his face and body as he ascends to the top of the tower and his destiny.

He reaches the top of the tower in less than ten minutes. He figures he's about seventy-five feet in the air, and the view is breathtaking. The cars look so small from this viewpoint. He can barely hear the sounds they make as they pass below him.

All these people, he thinks, *are on their way somewhere*. To him, every destination is unknown, and he thinks that's okay by him. *They may not care about me now, but soon, real soon, the whole world will know who I am.*

The warm air feels so good to him. It has a calming effect on his mind and body, like that of a lover. He closes his eyes and enjoys that sensation as he sits atop his tower.

Charles opens his eyes and decides it is time, time to meet his fate, time to go to a glorious death with no fear in his heart, He will face his death with courage and honor as he stands and prepares to throw himself into the traffic below.

He looks to his left at the traffic coming toward him and then across the bridge to his right at the cars going away from him. He decides to play one last game before he dies.

He decides he is going to try to pick a minivan to fall onto. It'll probably be filled with a family going to or coming from some place. He is beyond caring about anyone else his actions may hurt. Like the doctor said, "Fuck it if you kill someone else."

I'm gonna die, so I might as well fuck someone else's day up too. That thought makes perfect sense now, he thinks to himself. Besides, Charles feels that these little insects scurrying about are now beneath his capacity to care about. He now feels he has the power to grant life or take life, like a god. And this night, his power will be used to end the lives of a whole family as well as his own. It will be glorious.

He focuses on the vehicles to his right. He makes test runs in his mind on exactly when to jump so that he impacts at exactly the moment he wishes. He lets at least thirty minivans pass before he has the timing down in his head.

He tells himself he is ready. He sees his target, and he prepares himself to step off the edge at exactly the right moment. He almost can't wait to see his life played back in his mind when he steps off the tower.

He concentrates on his target. A red minivan. He focuses his resolve and steps off the tower. One micro second after he steps off the tower, he realizes he made a critical mistake. He was concentrating on the wrong side of the bridge, on the traffic that was moving away from him. He screams in his mind as he now perceives his last seconds of life in slow motion.

His eyes are opened so wide, they feel as if they are going to explode out of his skull. The air is ice cold as he plummets to his death. He can hear his heart beating as the noise of the traffic below him gets louder and louder, and still he sees everything racing toward him in slow motion.

He realizes that his life is not playing back in his mind. He feels the terror of death coming to meet him, and he screams. He feels the horror of what he committed himself to and he screams. He continues to scream as he plummets to his death and perceives it all in vivid slow motion.

As he falls, his intended target intersects with his location, just as he had planned. He falls, screaming until his body makes contact with the top of a moving vehicle with such force that the entire right side of his body is torn open. His blood splatters to the wind on impact

He crashes through the top of the vehicle and feels the pain of his body smashing into and through numerous hard objects. He feels the excruciating pain of his ribs, back, and legs breaking on impact as they make contact with the vehicle's cargo containers.

His fall comes to a stop, and Charles realizes he is barely alive. He cannot move and can barely feel his body. Seconds later, he is only semi-conscious but realizes he isn't alone. He can barely perceive a foul odor in the vehicle, and he hears sounds he can't make out.

Something moves under him, something he's laying on. He's lying in his own warm blood, but he doesn't know it. There is almost no light so he can't see what's going on inside the vehicle. Then something pulls at his legs. He can't feel anything but he knows something is pulling on him.

Whatever it is under him starts to move violently now, but he can't move away. His barely conscious mind and paralyzed body can do nothing except lay where it fell. Then, out of the darkness, something pulls on his arm, then his legs again. Something attacks his face. He see's a mouth full of teeth, and he smells the creatures foul breath, but he doesn't know what it is.

Charles realizes some kind of animals are attacking him. He doesn't know what they are, and he can't call out for help. The animals are not just pulling on his arms and legs, they are biting chunks of flesh out of his body, tearing him apart. He sees many of the creatures now at his stomach, eating and pulling his intestines out of his abdomen and drinking his blood. He can barely feel the pain, and what he see's drives him insane. He watches horrified as he is eaten alive.

The truck continues its journey down the highway. The lettering on the side of the truck reads. US Military Animal Research Center. He will be one of the thousands who go missing each year. His ultimate fate will never be known as Charles' silent screams can be heard by no one.

***

Earlier that evening, at 6:30 PM, after the last patient has left the doctor's office, the doctor's assistant lets him know over the intercom that the last patient has just left the office.

"Okay baby, get that fine ass in here," he says.

"Coming, Doctor," she replies. She comes into his office and walks toward him with her arms open to hug him. They embrace and kiss passionately.

"Baby, did you listen in on that last motherfucker?"

"Yes and that bastard was truly fucked up. I almost fell out my damn seat when he said what he did to his mother."

"I wish I could have seen his face when you told him you were going to talk to the police about what he'd done to his mother and his punk ass was going to prison," she says.

"He was in here crying like a little bitch," he tells her.

"All right, baby, we have to get this office cleaned up. Get that liquor out of the fridge and wipe down everything. I'll take care of the furniture and the ashtrays. I already re-set his computer the way he had it and erased our history."

"You got it, baby."

"I also confirmed our reservations on the red-eye back to Vegas. Our flight leaves National at 9:30 PM," she says as she cleans out the refrigerator and replaces the liquor with bottled water.

"Good. That'll give us plenty of time to get out of town," he responds. "T, are all the letters ready to go?" he asks.

"Yes, we can mail them on our way out of town. I had everything else you prepared and wanted sent by courier delivered. I confirmed all the packages and letters were received this afternoon.

"I also made all the phone calls you requested and those special calls concerning that dirtyass cop's activities to some very interested brothers in the hood. I'm sure that dirty bastard is six feet under by now," she says.

"Either that or floating in the river," he responds.

"We did it, baby. We burned his ass good," T says.

"I've waited for this for a long time, baby. Because of this no good, sanctimonious asshole, I spent eight years in jail. My own fucking big brother wouldn't testify at my trial or help me with my defense, and it cost me eight years of my life," Jeff explains.

"I'm going to love every minute of this. His practice will be ruined when these letters go out. I'm going to enjoy watching the great Dr. Feelgood trying to get his ass out of this mess."

"By the time he's done answering inquiries from the American Psychiatric Association and paying out lawsuits he'll be disgraced, broke, and stripped of his license to practice medicine. And if it all goes right he'll spend the rest of his hypocritical life in prison."

"Jeff, you were always as smart as him. You used your time wisely, and earned two degrees in prison, psychology and computer science, and you've done very well for years, so fuck him," T says.

T picks up a picture on the doctor's desk and says, "You two could be twins, even though you're five years apart. It would be hard as hell to tell you two apart in person."

"We don't have to worry about that," Jeff says.

"What I'd love to see is him explain to his tight-ass wife how he was in Europe for two weeks with his girlfriend when he was supposed to be at a conference in New York when all this shit kicks off," T laughs.

"When his wife gets the contents of his office computer and copies of all the letters he wrote to his little white playmate, she might kill his ass," Jeff says.

"Jeff, have you ever met your brother's wife?" T asks.

"No, I haven't seen or spoken to my brother in eighteen years. Our mother died while I was in prison, so after my release I changed my last name so I wouldn't be reminded I'm related to his ass. So I've never met his wife or any of their kids, but I've been able to keep track of his ass via the Internet and his computers, You know, baby computers are a wonderful thing. It's amazing what you can accomplish with them if you know what the fuck you're doing."

They both laugh as they leave the office, closing the door behind them.

***

8 PM that same evening, Channel 13 news late evening report

"This is Virginia Summers, Channel 13 news, coming to you live tonight with two exclusive stories. Our first report concerns corruption and police misconduct of an extremely brutal nature within the Prince Georges Police Department."

"Our second report concerns mysterious patient deaths at Mercy General Hospital. We have confirmed reports that Nurse Rashanaria

Williams, an employee at Mercy General Hospital, is suspected of having caused the deaths of at least four patients."

"We will show you hidden camera video of the nurse injecting unknown substances into a patient's IV. We would like to caution viewers that this footage may not be suitable for children." The report continues.

***

That night at the home of Jimmy and Rashanaria

Jimmy sits in front of his TV in stunned silence. He can't believe what he's seeing. He doesn't want to believe the report, but since Rosh won't talk to him about what's going on at the hospital, he doesn't know what to think.

He wants to talk to her, but he can't tear himself away from the TV. Even as his phone rings, he sits in front of his TV like a man possessed and watches the reports.

The news report is over at 9:30 PM and Jimmy decides he has to hear from Rosh that she is not involved in this, that they have the wrong person. *That might not have been her on the video*, he lies to himself.

He decides that no matter what, he's going to stand with his woman. There is no way the woman he loves could be a part of murdering patients, not the love of his life.

Jimmy goes upstairs to the bedroom. The only thing he can think is that this has got to be a mistake. He'll believe whatever she tells him. He loves her, so it doesn't matter what they say.

He opens the door to their bedroom, and he sees that she is asleep. He decides not to bother her. *She looks so beautiful when she sleeps*, he thinks to himself, *like an angel, his beautiful angel.*

He crosses the room to go to his side of the bed and sits down next to her sleeping body. He touches her face, and his love for her is confirmed in his heart.

He looks on his nightstand and sees an envelope. "To my baby" is written on it. He picks it up and smiles as he opens the envelope. As he reads the letter, his smile and the happiness he feels intensifies.

He continues to the second page, and his happiness quickly fades, and is replaced with blind panic and fear. He throws the letter to the floor and reaches for his woman, screaming at her to wake up.

He holds her in his arms, crying. Her body is still warm, but she won't wake up. He screams her name, "Rosh, baby, wake up! Don't do this! Baby, we can work this out!" He reaches for the phone and dials 911 as he holds her.

He cries loudly and furiously as he holds his baby in his arms, trying to wake her. The tears flow down his face and onto hers as he calls her name and holds her to his chest tightly. She won't move, she won't respond to his voice. She is pronounced dead shortly after the ambulance arrives.

***

9:30 PM, Jeff and T board their flight to Las Vegas

Two weeks later at the Mirage Hotel on the Las Vegas Strip

Jeff and T are relaxing by the pool on a sunny hot Las Vegas morning when a copy of that day's *Washington Post* is brought to their table.

The front-page story in the metro section catches his attention. A nurse at Mercy General Hospital who was suspected of killing patients committed suicide two weeks ago. Her autopsy revealed she was six weeks pregnant.

Senator Charles Kirkland of Maryland is being questioned about the whereabouts of his son. The story is still under investigation, but apparently it involves some type of sexual assault against his wife. The article goes on to say more information will be forth coming as the investigation proceeds.

The article that Jeff has been waiting for is finally out.

Noted Washington, D.C. area psychiatrist Doctor Y. Feelgood is scheduled to go before the American Medical Association and the American Psychiatric Association on several charges of physician misconduct and ethics violations in the coming weeks.

Speaking through his lawyer, the only statement the doctor would release as he came out of the district court house was. "He simply has no comment at this time. He needs to spend time with his family as these matters are being investigated. Thank you."

Jeff smiles as he puts the paper in the trash can and lays next to his sleeping beauty and thinks to himself, laughing, "I got you, motherfucker. I got your ass."

We all know family fucks you first. They aren't afraid of you, but your friends are, and they lay in wait.

The Link

The girls meet at this particular restaurant almost every Friday after work before they take off to dance the night away and have fun at one of many clubs they frequent on the weekends.

This meeting is not like most. One of the group is pregnant and hasn't been able to drink or party with her friends for some time now. Unfortunately, her pregnancy isn't her only issue.

Lois is the first of the four to enter the restaurant. She is greeted by the hostess and taken to their usual table to wait for her friends to arrive. It'll be sometime before the others arrive. It's 3:30 PM. The others won't arrive before 4 PM.

She orders a glass of sweet iced tea and waits for her friends to arrive. She thinks to herself that they have been really supportive, standing by her all these months during her pregnancy. She just wishes her baby's father could be equally supportive. She rubs her stomach and silently tells her baby everything will be okay.

She tried again last night to talk to Vic on the phone about the baby, for the thousandth time, it seemed to her. Their conversation went like it had in the past, which is not well at all, with both of them saying mean things to the other. She replays their latest conversation back in her mind.

After she arrived home last night and settled in for the evening, Lois decided to call Vic for the third time that day to see if he would be willing to come over to her place so they could talk face to face.

Lois picked up the phone and dialed his number. It rings five times before he answered.

Lois: Hello.

Vic: Hey, Lois, can I call you back? I'm kind of busy right now.

Lois: Vic, you always say that, then you never call back. I just want to talk.

Long pause

Vic: All right, Lois. Hold on for a few seconds. I'm gonna change phones.

Thirty seconds later, Vic returns to the phone.

Vic: Okay, what's up?

Lois: How are you doing?

Vic: I'm fine.

Lois: Vic do, you think we can get together so we can discuss the baby?

Vic: What is there to discuss, Lois? I told you when you first came to me and told me you were pregnant that I didn't want to have a child, not now, not ever. I offered to pay for an abortion, you said no, so what do you want to talk about that's new?

Lois: Vic, I told you then that I don't believe in abortions. I can't just kill our baby, I want the baby, and I just want to know if you'll be a part of our child's life.

Vic: Lois, please don't take this the wrong way. I'm trying my hardest to be nice, but I told you months ago how I felt.
I told you when we got together that I had someone. You told me you didn't care. You said that one night we had sex was about us, no strings. You even said you were on birth control and insisted I didn't have to wear a condom. You remember that? So you lied to me.

Lois: I remember we were both twisted and wanted each other that night. I didn't plan to get pregnant, Vic.

Vic: Well, that's the way it looks to me. Why do you want to ruin my life? I don't want kids in my life. Your forcing this shit on me.

Lois: Vic, I do want a child. Getting pregnant was an accident. It wasn't on purpose. Since I am pregnant, why can't you be in our lives?

Vic: Lois, I don't want you in my life or a baby. Look you're a very attractive woman. Any man would be proud to have you as his lady. Why do you want to be with someone who doesn't want to be with you? That's what I can't understand.

Lois: Vic, I'm not trying to trap you if that's what you're trying to say. I just don't want to do this alone. I didn't get pregnant alone.

Vic: You didn't have to be pregnant at all. I'm not gonna change my lifestyle for you. Lois. I have open relationships, and I told you that, you're twenty-seven, I'm thirty, neither of us is married. I don't want to be tied down with a damn family. I have someone in my life that I want to be with. You and me were just about fun, that's it.

Lois: Well, Vic, you didn't have to fuck me. You made that choice and now you can't face up to your responsibility.

Vic: How many times can I say I don't want to be with or have any responsibility to you. I've never tried to mislead you or run game on you. Hell, Lois, we haven't been together since that first time. That should tell you something. It was fun but that's all it was.

Lois: Like I said, you could have said no.

Vic: You practically dragged me to that damn suite in the hotel where you work. You had that shit set up in advance to take someone there. It just happened to be me that night.

Lois: I don't remember forcing you to do a damn thing you didn't want to do.

Vic: Like you didn't want to get fucked. Don't lay all this shit on me. Yeah, I know it's partly my fault, but you came on to me.

Lois: Vic, you don't have to be with me. All I'm asking if you are just willing to be a part of the baby's life.

Vic: When the baby's born, I want a DNA test. If it shows I'm the father, then we'll see, okay?

Lois: No, that's not okay. Why are you doubting it's yours now? I told you I hadn't been with anyone for months prior to you, and I haven't been with anyone since you, then I found out I was pregnant, and I sure as hell haven't been fucking anyone else.

Vic: How am I supposed to know that? I barely know anything about you. How am I supposed to know what you and your freak-ass girls do, or have you forgotten how you all were acting the night we met? You need to check your girl Monique. She told me some crazy shit about all you bitches.

Lois: What about her? What did she say to you?

Vic: She's as easy as you. Talk to her.

Lois: Oh, so now I'm a whore that goes around just fucking everybody?

Vic: I didn't say that, you did. Look, I don't know what else to say to you. When the kid is born we can get the DNA test. I'm not gonna let you stick me with someone else's kid.

Lois: I'm not trying to stick you with anything. I'm carrying your kid.

Vic: Whether I want a baby or not, your gonna make that decision for me. How is that fair to me? I could see if I felt the same as you.

Lois: Why can't you give this a chance? I'm not asking for a lot. Why can't you give us a chance, Vic? I could make you happy.
Do you know how many months I am? Do you want to know what the baby's sex is.

Vic: I don't care.

Lois: Nigga, I'm seven-and-a-half months, and it's a girl!

Vic: Lois, you just don't get it. Over the last few months, you've made me miserable, ever since you told me you could be pregnant with my kid. You don't care that I don't want kids, and you say you're not forcing this shit on me, but what the hell would you call it?

Lois: I love you, Vic. Is that wrong?

Vic: How the fuck can you love me? You don't know anything about me. This really bothers me. Lois. For all I know you could be a damn psycho, and you've sounded like one for months. That's why I don't want to talk to you about this shit. Hell, for all you know, I could be a psycho. You don't love me, and I sure as hell don't love you, so please stop saying that.

Lois: I don't understand how you can be so cold to me. You won't even give me a chance. I'm all alone and pregnant and I'm scared.

Vic: Look, you should have thought about all that shit before you decided you wanted to have a baby. I have someone. I'm not leaving her for you. What goddamn part of that don't you understand?

Lois: I understand you have a baby on the way, and you're the father.

Vic: Why me? Of all the men out there why latch on to me? I'm not trying to hurt you. Why can't you leave me the fuck alone?

Lois: Because, nigga, I'm pregnant by you!
Do you remember all that shit you said to me when you were in this pussy? How good it was and all that other shit you were talking? You weren't thinking about that other bitch when you had your face buried in my pussy, were you mothafucka?

Vic: This is what I'm talking about. You sound like a fucking street ho now. I'm tired of you kirk'in the fuck out on me.

Lois: I wouldn't have to if you would man up and handle your business, nigga.

Vic: Bitch, you can go straight to hell, you and your damn baby.

Lois: Nigga, fuck you!
Vic: Okay, that's it. I don't have anything else to say to your desperate ass. Don't call me anymore. I guess I'll see you in court, bitch. Bye.

Vic hangs up the phone. Lois puts her receiver in the cradle and lays down on her bed. She wants to cry, but she knows her stresses are not good for her baby.

The tears come anyway as she drifts off to sleep telling her baby that Daddy didn't mean those ugly things he said and thinking that she really does love Vic. But she can't help wondering what he meant when he said she should talk to Monique.

***

The arrival of Terri and Bernice snaps Lois's attention to the present. They greet each other, and the two arriving friends take a seat at the table.

"Terri, where's Monique?" Lois asks.

"I don't know. She called me earlier at work and said she'd be here," Terri responds.

"Girl, you know Monique's ass is never on time. She'll be here. We're not going anywhere for a while," says Bernice.

"That's true," Lois says.

"Lois, have you been able to reach Vic? Is that nigga still trippin?" asks Bernice.

"Yeah, I talked to him last night finally. It didn't go well. He's still insisting he isn't the father, and he doesn't want a baby." Lois goes on to tell her friends about her conversation with Vic and how upset it made her.

"That sorry bastard. Girl, what you need to do is take him to court when the baby is born. I told you I can hook you up. I am a paralegal. You have to make him at least pay child support," says Bernice.

"Lois, as much as you might think you want this guy, you can't make him be with you if he insists he doesn't want the same thing. Girl, as pretty as you are, finding a man won't be a problem. The hell with him," says Bernice.

"That's right, Lois. Your baby will have us, so you don't need that sorry ass nigga. We'll be with you and the baby. What fuck'in man doesn't want to know the sex of his baby?" Terri continues. "What that mothafucka needs is his ass kicked. We should get some guys to fuck him up." All the women laugh at that statement.

"That sounds good, but I don't think it would accomplish anything," Lois says.

"It might not, but he needs to know he can't just walk away from this. I wonder if that bitch he's seeing knows he has a baby on the way?" Terri says.

"I doubt it, I don't think he would have told her," says Lois.

"Well, maybe we need to find this bitch and clue her in to what her man has been doing. Bernice, you can track that bitch down for us. You have that kind of access," Terri states.

"Terri, you're violent as hell. What good would that do Lois? If we did that, would it make him want to accept Lois and his baby?" Bernice asks.

"It'll let him know he can't go around fuck'in people over, especially our girl. I bet he wasn't complaining when he was making that baby," Terri says.

"No, he damn sure wasn't," says Lois.

"Well, we want to make things better for Lois, not worse. Maybe he'll have a change of heart when he sees the baby. This nigga might be just talkin' shit like most men do," Bernice continues.

"You've seen those bullshit shows on TV where niggas and their mamas want to deny they're the daddy until the damn test is read. When dude says, □When it comes to so and so, Vic you are the father.' Then after talkin' all that shit they get soft as a mothafucka," Bernice says. All the women laugh.

***

One hour later, at 5:30 PM Monique comes in and goes right to their table.

"Hey, y'all. Sorry I'm late. I had to stay a little later at work, finishing some memos for my boss, then I got caught up in damn traffic. How is everybody doing?"

The friends brought Monique up to speed on the conversations of the last hour. They order drinks and dinner and talk about their plans for the rest of the evening.

"Terri, what are your plans for tonight?" asks Lois.

"I'm going to a movie with Kenny about 9 PM and then probably back to his place to fuck like rabbits." All the women laugh.

"Damn, girl, that was a little too much info," Bernice says.

"You know I say what's up. Why bullshit with it? Since when have we been shy with each other?"

"True that," says Bernice.

"What about the rest of you?" asks Terri. "I can't hang tonight. I have some damn legal briefs I have to finish for Monday, so I'll be tied up with that shit all weekend," says Bernice.

"What about you Monique?" Terri asks.

"I don't really have any plans after we leave here. Phil is out of town, and I don't feel like being bothered right now with any strange dick. I'm not gonna lie though, I could use some head." Again they all laugh.

"Well, in my condition, I'm not going to be doing anything but going home and sleeping," Lois says.

"No fuck that, girl. How about you and me go to a move? But not at the same theater Terri's going to. We wouldn't want to inhibit her," says Monique.

"Inhibit me? I don't think that's possible. If I want to suck that nigga's dick in the theater or driving down the highway, it's gonna happen, and I get mine the same way. So you're both welcomed to join us." There's another round of laughter from the table.

"Girl, you're a mess," says Monique.

"Aren't we all?" Terri responds.

"Yeah, I guess so," Monique says. "Lois, do you want to go see a movie? It's better than sitting at home alone all night," Monique says.

"Yeah, Monique, that'll work, but you have to follow me home so I can drop off my car," says Lois,

"No problem. That'll give us time to talk," Monique responds. The four friends say their good-byes after dinner and take off for their evening's activities.

Twenty minutes after leaving the restaurant, Lois and Monique arrive at Lois's townhouse and go inside.

"Monique do you want something to drink?"

"Do you have any white wine?"

"Yeah, give me a minute," Lois responds. Monique settles into the living room and turns on the TV. Lois goes into the kitchen and comes back with a glass of wine for her friend.

"Lois, you look a bit tired. Are you sure you're up for a movie? We can just sit here and talk if you like. The movies will be there another time," Monique says.

"I am feeling a little beat. If you don't mind, we can just stay here and talk. I'd like that," says Lois.

"Monique, I'm just so confused right now. I'm seven-and-a-half months pregnant, and I had to pick a nigga like Vic. I mean, he talks like I'm trying to trap him. I didn't get pregnant on purpose, but he swears that's what I did."

"Lois, I know that wasn't the case, and it's a damn shame he's treating you like this, but if he won't even talk about things with you, the only thing you can make his sorry ass do is pay child support."

"But, Monique, that's not even the issue. I don't need his money. I've tried to tell him that. He's a physical therapist, and he makes good money I guess, for that kind of work, but I get paid more than him. I don't need his fuck'in' money."

"That may be true, Lois, but it's like Bernice said, making that fucker pay support is not about you, it's about the baby. He helped to make the baby, and if he's not going to emotionally support her, then that bastard should be made to pay support."

"Monique, I just don't know what to do. I have feelings for Vic, and he won't even acknowledge me. I'm not trying to ruin his damn life. That one night we were together was good. That nigga has some good dick, but for me, it's more than that," Lois continues

"He told me he loved me. I know he said it when we were fucking, but he made me believe he could love me. We only had sex one time, but we did spend time together after that, and we'd talk on the phone a lot until I told him I was pregnant."

"Lois, you know when a man is in some good pussy, you can make his ass quack like a duck or say anything you want his ass to say. Baby, that's probably all it was. We both know men lie, especially when their dick is hard and they want to fuck."

"I'm not saying your feelings for him are misplaced. I believe you do love him, and he's an ass for treating you this way, but, Lois, you can't make him love you."

Lois puts her hands to her face and starts to cry. In a shaky voice, she asks Monique why she had to fall in love with a man who won't love her back. Monique holds her friend until she calms down.

"Lois, baby, don't cry, We can't help who we fall in love with. Your love for him is real, but he wants to be an ass, I know he told you he has someone, but look at what he did behind her back. He's not worth your tears, and he's not worthy of you. Terri was right, you have us, the hell with him." Lois stops crying and composes herself.

"Monique, last night when I was talking to Vic on the phone, he said a lot of things to me that hurt, but he also said something about you too. I have to ask you something concerning some of the shit he said last night."

"Sure," Monique says.

"Vic said to me that you were easy and that you told him shit about us— Terri, Bernice, you, and me. When I asked him what he was talking about, he said I need to talk to my girl Monique. He wouldn't say what he meant."

The look on Monique's face turns somber. Her eyes start to water and her hands start to tremble as she begins to speak.

"Lois, I don't know how to tell you this," she pauses. "There is something I need to tell you, and I really don't know where to begin." As Monique speaks, her mind drifts back to that day.

She tells Lois how she went to the new Gaylord Hotel Complex in February after work to have a drink at one of the bars before going home to check the place out since it was recently completed.

She didn't plan on staying long. She was sitting at the bar and saw one of the guys who was with Vic the night they all met for the first time, but Vic wasn't with him.

About an hour later, Vic comes up to where she was sitting and sits next to her. He remembered who she was but not her name. They sat there for a while talking about their jobs and how nice the Gaylord is. All the while, he was buying round after round of drinks.

During the course of the evening he got a brochure from the bar that showed the room rates and configurations. She says she was shocked when he asked her if she would like to check out one of the rooms with him.

She told him "hell no," and asked him "Aren't you with Lois?" He went on to tell her that he and Lois were not a couple and that he has no ties to her. She reminded him that Lois was pregnant with his baby and that she doesn't fuck around with her friend's men, ex's or otherwise.

By about 8 PM Monique knew she was past twisted and needed to go home. She gathered her purse and jacket to leave, and Vic insisted she was too intoxicated to drive.

By this time, Monique's resistance was shot, and he easily persuaded her to go to a room with him. All the while, she was insisting that he wasn't going to fuck her. He led her out of the bar and into a room he had booked.

As Monique tells Lois what happened that night, she rests her head in her hands and silently cries, but she continues the story.

They got to the room and Monique remembers how nice and spacious the room was, and she also remembers saying to herself, *Fuck it. I'm here now and twisted. I may as well get my freak on.*

As she tells Lois what happened between her and Vic, she does not describe what they did in vivid detail, but the events play back in her mind as she speaks.

She took her clothes off and got in the shower. Vic joined her. She remembers the water was hot and so was his body as he pressed against her back and cupped her breasts in his hands. He took the soap and washed her body.

She turned to face him in the shower and kissed him as his hands found their way between her legs. She remembers how good his hands felt as they worked her pussy. She began stroking his dick. He was long and hard. She sucked his dick in the shower, then turned around to receive him from behind.

They then moved to the bedroom. Monique sat on the bed facing him as he came toward her, his long, hard dick leading the way.

She took his dick in her hand and took as much of it as she could in her mouth. She sucked his dick until he came. She let him spray cum all over her breasts. She wiped his cum off her breasts with a towel and turned around on her hands and knees and let him take her again from behind.

She felt his long dick make its way deep into her pussy. She moaned loudly with pleasure as it filled her pussy completely. She asked that he stroke her pussy faster. He complied and was soon thrusting his long dick in her harder and faster.

She moaned louder and louder, almost screaming with every stroke of his dick. She begged him not to stop as he pushed faster and faster. She pushed onto the dick as she came with such intensity her whole body spasmed with pleasure.

Dripping with sweat and holding her tight against his dick she screamed as Vic came deep in her pussy. When Vic was done, Monique turned to see another man had entered the bedroom carrying a bottle of liquor. She smiled and said, "Bring it on." All three of them fucked and talked for hours.

As Monique finishes telling Lois what happened between her and Vic, she can't stop herself from crying. "Lois, I'm so sorry, I never meant for that to happen. I don't know what else to say except I'm sorry. I think Vic and his boy set me up from the moment they saw me at the bar."

Lois looks at Monique through bloodshot eyes and honestly doesn't know what to say. All she can think of is *How could my girlfriend of over six years have done this to me?* Lois thinks to herself, *Just calm down. It happened and it's done. There is nothing you can do about it now.*

"Monique, I have to know, how could you do that to me? I know how freaky you get when you're fucked up, but knowing I love him, how could you do that?" Lois asks.

"Lois, all I can say is I got fucked up, and it happened. I didn't fuck him to hurt you. I would never do anything to intentionally hurt you. I'm sorry it happened. I only ask that you please try to find a way to forgive me."

Lois is now more confused than ever. Her emotional state is almost shot. She feels extreme anger toward Monique for what she just told her concerning Vic. She thinks to herself, *How could this bitch betray me like this? And what else did she tell Vic*?

Lois shouts, "Monique what else did you tell him? He mentioned something about us. What did you say to him? What does he know?" Monique starts crying again as she wraps her arms around herself.

"Lois, I think I told him," Monique says.

"Monique, please God tell me you didn't. You say 'you think.' What the fuck does that mean? Did you tell him or not?

"Yes," she responds.

"How the fuck could you do that? We all swore to never even talk about that again. If you did run your fucking mouth to Vic, who the fuck else knows? And what are you gonna say to Bernice? And you know how crazy Terri can get."

Monique sits back in the chair and cries as she faces her friend of many years and thinks to herself. *What have I done*? She knows saying I'm sorry won't help the situation, and at this point she really doesn't know what else to say.

"Lois, what are you gonna say to Bernice and Terri?" Monique asks.

"What the fuck do you think I should say, Monique? You betrayed us all, not just me." Lois continues

"I could almost forgive you for fucking Vic, but I'm pregnant by that nigga and in love with his sorry ass, and on top of all of that, you told him our secret. Monique, I'm not feelin' you right now. Please leave." Lois asks.

Monique begs Lois not to tell the others what she's done. She apologizes to Lois again and then leaves her home.

Confused, hurt, and betrayed doesn't even come close to describing how Lois felt at that moment. Being alone and pregnant was enough for her to have to deal with. Now she has to cope with the knowledge that other people besides those involved know her secret. She can't guess the implications that might have for her life, but they won't be good.

Lois thinks to herself, *This has been a horrible day*. And she knows the only way she can keep from stressing out further is to go to sleep, but how can she sleep after what was just revealed to her? She thinks she'll have to try. She doesn't want to hurt her baby.

Lois lays in bed on her side with her night light on. She is feeling profoundly sad. She knows these up and down feelings she's been having can't be good for her body or her baby, but she can't help herself.

Her mind can't focus on anything except her conversation with Monique and the impact that revelation is going to have on her friendships. She knows it won't be good.

Lois lets her mind drift back to a day two years ago that she and her friends all swore to keep secret forever and the events that occurred on that day that made their oath necessary.

The four friends had agreed to meet at Monique's one particular Friday evening after work. They had planned a long weekend of partying and possibly going up to Atlantic City Saturday morning, so everyone would be staying together at Monique's house.

The rule for the weekend was leave the boyfriends behind. None of them was married or had kids so that wasn't a problem. The girls had planned a weekend just for them, and they didn't want men around to complicate shit.

Monique had taken Friday off so she could be free to make preparations at home for her friends. She had a three-bedroom, two-and-a-half bathroom house, so she had plenty of room for everybody.

Terri and Bernice arrived at Monique's about 5: 30 PM, suitcases in hand. After they were settled in, they all went into the living room and had a glass of white wine and waited for Lois to arrive.

Lois got to Monique's about 6 PM, After they all greeted each other and had more wine, it was time to decide where they would go for dinner and which club they were going to hit.

All the women had settled in and put away their things. They gathered around the dining room table, each with a glass of wine and started talking and having a good time, discussing what their plans were going to be for the evening.

"Okay ladies, what are we gonna do tonight?" asks Monique.

"Lets decide where we're gonna have dinner first," says Bernice.

"How about that Italian place Carrabas. I hear the food is good," says Lois.

"That's fine with me," says Terri.

"Okay is that place good for dinner with everybody?" asks Lois. They all agree on Italian for dinner.

"What time should we head out for dinner then?" says Bernice.

"We need to be at the club before 10:30 PM or our asses are gonna be standing up all night," says Terri.

"How about we take a quick shower, change up, and be out of here by 8 PM? It's seven now, so that should give us plenty of time," says Monique.

"That's cool", they all agree.

"Hey, Monique, make some of those kick-ass strawberry daiquiris right quick," Terri requests.

"Already done," says Monique.

Monique goes into the kitchen and comes out with a tray of four tall glasses filled with the requested drink. They each take one.

"Okay ladies, we said no guys tonight. This weekend is all about us, right?" says Bernice as they drink their daiquiris.

"Yeah, but what if I get that itch, and I need some dick?" says Monique.

"Have a dude scratch that ass Sunday night," laughs Lois.

"Or go out to the parking lot and get your freak on in his car," says Terri. They all laugh.

"No seriously, we said no guys this weekend, right?" Bernice says again.

"No guys, Bernice. It's about us this weekend. But we can think about fuck'in', can't we?" Terri laughs.

"Yeah, you can think about it. I'm gonna hold my shit till Sunday and wear Carl's ass out when we get back," Bernice says.

"But what if you meet a fine nigga in Atlantic City, and you wanna ride that dick? You gonna walk away?" asks Monique.

"I'll cross that bridge when I come to it," Bernice says.

"Oh, bitch, stop lying. Your ass will be the first one on some dick, and you know it. Remember the cruise?" Terri says.

"Yeah, well, what's a girl to do when she see's a fine nigga's dick bulging in his swimming trunks? I couldn't resist it. How was I to know he liked the feel of his own hand?" Bernice says smiling.

"Yeah, wasn't that the mothafucka who came as soon as he took his dick out his trucks?" Lois asks. They all laugh.

"Yeah," says Bernice. "I'm in his cabin on the bed, pussy good and wet. I open my legs, this nigga takes his shit out, and nuts everywhere. Never touched the pussy. Then he couldn't get it back up and gonna say some shit like, 'Baby, can you suck on it for a minute? It'll get hard again.' "I was like, 'Nigga, please. I don't give head to little boys, and I only suck on hard dicks,' and walked out his cabin.

"You talk about a bitch being frustrated. I wanted to grab the first dick I saw. I had to go take a cold ass shower after that shit." The women all laugh.

"Then for the rest of the damn cruise that mothafucka had the nerve to keep bringing his ass around me," says Bernice. More laughter. "Until I told his limp-dick ass to come back with some damn Viagra," laughs Terri. They all laugh so hard, Lois and Monique almost spill their drinks.

"Hey, y'all, we need to get our happy asses in the shower so we can roll. It's a quarter past 7 PM now," Monique says. As the women get ready to leave the table, a loud clap of thunder stops their conversation.

"What the fuck was that? Please don't tell me it's getting ready to fuck'in' thunderstorm out here now," says Terri. The women all go to the patio door and onto the deck.

They all look up to see ominous black clouds moving toward them in the sky. The rain starts slowly at first, then after a few minutes it starts to pour heavier. A bolt of lightning sends the four friends running into the house.

Monique goes to the TV and turns on the news. The friends gather in the living room in time to hear the weatherman say that the entire viewing area is under a severe thunderstorm warning until 11:30 PM tonight and people are cautioned to remain off the roads if possible.

"Get the fuck outta here. This shit would have to happen now," says Lois.

"Well, at least the shit kicked off before we left," Terri says. A loud clap of thunder startles the ladies as they decide on a new course of action.

"Well I know I don't want to drive in this shit," Bernice says.

"I'm not either" says Monique.

"Well, I guess our asses are stuck in the house tonight," says Bernice.

"Well, seeing as how that might turn out to be the case, why don't we just fix dinner here and get fucked up. I went to the store today, so I have plenty of food and liquor," says Monique.

"That works for me. We can watch videos, talk shit, and drink till we pass the fuck out, get up in the morning early and head to Atlantic City," Terri says. The ladies all agree on the change of plans.

"Hey, Bernice, since you and Lois are the cooks in the group, why don't you two fix dinner? 'I'll take care of the drinks, and, Terri, you can call Caesar's in Atlantic City and confirm our reservations for tomorrow. And since you two cooked, Terri and I will take care of the clean up," Monique says.

The women all agree on the new change of plans and get busy on their assignments.

At 9:30 PM, the women sit down to a dinner of steaks, mashed potatoes, string beans, and Caesar salad. As they eat dinner, they enjoy more conversation and laughter.

After dinner, Monique and Terri cleaned up the kitchen and dinning room while Bernice and Lois went to take showers. When they were done, Monique had more daiquiris waiting for them, and she and Terri showered.

After the women had all taken showers, they came into the living room to settle down and have more drinks while Monique searched for a movie for the group to watch.

"This is really fucked up. We're supposed to be at the damn club getting our party on," Terri said.

"We can do that tomorrow, Terri. It's just fucked up it had to rain on our asses today. Besides the clubs are better in Atlantic City anyway," Monique said.

"What are you gonna have us watching, Monique? Please no scary shit," says Bernice.

"Girl chill out. You're the only one in the group that doesn't like a good scary movie," says Monique.

"It's not that I don't like them. I need my man next to me while I watch that shit," Bernice says.

"Well, we can't call his ass over here now, so you're stuck with us. Your rule, remember? No dicks this weekend," Terri laughs.

"How about we drink something a little stronger? Bartender, we need four strong Long Island Iced Teas," Lois says.

"Coming right up," responded Monique.

"After two of those, you won't give a damn what we watch," laughs Lois.

The four friends settle down with their iced teas and watch the first movie, which they agreed should be a comedy, a Tyler Perry movie, and then they would watch a scary movie and drink some more.

"Hey, y'all, since the movie is almost over, I need to go smoke one. I'll be right back," Terri says. Terri goes to the balcony to smoke as the others finish the movie.

Terri comes back to the living room just as the credits start to roll on the movie they were watching, and everybody stands to stretch their legs and arms.

"Does anyone want another drink?" asks Monique.

"Sure, why not? It's barely midnight," says Bernice.

"Yeah, it's still early," says Terri.

"Lois, put another movie in while I fix the drinks," Monique asks.

The others follow Monique in the kitchen as Lois looks through the collection of movies in the horror stack and selects a DVD titled *Dark Secrets*. She puts the DVD in the machine and goes to the kitchen with the others. When the ladies return to the living room, the DVD has started to play.

"What the fuck is this? Lois look what you put on," Terri laughs.

"Oh, damn. I didn't know this was a porno flick," says Lois.

"That bitch got her face all in that other ho's pussy," says Terri. The others gather around the TV.

"I don't mind watching a porno if I have to, but that shit makes me horny as hell, and I don't see any dicks in here," laughs Bernice.

"Your rules, bitch," says Lois.

"Damn, that white bitch is eatin' the shit out that sister's pussy," says Terri.

"Those hos get paid big money for that shit," say's Monique. The women watch the movie and laugh with an almost disgusted fascination.

"I wonder if those bitches are gay," Terri says.

"Probably swing both ways. They get paid to fuck whoever's in front of them. They probably take it as just another job," Bernice says.

"Well, looking at the way them bitches are eatin' each other out, I figure them for straight dykes," Terri says.

"Shit, I wish nigga's would take time to work a pussy like that," Monique says.

"Yeah, they want to give just enough head to make you wet so they can put the dick in," laughs Lois.

"But the motherfuckers want us to suck their dicks for hours at a time," laughs Monique.

"I tried that one time, I said I'm gonna suck the skin off this nigga's dick. I'm gonna make him cry like a bitch. The nigga came twice and whined like a little girl, "talking" bout how I sucked it too good cause he couldn't get it back up," continues Terri. "I was like, 'Fine, then you can eat this pussy for a while,' cause my jaws were hurtin' like shit," Terri laughs.

"Maybe if you mean bitches taught your man how to eat the pussy, you'd be a little less frustrated," Bernice slurred.

"Niggas think they know how to eat pussy and get all fucked up when you try to show their ass something," says Lois.

"Oh, I guess you taught Carl how to eat you out?" asks Terri.

"I damn sure did. Practice makes perfect, goddamnit," Bernice laughed. The women return to watching the video.

"See, after all that, I'd need some dick, a dildo or something. Head is good, but I need something in my pussy besides fingers and a tongue," Monique says as she watches the two women on the video pleasure each other.

"Since Lois has us watchin' this shit, I have a question," Monique says.

"Hey, I thought this was a scary movie. It's your video," Lois laughs.

"I forgot it was there. Mike brought that shit over here," says Monique.

"Yeah, yeah, tell us anything," Terri says as she nudges Bernice. They both laugh.

"Is there something you want to tell us, Monique?" Bernice says laughing.

"Hell, no, ain't no dyke bitch here. I like dicks of all shapes ands sizes," Monique says laughing.

"I need another drink," Terri says.

"Seriously though, I want to ask you hos a question. Have any of you ever been eaten by another woman?" Lois and Bernice look at Monique and say almost in unison, "Hell no."

"But you know dyke bitches are always hitting on straight women, asking can they do that shit to you. I get that shit at least once a month," says Bernice.

"I had to tell one bitch that wouldn't take no for an answer that I would let her eat me after my man came in the pussy. That dyke bitch hauled ass away from me," said Bernice. All the women were laughing when Terri stumbled in the living room with another drink.

"What did I miss?" asks Terri.

"Monique asked have we ever let a bitch eat our pussy, and I told her that I had to tell one dyke she could after my man came in me." They all laughed again.

"Damn, girl, you nasty. And yall talk about me. Bernice ass can get raw too," Terri says.

"But you know what? I'd let a bitch eat my pussy. As much as I love head, a bitch could eat my pussy all day. I know I'm not a fuck'in' dyke, but I'd give that ho a mouth full of pussy juice." Terri laughs so hard she spills her drink.

"But by letting a woman eat you wouldn't that make you gay too?" asks Lois.

"No, because we can do that type of shit. For women it's called experimentation. For a man his ass is gay," Terri says.

"Which one of you bitches brought that shit up anyway? This freak ass movie got you hos pussy's tingling," says Terri.

"Blame Lois for putting that shit on without dicks in the room," says Bernice. Terri laughs.

"Monique, what about you? Have you ever gotten head from a women?" asks Lois as she finishes her drink.

"I did one time in high school. I was taking a shower after gym and changing my clothes. I noticed this girl kept looking at me on the sly."

"I asked her what she was looking at, and she said I was pretty. I said thanks and didn't think anything of it. Then she comes over to me and asks if she can kiss my stomach. I knew what she wanted and I was curious, so I dropped my towel, stood in front of that bitch, and she went to work right there."

"We damn near got caught by the gym teacher because when I came, I made a little too much noise. We heard the door open to the locker room, and she got off my pussy just in time.

"That was the only time I ever let a woman touch me like that. I never saw her again after that, but the bitch gave good head," Monique finished. "See, like I said, I'll let a bitch eat me," says Terri again.

"Don't you hos get tired of not having your pussy's eaten the way it should be? Tell the truth. How many times have we complained that our men don't eat us right?" asks Monique.

"All the time, but that doesn't mean I'd necessarily let a women do it, even though I have been curious about what it would feel like," said Lois.

"Why not? Head is head, and the shit feels good, especially when you're fucked up and horny like all our asses are now," says Terri.

"What are you saying, Terri? We should experiment with dykes to see how it feels to be eaten by a women? I don't know if I could do that," Bernice says.

"No fuck that. I wouldn't let one of those nasty bitches touch me either, but now that you hos brought this shit up, I have been curious about it," Terri says.

"Okay, so we're curious about what it feels like to get head from a woman. The only one of us that has experienced that shit is Monique. So should we let Monique give us all some head?" Lois laughs.

"I'm not eatin' all you bitches, and remember, I was on the receiving end. I didn't give shit," Monique laughs.

"Then let's give each other some head, and kill the fuck'in' curiosity. Who the fuck is gonna find out? What the fuck? My pussy is wet, and now I'm horny as hell," Monique laughs. The words leave her mouth before she has time to think about what she said and they catch the other women totally off guard. No one says a word for a few seconds.

"Are you serious, Monique? Did you just hear what your drunk ass just said? We should give each other head," Lois says. "Girl, we're all best friends. How the hell can we eat each other?" Lois says.

"Because we're all horny as hell after watching that freak-ass video you put on, and drunk with no men to fuck," Terri says.

"You bitches have had a little too much to drink. I'm curious, but how do we do that? Like Lois said, we are best friends, and we're gonna eat each other?" Bernice laughs.

"We agree to do this one time to see what it's like and carry our horny asses to sleep," Monique says.

"Are you serious, Monique?" asks Lois.

"Yeah, why the fuck not? Because we are all friends, we can make each other feel good, and it'll be our secret for life. We never have to do the shit again if everyone agrees to it," Monique says.

"What, we partner up, go to a bedroom and eat each other?" Bernice says.

"If we're gonna do this shit, I say no hiding behind closed doors. We can get our freak on in front of each other and get it over with," Terri says.

"Okay you bitches figure the shit out. I need another drink," Lois says.

"Hold the fuck up. I didn't agree to do this," Bernice says.

"Oh, bitch, come on. What, you gonna watch?" Monique laughs.

"I can do that. Maybe that and another drink will loosen me up, I don't know," Bernice says.

Lois returns with another drink and enters the conversation.

"Look I'm getting tired, and I'm fucked up. This is some crazy shit we're talking about, but if we are gonna do this, y'all better make up your minds because I'm getting sleepy," Lois said.

"I know. We can do a link," says Monique.

"What the hell is a link? asks Bernice.

"We can do this at the same time, all at once," Monique says.

"How?" asks Terri.

"There are four of us. We line up, two lay down and two on our knees. It's called a link," Monique says.

"But it's not all at once. The last person will be left out if it's done that way, unless somebody is flexible as hell," Lois says.

"If that's the case then somebody has to switch because the first person lying down won't have a pussy to eat," Terri laughs.

"Ok, the last person in line will get eaten by the first person in line. How's that?" says Monique.

"You bitches are crazy. We're sitting here talking about how we're gonna eat each other's pussy. This is some crazy shit. Are we really that drunk and horny?" asks Bernice.

"You gonna back out now? Three of us want to try it. What the fuck, Bernice? Be a little adventurous," says Terri.

"Oh, bitch, your little ass is always horny," says Bernice.

"What the hell? Why can't I just watch you three?"

"Because we all do this shit together or forget the whole thing and go masturbate our asses to sleep," Monique says.

"Alright, you horny bitches, come on before the alcohol wears off. I can always claim I was fucked up and didn't know what I was doing," laughs Bernice.

"And by the fuck'in' way, Monique, how the hell do you know about this link shit?" asks Lois, laughing.

"Watching those freak ass porno movies with Mike. "

"Yeah, okay," says Terri.

"No bullshit, I never did this before, but the link thing I just made up. It makes sense, like a chain all connected together," laughs Monique.

"Before we do this, we need to get one damn thing straight. As long as our asses stay black, we will never tell anyone what we did here," states Bernice.

"Hell, yeah. If anybody lets this shit out, the rest of us will fuck that ass up," adds Terri. The women all look at each other and agree.

"Lois, help me bring some blankets and pillows down here so we can make a big bed on the floor down here," asks Monique.

"I'll move the furniture around and dim the lights. Give me a hand, Bernice," Terri says.

"I swear, I don't believe I'm getting ready to do this."

"It'll be different. What the hell, Bernice? It'll be a new experience for all of us. Now we'll see for ourselves if it's true or not that women know what women want," Terri says.

Monique and Lois return with the blankets and pillows. Everything is laid out on the floor. The furniture and tables have been moved to create a space large enough on the floor for everyone.

"Okay, are there any rules we should know about, shit we should or shouldn't do?" asks Lois.

"I don't want to do any kissing," says Bernice.

"Is sucking titties okay" asks Terri.

"No dildos allowed," says Monique.

"Okay, no kissing on the lips," says Monique.

"Which ones?" laughs Terri.

"No kissing on the mouth, smartass. Okay, here it is. No kissing on the mouth by anybody, no dildos, and tits can be sucked. Ready to get started, y'all," says Monique.

The women all look at each other and slowly begin to take off their clothes. When they get to their underwear, they stop to decide what the order will be.

"Okay, who is gonna do what to who," asks Lois.

"It doesn't matter. Everybody is gonna get done," says Terri.

"How about this? Bernice you lay down first since we have to loosen your ass up. Terri will eat you laying down. I'll get under Terri, and Lois will do me while I lay down. She'll be on her knees. When we switch, Bernice you do Lois, I'll do you and Terri does me," Monique explains.

"I have a question. Is there a time limit on this?" asks Bernice.

"No, but we do want to make each other cum, otherwise what's the point?" says Monique.

"How about those eating go until they get tired or her partner cums and then we switch," says Terri. The women all agree.

"One last thing. Does anyone want to shower up real quick? We wouldn't want our shit to be too tart seeing what we're getting ready to do," Terri says laughing.

"We already took showers. We didn't do anything except sit here and watch a movie. It's getting late. I suggest we get busy before our asses go to sleep and I back out of this crazy shit," says Bernice.

The women stand in a circle and all remove their underwear tossing the garments to the side. They are all in there twenties, and all of them have firm bodies and full breasts for their height.

They all look at Bernice. When her underwear is removed, and though none of them say anything they all think the same thing. Her fuck'in' body is gorgeous. Bernice is the oldest of the group at twenty-nine and the tallest at five feet eight inches.

Her skin is beautiful and flawless. The muscles of her arms and legs are well toned, her breasts big and firm. She has a defined abdomen, and the hair on her pussy is shaved close and tapered.

Terri thinks to herself when she sees Bernice's body, *No wonder that nigga sprayed nut everywhere when he saw that bitch naked. I see why now. I wonder if her pussy tastes as good as she looks naked. I guess I'll find out in a minute.*

Bernice lays down on her back and spreads her legs. Terri goes down on her and starts to eat her pussy. Monique gets under Terri and positions herself. She pulls Terri to her so she can eat Terri. Monique opens her legs and Lois goes down on her.

Bernice moans with extreme pleasure as Terri works her pussy with her tongue, circling the lips of her pussy and her clit, playfully teasing her as Bernice moans louder and louder. Bernice cups and squeezes her own breast, making her nipples hard as Terri pleasures her pussy with her tongue and lips, gently working her clit. Bernice feels the warmth of her pussy increase as her juices begin to flow.

Terri finds that the combination of eating pussy and being eaten at the same time is overwhelming. She finds it hard to concentrate on Bernice as Monique licks and gently sucks her clit, her moans get louder and her breathing gets harder. She gently responds to Monique's tongue by pressing and sliding her pussy against it.

Monique squeezes Terri's breast even as she eats her pussy. Monique feels the wetness and pleasure of Lois's tongue working her pussy. Lois's tongue is fast and gentle as she teases Monique's clit with her tongue and lips. She feels Lois insert her fingers in her pussy as she eats her. The feeling is phenomenal as she feels the double pleasure of the tongue and fingers inserted into her pussy.

Lois feels like electricity is running through her body as she feels herself getting wet and extremely excited. She uses her free hand to play with her pussy as she eats Monique. She moans gently as she feels the warmth between her legs increase.

The women pleasure themselves and their partners for the next hour. No one moves from their position as they enjoy what they are sharing, As one, they are all happy and enjoying the feelings and pleasure they are sharing as what they are finding here on this night transcends what they thought they knew about sex.

Monique comes first, as Lois gently teases her clit. Monique's spasms with pleasure as she lays under Terri licking her pussy. She puts both her hands on Terri's hips and squeezes as she comes again. As she does so, Terri comes as she grips Bernice's wet soft breasts in her hands, almost screaming with pleasure.

The next hour was more of the same awesome sex as Bernice, who didn't come the first time, admitted she had had the strongest orgasm of her life while she gave Lois head and Monique ate her.

Lois remembers that it was magical. They all had an orgasm at the same time, even Terri, who was on the end. She remembers they all screamed at the same time as they came as one. She had never experienced anything like that before or since, and probably never would again.

Lois remembers these events like they happened yesterday as she lays in her bed trying to go to sleep, but knowing that's going to be so difficult now that she knows what Monique has done, and she can't help crying because the magic they experienced that night together has been destroyed.

Lois drives home from work thinking that she can no longer keep this to herself. It's been two weeks now since Monique told her that she told Vic their secret after having fucked him and his friend. Lois hasn't spoken to Monique since she confronted her about what Vic had said to her that night on the phone.

Lois also knows she can no longer avoid Bernice's and Terri's calls. They are just worried about their friend, and they know Lois had been having a hard time with the whole pregnancy situation.

I'm due to have my baby in a month and I don't know how to get through to Vic. He probably hates me but right now, I don't care. I've started my twelve-week maternity leave, so I don't need to worry about work for a while. I need to talk to my girls.

Lois gets home and thinks how much nicer her home would be if Vic would share it with her and their baby instead of being with that other women. She parks her car and goes inside, puts her purse on the table, and sits in front of her wide-screen TV. She thinks, *Vic would love this TV. All men like watching their sports on big screens. Maybe I'll invite him over soon*. She decides to take a quick nap and call her friends about 5 PM.

Lois rubs her stomach and tells her daughter that everything will be okay. *You'll be born soon, and Daddy will be with us*. As tears fall from Lois's eyes, she thinks that would feel so right, to have him in their lives. *I'm gonna make it happen, one way or another*. She sets her alarm for 5 PM and goes to sleep.

***

Lois wakes up when the alarm goes off at 5 pm, takes a shower, and fixes a light dinner. As she eats her meal, she tries to decide the best way to break the news to her friends. This is not something she wants to do, but she has to.

Monique put herself in this situation. It wasn't bad enough that she fucked my man behind my back. She had to run her fuck'in' mouth about what we did. And there's no telling who Vic may have told. He obviously believes it or he wouldn't have said what he did to me. Lois thinks to herself that she really doesn't want to do this, but she has no choice. The others have to know.

Lois calls Bernice and Terri and tells them she has to talk to them about something important and asks if they can come to her place about 8 PM. They both said they'd be over at eight. Bernice arrives at Lois's at 7:45 PM. Terri gets there minutes behind her.

After Bernice and Terri arrive at Lois's, they go into the living room so they can talk.

"Lois, is everything okay? How are you and the baby doing?" asks Bernice.

"We're okay, I took my maternity leave, so I'll be off for the next twelve weeks. The doctor says I'm right on schedule."

"Any news from Vic's sorry ass?" Terri asks.

"No, I haven't heard from him in weeks, and I don't plan on calling him either, not until the baby is born," Lois says.

"Well, whatever you decide to do, we got your back. Now why the hell haven't you returned my calls in the last couple days? Girl, you had me worried," Terri says. Bernice agrees.

"I've had a lot on my mind the last couple of weeks, and I have been trying to work some things out, that's all," explains Lois.

"Is everything okay at work? I know how employers trip when a women has to take that much leave," Bernice says.

"No, my supervisor is cool with my leave, she told me to take as much time as I need. My whole twelve weeks will be paid, so that's not an issue," Lois explains.

"Does anyone want anything to drink?" asks Lois.

"Do you have any soda?" Bernice asks.

"Yeah, I'll get it," say's Lois.

"No, girl, you stay there. I'll get them," Terri says. Terri leaves the room to get the women sodas.

"Lois, what's bothering you? I can look at you and tell something isn't right," Bernice says.

Lois feels the tears that want to fall start to well up in her eyes when Bernice asks that question and fights her hardest not to cry in front of her friends. She doesn't want them to worry about her.

Terri returns with drinks for them all, and she too notices the look in Lois's eyes.

"Lois, what's wrong?" What did you say to her, Bernice?" Terri asks.

"I asked her what's wrong," says Bernice.

"Okay, you two stop. We need to talk, and what I have to say isn't easy," Lois says.

"You can tell us anything. You know we're here for you no matter what. By the way, is Monique coming by?" Bernice asks.

At the mention of Monique's name, Lois again feels a sadness that makes her want to cry.

"No, I didn't call her. She's the reason I called you two."

"Lois, what's going on? Now I'm starting to get worried," says Bernice.

"I really don't know where to start with this shit," Lois says.

"Take your time, girl, we're here," Terri says. Lois begins her tale.

"Remember when we were together two weeks ago at the spot, and Monique and I were gonna go see a movie? Well, we didn't make it. We came back here to talk because I didn't feel up to a movie.

"The last time I talked to Vic, he said something to me that really bothered me, but he wouldn't explain what he meant."

"But it concerned Monique. When I asked her what the hell Vic was talking about, she told me." Lois pauses before going on. "She told me she fucked Vic and one of his friends at the Gaylord Hotel in February."

Bernice and Terri are shocked into silence by Lois's last statement. Both their mouths drop open, and their eyes get big in stunned disbelief as they listen to what Lois has to say.

"She told me Vic got her drunk, they went to a room, and she fucked him and his boy." Lois starts to cry.

"Don't cry Lois. I'm gonna kill that bitch. How the fuck could she do some foul shit like that?" Terry says.

"That's not all of it," Lois continues. "When I talked to Vic, he also said Monique told him some freaky shit concerning us."

Bernice interrupts, "Lois, don't tell me Monique ran her fuck'in' mouth about us. I know she didn't tell that mothafucka what happened between us."

"Yes, she did, Bernice. She said she was fucked up, and she told him everything," says Lois.

"Where's that bitch now? I'm gonna fuck her up. We swore we would never tell anybody that shit. I don't give a fuck that she was drunk," Bernice says.

"Now we haven't talked about that night in over two years, and she decides she wants to run her fuck'in' mouth now? And on top of that, she fucked Vic too, knowing how much you care for that nigga. I'm gonna fuck that bitch up good," Terri says.

Bernice shakes her head with a disgusted look on her face. "How the fuck could she have done this shit to us?" Bernice asks.

"I asked her the same damn question," Lois says through tears. "All she could say was she got fucked up, and it just happened, that Vic and his boy set her up. And she asked if I could forgive her for what she did," Lois says.

"I'll never forgive that bitch. She fucked Vic, told our goddamn secret to him and his boy, and who knows how many other fuck'in' people. Monique deserves a serious beat down, and I'm gonna give it to her," Terri says.

"What good would kicking her ass do us now, Terri? The shit is out there now. Why do we have to make it worse by beating on her? I'm pissed too, but aren't we too old for that shit?" Lois says.

"I don't know, Lois. I want to kick her ass too," says Bernice. "We've known each other for years, and as much trash as we talk, we have remained close and loyal to each other, especially after the link. Now Monique has fucked that up. I want to fuck her up too," says Bernice.

"Please don't do this. Let's get together, and we'll all sit down and talk about it, okay? Lois implores the others as she puts her hand on her stomach.

"Lois, we don't want to upset you, but hearing what you told us is fucked up. I would have never thought Monique of all people would do some shit like this," Terri says.

"She had to know we'd find out sooner or later, because whoever she told would run their mouths about what they heard, and we hang out at a few spots together and know a lot of the same people," Bernice says.

"Look, y'all, it's been more than three months since she told Vic, and none of us has heard anything. Why don't we just get together and talk to her? I'm pissed too, but we don't have to beat on her, do we?" Lois asks.

"We made a promise to each other, Lois, and we agreed to never even talk about what happened. We also agreed about what would happen if anyone ran their mouth about it. What good would talking to Monique do? She can sit here and say she's sorry all day, it won't change shit. That bitch still betrayed us," says Terri.

"How do we trust her again Lois? Why would you want to be around her after she fucked Vic? She knew what time it was. According to what she told you, she wasn't so fucked up that she forgot you're pregnant by that nigga," Bernice says.

"I'm so pissed, I really don't know what to say at this point, but I can tell you this, I'm done with Monique. I never want to speak to her again," says Bernice.

"Well, I still want to put my foot in her ass, but you know what? Fuck it. I don't ever need to see her again, but she is going to know how I feel about her ass," Terri says.

"I honestly didn't want to tell y'all what she did, but I had to, and it wasn't to ruin our friendship," says Lois.

"Lois, you're not the one who told our secret or fucked any of our men. Monique's nasty ass did that," says Bernice.

"So what are we gonna do? Let that bitch get away with what she did?" states Terri.

"For now, why don't we just let it go and say the hell with her? This is hard enough to deal with as it is. I don't want to have to deal with any violent shit okay? The baby has lost one aunt already," says Lois.

"Only because you asked me to. You saved that bitch a serious beat down," says Terri.

"It's getting late, Lois. I need to get home. If you need anything, girl, call me. I don't care where or what time," Bernice says.

"Yeah, I'm good and pissed. Let me get out of here too. Same thing goes here. If you need me, call," Terri says. The women all hug and say good night.

As Terri and Bernice walk to their cars, they stop to talk when they get far enough away from Lois's front door.

"I didn't want to upset Lois anymore, but there is no way Monique is gonna get away with what she did. No fuck'in' way," says Terri.

"I agree. Call me when you get home, and we'll discuss it," says Bernice. They get in their cars and leave to go home.

After her friends leave, Lois tries to relax in front of the TV and tries her hardest not worry about the conversation she just had with her two best friends. Feeling confident that no harm will come to Monique at the hands of Terri and Bernice, she tries to relax away the tension.

Watching TV is not what she really wants to do though. She needs to talk to Vic, even though she knows he doesn't want anything to do with her or the baby. But that thought makes her angry, knowing his daughter is due in four weeks and he still hasn't committed to be a part of her life.

So Lois decides to call him, to try again to talk some sense into him. She decides she will make him listen to her whether he wants to or not, not for her sake but for her daughter's. Even if she has to go to his house, he's going to listen to what she has to say.

Lois calls his number repeatedly for the next hour and a half. She leaves many messages for him to please call her. None of her messages are demands or threats but simple pleas for him to call her at his earliest convenience. She sits and waits for a call she's not sure is going to come until 11 PM and decides he's not going to call, and she prepares herself for bed.

Lois's phone rings about 11:45 PM. Her heart beats just a little faster. She actually feels a bit of joy thinking it might be Vic calling her back. She lets out a sigh of relief when she picks up the phone, thinking at least he called back. That's something at least.

As Lois picks up the phone and greets the caller, an unknown female voice responds.

Caller: Hi, my name is Kim. I don't know you, but why are you repeatedly calling this number?

Lois: I was calling for Vic. I'm sorry do I have the wrong number?

Kim: No, the number you were dialing does belong to Vic. I just want to know why you're calling him?

Lois: Can I ask who you are?

Kim: I'm his woman. Now can you please tell me who you are and why you're calling him?

Lois feels her heart sink in her chest. This is the woman Vic claims he loves, that he is denying his baby for, and I have that bitch on the phone.

Lois: My name is Lois, and I need to speak to him.

Kim: Vic is not in right now. He left without his cell phone, but you can tell me what you want him to know, and I'll be happy to pass it on.

Lois: Kim, is that your name? Well, what I have to tell Vic is between him and I. I don't mean to be disrespectful, but it has nothing to do with you.

Kim: Lois, when another woman calls my man and won't tell me what she wants, it becomes my business. What would you say if our positions were reversed?

Lois: Well, I need to talk to Vic about some very important issues.

Kim: You're not woman enough to discuss these issues with me.

Lois: Bitch, my issues have nothing to do with you.

Kim: You're a very angry child, aren't you? I didn't call you nor have I used profanity when speaking to you. You may not respect yourself, but when you talk to me, please try and act like your mother taught you better.

Lois: Where is Vic?

Kim: Why should I tell you that? If he wanted you to know where he was, he'd have taken one of your calls before now.

Lois: I don't have time to sit here playing games with you. I need to talk to him.

Kim: Well, as I said earlier, why don't you tell me what you want, and I'll tell him.

Lois: Alright, you can tell him is daughter is due next month, and we need to talk.

Kim: Are you saying you're going to have Vic's child?

Lois: Yes, I am, which is why we need to talk.

Kim: Does Vic know that you're pregnant with his baby?

Lois: He knows. I told him months ago when I found out I was pregnant.

Kim: Obviously he doesn't believe he's the father because if he did, you wouldn't need to call him so close to your due date needing to track him down, and I'd have known about you.

Lois: How long have you known Vic?

Kim: That, my dear, is none of your business, but I'll tell you anyway. I've been with Vic for just over three years now.

Lois: Then you and he were together when I met him.

Kim: Yes, we were, We have a unique relationship. I don't mind Vic having his little playmates, as long as he doesn't bring me anything he didn't leave here with. We both have that freedom, although he exercises his freedoms more that I. Did he ever tell you that?

Lois: He told me he had someone and that he wasn't going to leave her.

Kim: Then why did you continue to pursue him?

Lois: I probably wouldn't have if I didn't get pregnant.

Kim: Lois, you have to understand something. I'm not angry with you. I know what Vic does in the street, and I'm fine with that because we both have that understanding, but you need to know someone like Vic will never be faithful to you or anyone else. And did you know he doesn't like being around children?

Lois's heart breaks when she hears that statement from the woman he's been with for years.

Lois: He told me he didn't want to have any kids.

Kim: But you do.

Lois: Yes, I want my baby.

Kim: Lois, did you think having his baby would somehow bring him into your life and change the person he is?

Lois: I don't know. I just wanted him in our lives. He thinks I got pregnant on purpose, and that wasn't the case.

Kim: Did you get pregnant on purpose?

Lois: No, I didn't, but when I found out I was, I wasn't going to have an abortion.

Kim: Lois, are you sure he's the father?

Lois: Yes, and I tried to explain that to him, but he wouldn't listen. He wants to take a DNA test after my daughter is born.

Kim: Of course he wouldn't believe you. A man like him, Lois, doesn't need children. He enjoys his freedom too much, and he won't let himself be tied down with a child or a family. So no matter what you do, he'll never be with you.

Kim hears Lois start to cry on the phone, and she tries to calm her down.

Kim: Lois, don't cry. I know this is upsetting, but that is the man you chose to have a baby with.

In a trembling voice, Lois responds to Kim's statement.

Lois: I just don't know what to do.

Kim: Lois, honestly, there isn't a lot you can do. But I'll tell you this, I enjoy my freedoms and my lifestyle just like Vic, but I'm coming to a point where I need a change in my life as well, and whether or not this turns out to be Vic's child, I don't know how much longer I want to stay with him.

Lois: Are you saying you and him are breaking up?

Kim: I'm saying it's going to happen regardless of what happens in your situation. I'll clue you in to something. Vic is not a violent man, but Vic is the kind of man that responds to actions. Words don't have much effect.

Lois: Does he know you're leaving him?

Kim: It doesn't matter what he knows. I, like him, can come and go as I please. But I'll tell you this, I'll talk to him concerning your situation, and I will try my best to persuade him to speak with you. I can't say that he will, but I'll try.

Lois: Kim, can I ask you why you would do that? I mean, get him to talk to me.

Kim: Because if he is your baby's father, he needs to do right by his child. And I don't want to be with a man who has the responsibility of children, and it's time he and I go our separate ways anyway, not because of your situation, but because I'm ready to move on. And the fact that my father wasn't in my life, I personally know how terrible a thing that can be for a child.

Lois: Do you love him?

Kim: Not in the way you think of love, but I'm not married to him and am under no obligation to remain with him forever. Besides, I've never had a man with kids, and I'm not about to start now.

Lois: Thank you for your help.

Kim: Don't thank me yet. I just want what's best for the baby, because no matter what happens between you two, it's not the baby's fault. If this is what needs to happen for him to talk to you concerning your baby than I don't have a problem with it. So expect a call from him soon.

One last thing, Lois. If you really care for Vic, you have to give him his baby in a way that will shock him into letting him know how much you care. You have to do something that will make him want his baby.

Lois: Well, thanks anyway. Good night.

Kim: Good night and good luck with the baby.

After they hang up, Lois gets in bed and thinks to herself that Kim doesn't give a damn about Vic. *She's gonna leave him, and he doesn't know how she really feels. She's a cold-hearted bitch because she never loved him, not the way I love Vic*. Lois decides now is her opportunity to really show Vic how much she really cares about him. She can take him away from that ice-cold bitch he's been dealing with. That thought makes her smile as she turns off her phone and drifts off to sleep, even though her last thoughts before going to sleep bothered her.

Lois thinks to herself, *I can accept that he doesn't want me, but our baby deserves to have her father in her life. I didn't have my father in my life either; and my daughter will not be put through the same shit I had to deal with. I know how to make him come to his damn senses' My daughter will have her father in her life. That nigga will have no choice but to accept his daughter. I'm gonna make sure of that. Nothing is more important than my baby's well being.*

Two days after talking to Kim, Vic still hasn't called Lois. Today is Friday.

***

Lois gets up Friday morning, and as she starts her day, she thinks to herself, *He still hasn't called me. It's been two days since I spoke with Kim and still no word from him. I guess I need to get it through my head that he'll never be with us, even after that bitch he's dealing with leaves his stupid ass.*

After she takes a shower and gets dressed, Lois prepares to go see her doctor one last time before the baby's due. She grabs her purse and her cell phone and heads out to her car.

She gets in her car and turns on her cell phone. Just as she starts the engine, her phone buzzes, signaling she has a message. She picks it up and sees it's Vic's phone number. She's so excited, she calls him right back. he answers immediately.

Lois: Hello, Vic, this is Lois. How are you doing?

Vic: I'm doing real fucked up right now. How could you call my girl and tell her the shit you told her?

Lois: I didn't call her. I called your cell number, and she answered. She wouldn't put you on the phone. She said you had stepped out.

Vic: I was home asleep the whole time you two talked.

Lois: How was I to know that, Vic? I called you a few times, and you never called me back, I just wanted to talk to you about the baby. I'm due in a few weeks.

Vic: What the fuck did you two talk about?

Lois: I told her I was gonna have your baby.

Vic: Do you have any idea how you have fucked things up for me by telling her that shit? We don't even know the baby is mine.

Lois: Vic, I'm sorry you're mad, but, look, I'm on my way to my doctor's office. I have an appointment at 11 AM. Can I call you back when I get home?

Vic: Yeah, we need to talk. What you did was totally fucked up and out of line.

Lois: I'm sorry you're angry with me, but let's do this. Why don't you come by for dinner tonight at my place about 8 PM and we can talk.

Vic: I'll be there at eight, but I don't want to have dinner with you. I just need to talk to you.

Lois: Alright then, I'll see you at eight. Write down my address.

Lois gives Vic her address and hangs up the phone. She realized his tone was hostile, but she finds it doesn't bother her. Maybe when he sees me again, pregnant with his baby, he'll finally have a change of heart. In any event, she thinks he'll have no choice but to accept his baby after tonight.

Lois leaves her doctor's office at 2 PM after having been examined and told everything is fine with her and the baby. She finds she can't wait to see Vic tonight. They have a lot to talk about, and she has a big surprise for him.

She briefly considers calling Terri and Bernice and having them there when Vic shows up but she dismisses that idea. It would spoil her surprise for Vic, and she doesn't think Vic will hurt her in any way. Besides, if they were there, she and Vic couldn't really talk the way they need to.

Lois gets home at 4 PM. At 5 PM, she starts to prepare for her evening with Vic. Even though he said he didn't want to have dinner with her, she prepares a nice meal for two. She remembers he ordered Patron when she met him, so she stopped on the way home and got a bottle.

At 7 PM, she has everything set up and ready for her baby's father. The meal will be ready by the time he gets there. The table is set for two. She'll pour him a drink while they eat dinner and talk about their child's future. She thinks this is her chance to turn everything around for them, and she intends to do just that.

She sits and waits patiently for Vic to arrive. It's 8:45 PM, and he hasn't called or gotten to her place yet. The dinner she prepared for them is being kept warm, but if he doesn't come soon, it'll be ruined.

She thinks maybe he had some last minute things to take care of, but he could have at least called her.

Lois hears her doorbell ring at quarter past nine. She knows it's Vic and she brightens up. She thinks to herself she can even forgive his being late. She goes to the door, opens it, and lets Vic in.

"Hi, Vic. I've been waiting for you. What kept you?" she asks. Vic enters Lois's home, and she sees a look of disgust on his face when he looks at her bulging stomach.

"I had some other things I had to take care of first," he says.

"It's okay, I kept dinner warm, We can eat now," she says.

"Lois I told you I didn't want to have any dinner. I just want to talk to you and leave," he says.

"Well, Vic, you're here now. We may as well have something to eat. Everything is ready. I was just waiting for you," she says. "Why don't we go into the living room and relax there," she says. Vic follows her into the living room, and Lois turns on the TV.

"How do you like my place?" she asks.

"You have a nice spot," Vic replies as he looks around her home.

"Vic, if you like, we can sit in here, and you can watch a game while we eat," Lois says.

"Lois, I don't want any of that. Can we please just sit down and talk without the TV on so I can get the fuck out of here." Vic insists. Lois is devastated by his words, and so she agrees to just sit and talk.

She sits across from Vic as he begins the conversation.

"Lois, I didn't come here to upset you or hurt you in any way, but why won't you stay out of my life? My damn girl is leaving me because of what you told her the other day," he says.

"Vic, that's not the way it is. I tried to talk to you, but you wouldn't answer my calls. I didn't tell her what's happening with me to make her leave you," Lois explains.

"Well, what did you think would happen when you told her you might be carrying my baby?" And I honestly don't know if the kid is mine or not. We went through all that. You knew exactly what you were doing," Vic says.

"Vic, it's not like that,. I just wanted to talk to you. I wasn't trying to cause trouble in your life. I just wanted you to know what was going on with me and the baby," Lois says as she starts crying.

"Look, don't do that. You don't need to be getting all upset and crying and shit. I just want to know what it will take for you to stay out of my life," Vic says.

"Vic, how is that gonna be possible? I'm having the baby in a few weeks, and all I've ever wanted is for her father to be a part of her life, the way my father never was. That's all I've ever asked," Lois says.

"Lois, you just don't understand. I know Kim told you I don't even like kids, so how can I be a father to your daughter? I wouldn't know how, and that's not what I want," Vic says. Something inside Lois snaps when she hears Vic make that last statement to her face.

"Look, Vic, I know you're probably not gonna be here much longer. Do you want a drink? We can talk for a little while longer, and then you can leave. I see now this just won't work out. Maybe it was a bad idea for you to come here. I really can raise my baby on my own. You still want that drink?"

"Sure what do you have?" Vic asks.

"I saw you order Patron when we met. I have that if you want," Lois says.

"That's cool," Vic says. Lois returns from the kitchen with a drink for him and one for herself. Vic takes his drink, and Lois sits back down where she was. "You're not drinking alcohol, are you?" Vic asks.

"No, silly, it's water. I haven't had a drink since I found out I was pregnant," says Lois.

"Lois, I'm sorry if it seems like I don't care what you're going through, but I've tried to make you understand I don't want kids in my life. I know Kim told you that because she told me everything you two talked about," Vic says.

"Did she leave out the part about her leaving you?" Lois says.

"No, she didn't, and it's because of what you told her about your baby," Vic says as he finishes his drink.

"Do you want another one? I bought that drink for you," says Lois.

"Sure, why not?" Vic responds.

Lois returns with another double shot of Patron for Vic.

"Lois, what do you want from me? Can you please tell me that?" Vic says.

"Vic, it's like I told you. I would like for you to be in our lives, but I know that's not going to happen. I guess I just had to hear it from you in person. Can we at least be friends for the baby's sake after we have the DNA test done? That's all I want," Lois says.

Vic finishes his drink, looks at Lois, and says nothing. Be sits back in his seat, drops his glass on the floor, and passes out. When he wakes up two hours later, he finds himself lying on his back with his head propped up, and he's cold, his vision is blurry, and his head feels as if it's splitting open. He tries to move his arms and legs but finds he is unable to do so.

Lois is sitting in the room at the foot of the bed when he wakes up. In a voice that's barely intelligible, Vic asks what's happened to him.

"I put a little something in your drink. I knew you wouldn't listen to reason, so I'm gonna make you listen." Lois goes into her bathroom wets a towel with cold water, and brings it to Vic. She wipes his face and forehead, then his chest and stomach.

Vic's vision becomes a litter clearer now as he realizes why he's cold and can't move. His clothes have been removed and his limbs have been tied to the bed posts. His first reaction is to panic, to try to break away from his restraints but he feels too weak and his head is still pounding, but his anger clears his vision as his eyes focus on Lois.

He also finds his voice as the panic in his mind becomes stronger and he pulls against his restraints with what little strength he can muster.

"Bitch, what the fuck are you doing? What the fuck did you do to me?" He tries to shout. Lois looks at her captive and moves back to the chair at the foot of the bed so she can face Vic as she speaks.

"All I've ever wanted from you since I found out I was pregnant was for you to be with me, So our child would have a family. I would have settled with you just being a part of the baby's life, but you don't even want to be a father to your own baby. And this is your daughter, Vic, no matter how much you want to deny it." Lois continues.

"Then, on top of all that, you had to fuck one of my best friends and you knew who she was when you fucked her," Lois shouts. "I loved you, nigga. My pussy wasn't good enough for you. You could have had this anytime you wanted, but instead you want to fuck every bitch you see," says Lois.

"Bitch, let me fuck'in' go. Untie me from this motherfuckin' bed. I'll kill your fuck'in' ass," Vic shouts with false bravado.

"Nigga, you can't do shit. I put enough shit in your drink to keep you here for as long as I want. And unless you're Spiderman, you're not breaking those straps," says Lois. " Now, like I said, you're gonna listen to me," Lois continues. "For fucking my friend, I should cut you dick off. You wouldn't be able to do shit about it. As she speaks, Lois pulls out a large knife.

Vic's eyes grow large at the sight of the knife in her hands, and his heart pounds in his chest as she looks at his naked body, focusing her eyes on his now limp penis. He shouts for her not to hurt him and for her to untie him. In a panicked voice, be begs her not to hurt him.

"Lois, don't do this. I didn't do anything to you," Vic says.

"You didn't do anything to me?" Lois shouts in anger. She reaches for his penis with her free hand, pulls it, and brings the knife closer it. He screams with everything he has as he watches the knife move closer. He pulls and struggles against his restraints to no avail as she brings the knife ever closer until its cold edge is almost touching the skin of his dick.

"Vic, how can you say that? You avoid my calls. You have rejected and embarrassed me every time I've tried to talk to you. You've called me names and disrespected me because you could. You cost me one of my best friends because you need to fuck everything you see, and you knew she was my friend when you and your boy fucked her."

Lois moves to sit on the edge of the bed and moves closer to his dick until her lips are barely touching it. Vic is in a panic. His whole body is trembling, and he is sweating profusely. Lois kisses the head of his dick and lets it go.

"Why shouldn't I cut that off, Vic? You don't want me to have it, but you have no problem using it on every other bitch you see. You don't give a fuck that I care for you, that I love your sorry ass, do you, nigga?" Lois shouts, her face now contorted with anger.

"Look, Lois, just let me go. I swear I won't tell anyone. Please let me go. I'll do anything you want me to do," Vic pleads.

"Let you go? No baby, I'm not done with you yet." Lois raises the knife over her head. Vic's eyes focus on the blade, and she slams the knife down onto the bed between Vic's legs with enough force to drive it into the mattress. Vic screams in terror as she leaves the knife stuck in the mattress.

"All I've ever wanted from you is to love me and our child, but you'd rather be with a cold-hearted bitch that you know is gonna leave your sorry ass anyway. I don't understand that shit. I could be everything to you. The bitch you're seeing doesn't even love you the way I do. Please explain that to me," Lois asks.

Feeling totally helpless and unable to free himself, the muscles of his arms and legs cramping, Vic trembles as tears of fear and terror pour from his eyes.

"Don't cry now, nigga. You're a badass on the phone. Answer my fuck'in' question," Lois demands. "Why can't you love us?" she shouts.

In a trembling voice, Vic responds even as he continues to cry.

"I don't know. I don't know what to say except give me a chance. I can change. Please, God, don't hurt me," he begs. Lois moves closer to him as he speaks. He sees a deranged look in her eyes that numbs him to the core.

"Do you understand how it feels now, mothafucka, to be rejected and belittled? Do you understand how it feels to beg someone for forgiveness when you've done nothing wrong, to beg for someone to love you and not hurt you? Do you fuckin' understand now how I've felt since the first time you fucked me?" Lois shouts.

"And you have the fuckin' nerve to ask me not to hurt you after the way you've treated me for months, and on top of all that, what you did with one of my best friends? You think you can use women however you please. Well, now it's my turn."

She moves to the foot of the bed, removes her sweat pants and panties, pulls the knife out of the bed, throws it in the chair, and climbs on top of him. She takes his dick in her hand and rubs it against her wet pussy.

"What's wrong, Vic? Can't get it up now, nigga? You can get it up to fuck everybody else. I saw how you looked at me when you came in my house. Do I disgust you because I'm pregnant? Come on, nigga, get it up for me.

"I need some dick sooo bad," she pleads. "I haven't had any since I found out I was pregnant with your baby." She continues to rub his dick against her pussy. Vic is too filled with terror to respond. His body can't stop trembling.

"PPPllease stop this Lois. Please let me go. Please untie me. I swear I'll never treat you badly ever again. I swear I can love you." He begs her with tears pouring from his eyes and his body trembling uncontrollably.

"I don't believe you, Vic," she says while still rubbing her pussy against his limp dick. "If what you said was true, I'd have your big dick in my pussy. You can't even get it up for me, so how can you love me? You love every other bitch's pussy, don't you? Just not mine. So we're gonna fix that right now."

"What are you gonna do to me?" Vic begs her continuously not to hurt him as she climbs off him.

"Baby, where's your dick? It slipped out of my hand. As big as I remember it, it looks like it crawled in your stomach. I'm sorry I scared you so badly. "Don't worry, baby, it's almost over.

"Oh, another thing. You can stop screaming. No one is gonna hear you down here. There are no windows, and I have music playing just loud enough to drown out the screams." Vic feels as if his heart is going to burst from his chest. He's so frightened, he's seeing sounds and hearing colors. He feels death approaching. He knows this crazy bitch is going to kill him, and there is nothing he can do about it.

Lois takes the knife out of the chair and sits down. She holds it in her right hand and rubs her stomach with her left as she speaks to Vic's trembling form.

"I can and I have accepted the fact that you and I are never going to be together I even felt the way you did about relationships until I got pregnant. Then I realized there is more to life than partying and fucking.

"My pregnancy and the fact that I was sexually abused as a young girl by family members with no father to protect me made me realize I needed a father for my daughter, and the lack of a father probably had a lot to do with my promiscuous attitudes.

"I don't want that for my daughter. I'm ashamed to admit it but if I raise her alone, she'll probably turn out just like me, fucking guy after guy looking for approval. I don't want that for her."

"What are you talking about? I won't let that happen. I promise we can do a good job raising her together," Vic says.

"Oh, nigga, please. I thought you didn't want kids in your life," Lois says. "Besides, I think you'd say anything right about now. Like you said you loved me when you were fucking me," says Lois.

Vic's hands and feet are so numb, he can't feel them anymore. He is frightened he's going to die unless he can convince Lois he wants the baby.

"Vic, all you had to do was give me a chance to make you happy. I know I could have," Lois says. Looking at her through bloodshot eyes, Vic tells Lois that all he can do is try, that he is willing to give their love a try.

"Oh, you love me now, nigga? Since when did you love me? See, mothafucka, I don't need you playing fuck'in' games with me. That's what you do. You know damn well you don't now and never did love me. I don't need lies. I only ever wanted to be loved by someone as much as I loved them," Lois says crying, looking at his prone body from her chair.

"You can't even get it up so I can fuck you, so I know you don't love me. Now I know what I need to do. Lois stands up with the knife in her hand and comes toward the bed. Vic sees the look in her eyes and panic overwhelms him. "Don't worry, Vic. I'm not gonna hurt you, but I'm not gonna let you walk away from our child either."

Lois drops the large knife at the foot of the bed. Vic watches as she turns, walks over to the dresser, picks up another object, and comes back to the bed. She knells between his legs the way she did when she tried to have sex with him. She rests on top of his penis.

"I don't want to fuck. You ruined that. I just want you to watch," Lois explains. She sets the object in her hand next to her, then she takes off her outer top and bra and throws them on the floor.

"You see, Vic, pregnant women are beautiful. We glow with the life that's growing inside of us." Vic stares at Lois, wide-eyed, not knowing what to say or do but too scared to move.

Lois takes the small object she laid next to her on the bed in her right hand and with her left hand rubs her large round stomach and smiles as she talks to Vic.

"Vic, I made a promise to our daughter that I'd make sure her daddy was in her life. Now we can do even better because you'll be here during her birth. Now there's no way you can deny her," Lois says.

"What do you mean, baby? You said you're not ready for a few weeks," said Vic through his terror.

Lois takes the object in her hand, which looks to Vic like a scalpel. She looks at Vic and cuts the bottom of her stomach below the navel from left to right about ten inches, screaming in agony as she does so. Vic screams for her to stop as loud as he can.

"What are you doing? Stop. Oh, my God, what are you doing?" he manages to scream, fighting against his bonds.

Her blood spills onto his body, all over his stomach and dick as she continues to cut herself. She screams as she finishes the incision. Bleeding more profusely now, she leans back onto her feet and screams again.

"Oh, God, it hurts, Vic. It hurts so bad," she says. Lois comes forward again and tries to insert her hand into her stomach, but it won't go in. Her blood is everywhere, all over Vic and the bed. He vomits uncontrollably.

Vic watches helplessly as Lois's blood pours out of her body. She is in agony and crying as she realizes she didn't cut herself deep enough. So she takes the scalpel, and with all the force she can muster, stabs it into the left side of the first incision, screaming as she does so, and pulls with what strength she has left across her abdomen.

Vic can do nothing but scream with all his might for her to stop. He pleads with her to let him go so he can get her help.

"Fuck!!! Lois, stop. Please don't do this. You're killing yourself!" She doesn't hear him as more and more of her blood pours out of her body. Vic vomits all over his chest.

With her head hanging down and her pain beyond description, she leans up and tries to insert her hands again into her abdomen. This time they go in. Blood and urine pour out of her like from a faucet and onto Vic. He screams like a man insane. Lois continues until she feels something in her move. She knows it's her baby.

She pushes her hands in harder. Her screams of pain are numbing. She pulls on the amniotic sack until it bursts The fluids shoot out onto Vic. He continues to scream for a God he never believed in and for Lois to stop, while continuing to vomit.

Through her pain and exhaustion, she manages to tell Vic, "I feel her. I feel the baby moving, Vic." Impossibly, Lois manages to smile. Vic can't scream anymore due to vomiting and spasms of his body.

Lois manages to get a hand on her baby and pull, but something is preventing her from coming out, and there is another scream of agony as Lois digs around in her abdomen to find her baby. She pushes down on something soft and round and more fluid shoots from her body onto Vic.

Lois tries again to feel for her baby, and this time she finds the small, wet body inside her, and Lois pulls until she sees the babies bottom. Through her pain, she pulls the baby straight out and again she smiles as the little body that was just folded in half tries to straighten out.

Lois brings the baby to her chest, holds her with both arms, and greets her as she starts to cry.

"Hey, Victoria, Mommy and Daddy are right here. You see, Vic, she's beautiful. She looks like both of us," Lois says in a weak voice as she looks at her baby. Vic doesn't respond to her question. He's choking on his own vomit. Lois doesn't notice he's stopped moving.

"Victoria, go to Daddy now. Let Daddy hold you. Now our family will be linked forever." Lois lays the crying squirming, newborn baby on Vic's vomit-covered chest, and she falls on top of him, cradling the crying baby, as she bleeds to death.

The following Saturday morning, Bernice calls Monique and invites her for a night out.

"Hey, Monique, what's up girl:

"Not a lot. What's going on with you?" Monique responds.

"Terri and I are planning on going out tonight, and we need to get together to plan Lois's baby shower. You know she's due in a few weeks, Bernice explains.

"Yeah, I know. That sounds good to me. Just let me know where we're gonna meet up," Monique says.

"We haven't been to the club at the Gaylord, so we want to check that out. I hear it's real nice there."

"Okay, that's fine. What time should I get there?" Monique asks. "We're gonna be there at 9 PM", Bernice says.

"Okay, I'll see you there."

"And, Monique, try to be on time," Bernice says laughing.

"I will be," says Monique.

At 8 PM that evening, Bernice and Terri are at The American Sports Bar inside the Gaylord hotel complex having a drink and waiting on Monique to show. At 8:45 PM, Monique walks into the bar. The friends all greet each other, and Bernice buys Monique a drink.

"Has anybody talked to Lois today?" Terri asks.

"No, I tried to call her yesterday, but I didn't get an answer," Bernice says.

"Well we need to go check on her," Monique responds.

"I'll drive by her place tomorrow afternoon. I'm sure she's fine, but we need to take care of our girl," says Bernice.

"We got her back. But tonight, we're gonna get our party on and get bent," says Terri.

"Okay, but before we do all that, can we make plans for the baby shower? It shouldn't take long," Bernice asks.

"Yeah, party pooper, I'm not going home tonight, so we can go upstairs and get that out of the way," says Terri.

"Somebody must have met a new guy," Monique says, laughing as she finishes her drink.

"Yeah, and I'm gonna ride that dick all night," Terri says laughing. "Bernice, order three more Long Islands. I'll pay for them and follow us upstairs, room 620. Let's roll, Monique," Terri says.

"Okay, no problem. I'll be right up," she responds.

Terri and Monique laugh and talk as they get on the elevator and then make their way to room 620. As they enter the room, Terri tells her how expensive the rooms are.

"Terri, how much was this room? This is nice, and the view is awesome," says Monique.

"You know, I really don't know. Mark, the guy I'm staying with tonight, is paying for it. He put it on his credit card," says Terri.

"I heard that this is a real classy hotel," Monique says. A few minutes later, Bernice knocks on the door.

"Monique, open the door. That has to be Bernice," says Terri. Monique opens the door and lets Bernice in the room.

"I paid for the drinks at the bar. They're gonna have room service bring them up," Bernice says.

"Okay, let's get busy with the planning of the shower so we can go back downstairs," Terri says.

Terri locks the door, and the women all go into the living room area of the room and take seats. Terri starts the conversation.

"Okay, first things first. So, Monique, how do you like the room?" Terri asks.

"It's real nice. Like I said, I'm gonna have to stay hear sometime," Monique responds.

"Are you sure you've never been here before?" asks Terri.

"No, this is my first time at this hotel," she responds.

"What would you say if I told you I know that's a damn lie?" says Bernice.

"Do you remember being here back in February with Vic and one of his boys and fucking them? Bernice says. Monique is shocked when she hears that. Her heart starts to beat a little faster, and she starts to get nervous. She realizes they know, that Lois had to tell, and she is scared. In a trembling voice, she begins to speak.

"Lois told you what I did. I'm sorry for what happened. I don't know what else to say," Monique says.

"Monique, how could you let Vic fuck you? Of all the goddamn guys out here, why him? You know Lois loves that nigga," Bernice says.

"Like I tried to explain to Lois, yall, I was fucked up and it happened. I'm sorry," Monique says.

"Look, I feel bad enough about this as it is. I'm gonna go home," Monique says. Monique stands to leave, and just as she does, Terri approaches her and smacks her hard across the face. Monique cries out and holds her face.

"Bitch, do you think we're just gonna let you leave here after what you did?" Terri screams at her. Terri hits Monique in the face with her fist, and she falls back on the couch. Terri stands over her, drawing back her fist to hit her again.

Crying now, Monique doesn't know what to do except hold her face in her hands and plead for Terri not to hit her anymore. Monique is no fighter, and she knows even though she and Terri are about the same size, she can't beat her. Bernice watches from across the room.

"Bitch, did you think that was cute, fuck'in' that nigga when you knew Lois loved his sorry ass?" Terri screams. Monique sits up on the couch, crying, and looks over to Bernice to help her.

"Don't look over here bitch. I'm not gonna help you. What you did was fucked up." says Bernice.

Terri smacks Monique again. She tries to cover her face with her hands and arms, but it doesn't do any good. Terri simply moves her arms out the way and punches her in her chest. Monique just cries as she takes the beating.

"Terri, stop hitting her face. We don't want that part fucked up," Bernice says. Terri moves away from a crying Monique. She wants to run, but she knows they'll stop her before she gets to the door and beat on her some more.

"Monique, not only did you fuck Vic, but what else did you do? Bitch, tell me what else you did. Tell us what you told that motha-fucka," Bernice shouts as she approaches the couch Monique is now crying like a baby. "Bitch, if you don't talk to me, both of us are gonna beat the living shit out of you," Bernice says.

Bernice pulls Terri away from Monique so she can uncover her face and look at them standing over her while she confesses what she did. Crying and wiping her face, Monique tells them what they want to know.

"Y'all, I'm so sorry. I'm sooo sorry. I told Vic about the link." At the mention of that, Terri rushes to hit Monique again, but Bernice grabs her just inches away from Monique's face and pulls her back. Monique throws up her arms in a defensive posture.

"Bitch, don't you raise your fuckin' hands to me. I'll kill your sorry ass in here," a furious Terri screams. Bernice pulls Terri away and stands in front of her.

"Bitch, do you understand how you've betrayed us? For all of us, the link was a magical experience. It brought us closer than anything could have, and you and your fuckin' drunk-ass mouth ruined it. And you think we're not supposed to be angry with you?" Bernice says.

"I'm sorry, Bernice. I'm sorry, Terri. I didn't mean for any of that to happen. If I could fix what I did, I would. I didn't mean to put our business out there like that," Monique says crying.

"Well, you did, bitch, and what we shared is now all fucked up. On top of that, you got Lois's head all fucked up, you fuckin' dirty skank. You should be lucky Bernice is here.That's the only reason why your ass isn't bleeding," a furious Terri says.

Monique is terrified and alone. She realizes these women who were her closest friends for years have just turned on her as if they never knew her. The, only thing she can do is beg their forgiveness.

"I'm sorry. Please don't do this to me anymore. I made a mistake. Please forgive me. I'll do anything. I said I'm sorry," Monique pleads as she crying.

"Ho, what the fuck can you do to fix what you've done to us?" Terri shouts.

"I'll do anything I have to. I can't beg anymore for yall to forgive me than I am now," she says sobbing.

"Take your clothes off Monique," Terri demands. Monique looks at her and repeats what she heard.

"Take my clothes off?"

"Yeah, bitch, take your fuckin' clothes off now or I will make your ass bleed," Terri says. Monique freezes for a second until Bernice orders her to remove her clothes again.

Monique completely undresses in the living room, and all three women walk to the bedroom, with Monique crying, leading the way. As they walk, Terri removes her shoes and belt. She stops briefly to take her pants off as they continue to the bedroom.

"Lay your ass on the bed," Bernice tells her. Crying, she does as she's told. Bernice sits in a chair facing the bed. Terri takes her panties off and walks to the bed.

"Open your fuckin' mouth bitch, she is told. Terri gets on the bed and positions herself so that her pussy is over Monique's mouth with Bernice looking on.

"Eat my pussy, bitch, And if you bite me, I'll pull your fuck'in' eyes out," Terri orders her.

Monique eats Terri's pussy, and the tears rain down her face. There is no joy in the act this time. For Terri, this is about payback. This action is about punishment and hate. Monique doesn't think anymore. She is too terrified, these are no longer her friends but her tormentors. Monique tries to push Terri up a little and is rebuffed.

"Bitch, don't touch me. Get your fuckin' hands off me. Just suck my pussy till I cum in your mouth. You can fuckin' cry all you want." Terri leans down, grabs Monique's head, and forcefully pushes her pussy onto Monique's tongue. "That's it, bitch, right there. All I better feel is your lips and tongue." Terri forces Monique to stay in this position for thirty minutes until she cums.

When Terri gets off Monique's face, Bernice has taken off her clothes, and she lays on the bed. She makes Monique go down on her face first. Terri takes the chair and watches as Monique eats Bernice's pussy for the next hour.

"Don't touch her, bitch. Keep your fuckin' hands to yourself. You lost the right to touch us when you ran you fuckin' mouth about the link."

When Bernice is satisfied, she pushes Monique away with her feet, gets up, and puts her clothes back on, then sits in the room with Monique. Monique is on her side faced away from Bernice, crying like a child whose mother has abandoned her.

Terri comes back in the room and closes the bedroom door. She looks at Bernice and gives her a nod. Terri walks over to the bed and puts a box on the dresser. Monique is still lying on her side but no longer crying but still shaking when Terri comes back in the room.

"Okay, bitch, this is the way it is, since you like to fuck and tell and you want us to forgive you. Look at me when I'm talking to your nasty ass," she orders Monique.

Monique turns to face Terri, shaking like a leaf in the wind. "Like I said, since you like to fuck and tell, you see this?" Terri holds up a box of ten condoms. "You said you'd do anything for us to forgive you, so you're gonna let ten dicks link with that pussy, then we can be friends again. And don't start crying, bitch. Your ass wasn't crying when you fucked Vic and his boy. You should feel lucky we won't let any of them fuck you in your ass."

Bernice opens the door, and the first of ten men walk in. Monique feels like a trapped rat and is truly terrified for her life. She cries anyway, covering her eyes and wishing she were dead, knowing now her life is ruined. She wishes for someone to save her, but she knows that's not going to happen as the first of ten unknown men put on a condom and fuck her as Terri and Bernice watch until the last condom is used and the bed is bloodied.